THE
RAVEN'S HONOR

Center Point
Large Print

Also by Johnny D. Boggs and available from Center Point Large Print:

And There I'll Be a Soldier
Top Soldier
Return to Red River
Hard Way Out of Hell
Summer of the Star
The Kansas City Cowboys
Wreaths of Glory

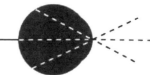

THE RAVEN'S HONOR
A Sam Houston Story

Johnny D. Boggs

CENTER POINT LARGE PRINT
THORNDIKE, MAINE

This Circle Ⓥ Western is published by
Center Point Large Print in the year 2017 in
co-operation with Golden West Literary Agency.

First Edition
December, 2017

Printed in the United States of America
on permanent paper.
Set in 16-point Times New Roman type.

ISBN: 978-1-68324-623-7

Library of Congress Cataloging-in-Publication Data

Names: Boggs, Johnny D., author.
Title: The raven's honor: a Sam Houston story / Johnny D. Boggs.
Description: First edition. | Thorndike, Maine :
    Center Point Large Print [2017] | Series: A Circle V western
Identifiers: LCCN 2017035380 | ISBN 9781683246237
    (hardcover : alk. paper)
Subjects: LCSH: Large type books. | GSAFD: Western stories.
Classification: LCC PS3552.O4375 R38 2017 | DDC 813/.54—dc23
LC record available at https://lccn.loc.gov/2017035380

In memory of Darrell C. Boggs,
1927–2009, the strongest man I've ever known;

and for Jack, who knows the story of
Sam Houston and the ring

THE
RAVEN'S HONOR

PROLOGUE

Virginian by birth, Tennessean by manhood, Texian for nigh thirty years. Sam Houston, the man who made Texas, had become legend long before the Year of Our Lord 1861.

This was the hero of the Battle of San Jacinto, where he had defeated Santa Anna's Mexican army and avenged the Alamo back in 1836. This ancient leviathan had been a friend of David Crockett, and of Andrew Jackson. A friend of the Cherokees, with whom he had lived as a youngster and as a middle-aged recluse. A friend of the people. An enemy to many.

People loved him. Despised him. Respected him. More than a few feared him.

Runaway. Schoolteacher. Hero of the Creek War. Indian agent. Lawyer. Prosecutor. Congressman. Governor of two states. Senator. Twice president of the Republic of Texas. An Andrew Jackson Democrat, handpicked by Old Hickory himself as one to fill Jackson's boots until the unthinkable had derailed Houston's political career, but only briefly.

The Cherokees had named him The Raven. He had also been called Old Sam, General Sam, Sam Jacinto, and The Big Drunk.

Countless times, his iron will had bested his

enemies. His wife, Margaret, however, had saved him from his worst enemy, himself.

Husband. Father. Christian. Slave owner. Divorcé. Drunkard. Hothead. Egomaniac. Soldier. Statesman. Manipulator. Blow-hard. Giant. Insignificant. Gutless. Valiant. Devoted. Disloyal. Honest. Liar.

He had been called every name in the book, often with good cause. He had lost battles, won wars, and bore painful reminders of both.

When well into his sixties, he recalled that he had tried—not always successfully—to live his life with his own brand of honor. He had endured. He had carved a reputation enemies kept trying—but always, eventually, failing—to smear. An old man, he had kept his self-respect. He still had his family. His legacy. His name.

Yet everything he had built, and all of his dreams, started crumbling, to test his honor, his endurance, and his faith.

Sam Houston brought Texas into the Union. Now, Sam Houston's Texas was leaving these United States to join the Confederacy.

As a new nation dawned, Sam Houston realized that his honor would be tested again as he fought his final war . . . against enemies and friends. What he could not understand yet was that he would have to conquer his ghosts, his family, his own countrymen, his demons, and himself.

CHAPTER ONE

March 16, 1861

Ink-slingers, pettifogging politicians, sky pilots, pathetic old biddies, and barbershop gossips would say that he had failed at all he had tried, seen everything come to ruin, and that what few victories he might have won came by luck and nothing else. Once the chair legs hit the floor, however, the big man knew they could never take this away from him. This would be his greatest victory.

Somehow, by himself, through sheer determination and not one iota of luck, he had gotten that damned chair from his office to the cavernous state Capitol's basement.

Struggling to catch his breath, the white-haired man leaned against the chair's back. Deep in the building's bowels, the air felt colder than he had expected, and above, through the thick ceiling, came muffled shouts, the stamping of boots on the floors of a hallowed hall. He had hoped to escape everything, but, alas, he had failed at that, too—and he lacked the strength to find another place to hide.

The old giant studied his chair.

Certainly a crate, box, or the cold floor itself

might have been just as comfortable. Plain, four simply turned legs, one loose, another uneven, with an arched backrest supported by six rods, the seventh having been broken six years earlier and never replaced. The seat, made of tanned cowhide, bore signs of age and scars. But he had made this chair himself. Now he removed the wooden walking stick that he had carried in the chair, and rested the crooked hickory against the wall. Finally, with a weary sigh, he sank into the rickety chair.

His lips trembled, his heart ached, but he refused to break down.

For a moment he sat there, not listening to the crowd above him in the state's *Confederate* congressional chambers or to the water dripping somewhere deeper in the basement.

He wore a coat that had been tailored for him twenty years earlier but could no longer be buttoned around his stomach. The cuffs of the fitted sleeves had started fraying long ago, and only a few massive buttons remained. Moths had eaten four small holes in the left side, and his wife always told him he should not be seen leaving his home in such a piece of garbage. He liked that coat, however, and always explained that such a coat befitted a man who worked and dealt with garbage. The vest? Well, even his wife never complained about it. Although he had not worn it in years, at least not in public, he had

13

prayed that it might bring him luck. "Leopard skin," he always called it, even if the skin came from a jaguar. "Leopards cannot change their spots," he was fond of saying. "Nor can I."

His shirt, like the vest, remained unbuttoned at the collar, for he hated anything tight against his throat. "Folks have wanted to put something around my neck for better than forty years, Margaret," he told his wife whenever she begged him to wear an ascot or some type of tie. "Damned if I'll do it myself."

Eventually, he reached inside his coat pocket, and withdrew the knife. As always, once he opened the blade, he lightly brushed his thumb across the edge. A keen edge was a dangerous weapon; a dull blade, even more so. Satisfied, he found a small piece of wood in another pocket. He pushed his chair back on two legs, brought the blade to the wood, and slowly shaved off a piece. He held the wood up to his eyes for closer inspection.

Pine, of course, had a softness to it, and he preferred harder woods when facing challenging problems. After wetting his lips, he started another pass of the blade, but stopped.

His head lifted toward the ceiling, and tears welled in his eyes. The leviathan summoned strength, shook his head, made himself block out the muted commotion above him. He made his next pass even lighter, watching the wood peel

14

as the knife came toward him. *Better. Take your time, make wood and edge last.* He cut again.

"What you carvin'?"

He lifted his large head, cerulean eyes glaring at a young boy in the hallway who stood underneath a lighted candle on the wall. The last thing he needed was some kid pestering him. He opened his mouth to roar at the boy and frighten him into a full-fledged retreat. A memory stopped him.

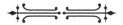

He was slightly older than this tyke, in the Tennessee woods, and had just come across an Indian leaning against a tree, knife in right hand, cutting on a sapling. "What are you carving?" he asked, and the lean figure jerked up, moving the knife into a defensive position, rage filling those black eyes. Fearing he was about to be butchered by a red savage, he stumbled, and fell onto his buttocks, but the Indian immediately relaxed. The stately looking Cherokee, who would adopt him as a son, even smiled before speaking.

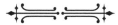

"Not carving," the old-timer said in as soft a voice as he could manage in answering the boy. "I'm whittling." It still sounded more like a bark. The behemoth settled back into his chair and slowly drew the knife toward him. Another shaving drifted silently to the floor.

"Ain't it the same thing?" the youngster asked.

His head shook as he trimmed off another shaving, staring at the youngster. Eight, nine, no more than ten years old, with long trousers, shoes that must have pinched his toes, a jacket, vest, starched shirt with paper collar and a cravat. Dressed up in his Sunday best, though today was Saturday, the kid started tugging at the tight collar with a finger.

"Whittling," the man explained, "is for thinking. Carving is for pleasure. And do not say *ain't*." He gave the kid his sternest look. "It ain't becoming for a distinguished young man such as yourself." He hoped the boy would go away. He knew better.

"I ain't dis- . . . um . . . I ain't . . ."

"Distinguished," the man said. "Means illustrious."

The boy frowned.

"Notable. Famous. Eminent." He nodded at the ceiling. "Like those folks upstairs. I figured, dressed as you are, that you were among our *new Confederate congress*." The last words came out as a bitter oath. His heart broke again. Seeing the kid step closer, the giant drew a deep breath, bottling up the emotions that tore through him.

"Nah," the boy said. "My ma made me come is

all. Says this is the most important day in my life. I figured it might be fun, but it ain't . . . isn't . . . fun at all. All they do is shout and spit and stamp their feet. All that speechifyin' is borin'. I could be rollin' hoops with Bucky and David."

"I wish I could roll hoops with you . . . Bucky and David, too." The old man shaved more wood, and, without looking away from his task, he asked: "Your pa up there among our fine Congress, or is he just part of the watching *horde?*"

The boy stared, not understanding horde, perhaps not even congress. His eyes, a deep brown, looked at his tiny shoes, and he said in almost a whisper: "My pa's dead."

"I am sorry," the man said. For a moment, the old-timer almost forgot what had brought him here, and all that the fools were destroying in the hallowed halls above.

The boy shrugged.

"I was just a few years older than you, I imagine, when my father was called to Glory," the old-timer said. "It is a hard thing. But your father will always be with you." He started to tap his chest with the pine, but thought: *Here you are, you old windbag, giving another damned speech.*

At least the boy didn't heckle him, or threaten to gun him down as a traitor to the Confederate States of America, to the state of Texas.

The boy swallowed. "My pa got killed . . . at the Alamo."

Leaning back, the old man studied the youngster. The kid would have to be in his mid-twenties to have a father who died with Crockett, Dickinson, Bonham, and all those others. Instead of rebuking the youngster, the leviathan offered the knife and wooden rectangle to the boy.

"Would you like to try?"

"Carve somethin'?"

"Not carve," the old man said. "Whittle."

"You don't carve?"

The man shrugged. "When the mood strikes me. Crosses. My wife likes crosses, likes to see me carve those. Hearts. Margaret likes those, too. Watch fobs. Buttons. Even small tomahawks. But when I need to contemplate, to think, to decide on something immensely important, I just whittle." He shook his hands, holding the knife and the piece of wood.

"How you do it?" the kid asked tentatively.

"Just . . . whittle," the big man said. "Whittle . . . and think. But you have to sit down to do a proper job. One does not whittle whilst on his feet."

The man stood to offer his chair to the boy, but the kid stepped back, his mouth hanging open.

"Are you . . . are you a . . . giant?"

For the first time in days, probably months, the ancient warrior smiled. "There are those who will say I have done big things, great things." Even now, as age and old wounds tried to shrink his powerful frame, he could make himself seem larger, more intimidating. A cheer above him ended the mood. So did other bottled-up memories. "Mayhap I have," he whispered. "But at times, I have been a very, very small man and done shamefully small things. Here." He thrust the tools at the boy.

"Careful," he said, after helping the youngster into the chair. "Do not cut yourself. The blade is sharp as a barber's razor." His massive finger pointed at the pine. "You see that. The grain. That's what you look for. Cut with the grain. If you carve against the grain, it'll go harder, and you're likely to split your wood. Put your thumb lower. Your ma would not care much for me if you returned to the chamber with a bloody thumb. There. That's good. Slowly. There. Pretty easy, isn't it? Now, did you do any good thinking?"

The kid looked up, glanced at the knife, the wood, and quickly thrust both back to the big man. "Here."

Frowning, saddened again, the giant took his tool and the wood, expecting the boy to leap down to the floor and skedaddle back to his mother—which is what the old man had wished for minutes ago. Instead, the boy stared at his hands and, after a long while, looked up. Tears brimmed in those brown eyes.

19

"My pa . . . he wasn't killed at . . . the Alamo."
He did not look up at the big man when he said
in a rushed whisper: "He ain't even dead."

Above them, the clamor reached a zenith,
causing the candle to flicker, and almost burn
out. The big man looked at the ceiling and finally
brought out a watch from the pocket of his
waistcoat. " 'Tis almost noon," he said absently.

"I'm hungry." The kid sniffled. "Ain't you?"

"I have no appetite this day."

The boy swallowed. "I . . . I reckon I . . . I
fibbed about my pa bein' dead and all."

"I have told some whoppers myself," the
leviathan said. "But . . ."—he tried to sound
stern—"do not make a habit of lying, young
man. Lies hurt. If you want to be a success in
this world . . . be honest, respect those older than
you, and do not lie. You won't always succeed in
doing those three things, but try your hardest to
make those three rules your creed."

"You won't tell my ma, will you?"

He shook his head.

"But you ain't got no food?"

In the chamber above them, a clock began to
chime, and, after the twelfth stroke, he heard
them call out the name, followed by applause.
The room above suddenly fell silent.

The boy leaped down off the seat, and said:
"You want to whittle? You look like you need to
do some thinkin'."

With a nod, the old giant sank again into the chair, kicking back, finding the grain, feeling the knife, liking the way the wood shaved.

"Basswood." He spoke just to fill the space, to forget. "That's what most prefer. But any wood'll do."

"You work here?" the boy asked.

Sighing, the giant did not answer. After another shaving fell, he again offered the knife and pine to the boy. "Here."

Above them, the name was called, and again the crowd roared.

When silence resumed, the boy said: "I reckon he don't hear 'em." The kid, having taken the knife and wood, sat on the hard floor, knees pulled up, head lowered, concentrating on his task.

The giant bit his lip, inhaled deeply, slowly exhaled.

The boy grinned at his accomplishment. He placed the wood on the floor and picked up his shaving. "Can I keep it?"

Blinking, the old man looked confused. "The shaving? Of course. What did you think? What problem did you solve?"

"I just thought it's good and long and funny-looking. The shaving."

"I have never seen any its equal," the man said, "and I have whittled a long, long time."

The boy frowned and looked up. This time, a

21

tear trickled down his cheek. "My pa . . . he . . . um . . . well, my ma . . . they . . . *divorced?*" The last word came out as a question. "But, Ma, she don't want nobody to know."

His immense head bobbed, and he rested his big hand on the young boy's shoulder. "I have experienced that pain as well, but not from your viewpoint, I must concede. Stand with your mother, lad. Yet do not loathe your father. Fathers, like all men, do foolish things. Try not to, when you are older."

"Should . . . ?" The boy squinted as if in deep concentration. "Should I add that to my . . . um . . . cree-?"

"Creed," the man said, emphasizing the d. "Means a statement of your principles, your personal rules, your beliefs."

"You must be a schoolmaster." Again, the lad turned to the pine.

"I cannot say I had much of an education, but I have taught school."

The boy examined his handiwork. "Wish we had you instead of mean ol' Miss Langston."

"Well . . ." He wanted to chuckle, but could barely smile. "Soon I shall be available for new employment."

The kid looked up, and his eyes saddened again. "My pa . . . he drinks."

"Yes." The old man's response came out like a sob.

"You're married," the boy said brightly, trying to change the subject, the mood. "I can tell."

The big man's blue eyes revitalized. "And how did you divine such knowledge?"

Pointing at the man's big hand, the youngster said: "That ring there . . . on your finger."

Sadly, he looked at the small gold band on his pinky, his own eyes misting once more. "Yes," he said, "listen to your mother, son. And always remember her."

Footsteps rattled down the dark chamber, and the big man fetched the cane for support, ready to do battle again with the man hurrying through the corridor. A well-dressed man with dark hair emerged from the shadows, stopping suddenly, breathing hard, his face damp with sweat.

"Jack, your mother has been worried sick." A young man to the giant, an old man to the boy, the newcomer spoke as a man with much education, and with an accent unlike what either the old whittler or the boy typically heard in these parts. "What are you doing down here?" The intruder straightened when the giant stepped into the light.

"I've been teaching Jack here how to whittle," the Goliath said, adding with a polite nod, "Reverend Baker."

"Governor," the minister said. He wet his lips. "Sir, they have called for you twice."

Hearing this bit of news, the boy slid away.

"The *hoi polloi* yell loudly," the governor said.

"I heard, yet chose to ignore such bidding."

The parson's face brightened, but no smile followed on such a solemn day. "I knew you would, sir. As Senator Throckmorton said the other day . . . 'When the rabble hiss, well may patriots tremble.'"

After a curt nod, the old man sat back into his chair.

Above, his name rang loudly for the third time.

"Houston! Governor Sam Houston!"

No applause followed this time. The silence did not stretch long, and whispers and hisses began creeping through the cracks into the basement. They would not call his name again. He had vacated his office, so those fire-breathing Secessionists would now choose a new governor for this *Confederate* state of Texas.

"Come along, Jack," the Reverend William Mumford Baker said. "Let us find your mother."

"Awe," the boy protested, but the preacher scowled, and the boy hurried toward him. After a few steps, the youngster stopped and looked back as the giant pushed back in the chair.

"Sir?" Jack asked timidly.

The giant's eyes found him. Before the boy could speak, the old-timer pointed at the stick and the knife that remained on the floor.

"Son," he said pleasantly, "why don't you take those with you? They might help solve your problems."

"I couldn't take 'em, sir," the boy said. "It's your knife and your wood, and you got to do all that thinkin'."

"I have plenty of knives and plenty of wood at my home, Jack," the giant said. "And I fear, lad, that in the coming years, your problems will be much more difficult and demanding than the ones I shall face . . . after today."

The boy hesitated, but the governor pointed. The child shot a respectful glance at the minister, who nodded his approval. Cautiously, the boy returned to where the whittler rocked on the chair legs, no longer looking at the boy or the preacher, but staring at the ceiling. If the boy had not known better, he would have sworn he saw tears in the old man's eyes. After retrieving knife, wood, and, for good measure, more shavings, the youngster stuffed all inside one pocket. He started again for the preacher, but stopped suddenly, and looked back at the old man.

"Are you . . ." he said, "really . . . Sam Houston?"

The man stopped rocking. Turning only his head, Sam Houston answered at last: "I am what's left of him."

CHAPTER TWO

March 18, 1861

Houston asked himself: *What are you doing, old man? You refused to take the oath to the Confederacy. You aren't governor of Texas anymore. Where do you have to go?*

He sat down on the four-poster bed to pull on his boots. He did not feel like using the rocking chair to finish getting dressed. Rocking chairs were for old men. And beds? This he contemplated before deciding that the rocking chair belonged to him, but the bed belonged to the State of Texas, courtesy of the state legislature and the bill it had passed in December of 1859 that approved $2,500 to be spent on furnishings for the new governor. He wondered what Ed Clark, the first Confederate governor of Texas, would do with the furniture.

Burn it, he guessed, using one of the bedposts to pull himself to his feet.

Downstairs, Margaret shepherded children and slaves as they packed up their possessions and prepared for the long trip to Cedar Point. Well, he had never liked the city of Austin, anyway. He had fought against the foul, polluted raw town— or fought Mirabeau B. Lamar back during the late

1830s and early 1840s—to prevent Austin from becoming the capital city, but to no avail. Texas's government should have been in Washington-on-the-Brazos, or, better yet, Houston City. Yet he did not feel the urge to leave Austin just yet. Grabbing his walking cane and hat, he left the bedroom and headed downstairs.

His boots, and that damnable cane, echoed in the mansion. He had never gotten used to this expensive palace of yellow bricks. By Jehovah, back in his day, he had lived in the Bullock Hotel as president of the Republic of Texas. And when he moved to Washington-on-the-Brazos, the president's home had been a small cabin. Even then, he had been unable to pay rent in advance so he and Margaret had lived with the Lockharts; Margaret would have disapproved of anything less than a good Baptist family.

"Wealth does not fit me," he told Margaret often. "Which is why we are poor."

Although he was anything but.

Jeff, his young personal servant, met him at the bottom of the staircase, holding an over-coat.

"Master Sam," the thin, young Negro said. "Joshua be hitchin' up the buggy, sir, to run you over to the Capitol this mornin'."

"Thank you, Jeff," he said, "but I'll walk this day."

"Master Sam . . ." The slave took the walking

27

cane and helped Houston into the coat. "You catch your death if you walk, sir."

"Catch my death?" Houston asked. "Or catch a bullet?"

Jeff ignored the remark or did not hear it. "It's a mite chilly this morn, and be lookin' like rain."

"I will be fine, Jeff." He took his cane, although the pain in his leg made him consider turning to the crutch. Pride prevented that, however. No one in Austin outside this house would see him using a damned crutch. A hickory cane was bad enough. He peered into the parlor, but Margaret had her hands full, ordering this and that to be done, so he moved toward the front door.

"Papa?"

His third child, Maggie, came toward him. "You have not taken breakfast yet, Papa." *Not yet a teenager,* Houston grumbled to himself, *and already just like her mother.*

"I shall eat upon my return from the office," he told her.

"Office?" She could not hide her concern.

"I did not get all of my belongings on Saturday, Maggie," he explained, which was what he had told Jeff earlier this morning. Which was true. He turned quickly to Jeff. "Where's that basket I asked for?"

The slave pointed toward the front door. Houston saw the basket and nodded at his daughter. "See. I shall fetch a few important things home. I should be back in time for dinner, likely famished."

If I can eat at all.

"Well, let me find my shawl and I shall accompany you."

He wanted no companionship this day. Not even Maggie, a sweet girl who prided herself on being her father's secretary and whose penmanship looked a hell of a lot better than his horrible scrawl. "I have no letters to dictate this day," he snapped, immediately regretting his tone. He frowned at his temper before gently squeezing her shoulder. "I will be back directly, my spring rose." He managed a pleasant voice. "But you must help your mother. We have much to do. And I promise I will feast on whatever Aunt Liza fixes for dinner *and* supper." He wanted to tell her: *Don't worry.*

Making herself brave, Maggie said—"All right, Papa."—and hurried up the stairs.

"How long you reckon they'll lets us stay here, sir?" Jeff had somehow beaten Houston to the door, and pulled it open.

"They are not burning me in effigy on the lawn." Houston pulled on his hat and grabbed the wicker basket. The door did not close behind him until he reached the street.

Reality punched him when he found Edward Clark sitting at the governor's desk. Clark had a rectangular head, big ears, a graying mustache and beard, and very little hair on the top of his head. What Houston saw was the bald head, beading sweat, as Clark bent forward, eyes squinting, reading the morning newspapers.

"Well, *Governor*," Houston said in a mocking voice, "you are an early riser."

Clark sat erect, and held his breath for a long while.

Sitting at my desk, Houston thought. *In my chair.*

"Yes." Clark found his own sarcastic tone. "*General.* I am illustrating the old maxim . . . 'The early bird catches the worm.' "

But, sir, you are the worm. Houston let that thought go unsaid. Instead, he pointed at the chair. "Well, *Governor Clark,* I hope you will find it an easier chair than I have found it."

"I'll endeavor to make it so, *General,* by conforming to the clearly expressed will of the people of Texas."

Houston wondered how he had managed to tolerate the blubbering fool as his lieutenant governor for all those months. Will of the people? The people favored Secession. The people favored war. Secession—and Houston's removal as governor—were entirely unconstitutional. And war?

"You are in for a long war, Governor." This time, he spoke in a serious tone.

"I suppose not," Clark said. "Being tempered from war, at Monterrey, as you might remember, where I had the honor and privilege to serve under General Henderson, I daresay that Texans always give their utmost, which will be more than enough to send Northern tyrants retreating back to Washington City to crucify Mister Lincoln, that Abolitionist zealot, for starting this ruction."

Working on his speech, Houston thought. *It needs work. Much work. And he knows nothing about war.* He pointed. "I'll not bother you, Governor. I merely came to gather the rest of my personal effects, if you do not mind."

"By all means, General." Clark returned to his newspapers, and Houston set the basket down. His copies of *The Iliad* and *The Odyssey* were so torn and ragged, he thought Clark might have thrown them out with the garbage, but, of course, Clark would have no reason to peruse a bookshelf. Houston cushioned the volumes, his most valuable treasures, with his gloves, grabbed a few trinkets he had carved, and two unopened letters. Recognizing the handwriting and return address on one, he immediately opened it, surprised that a letter from a damnyankee state like Connecticut could make it into the Capitol.

Save Texas for us, Lydia Sigourney had written, *if you can.*

"Oh, you Sweet Singer of Hartford," he said softly, "this, I fear, I cannot do."

31

Placing the letter from his friend and poet on top of his carvings, he closed the basket's lid. He opened the other letter, read a few lines, and crumpled it and the envelope and let them fall into the trash.

Clark kept reading the newspapers, and down the corridor someone cleared his throat. Glancing around the governor's office, Houston knew he did not belong here. If he stayed much longer, he might fall into myriad pieces.

"Good day, Governor Clark," he said at the entrance, his bow as exaggerated as his tidings. But Houston would be damned if he walked away without a final punch.

Clark raised his bald head and opened his mouth, but stopped when Houston pointed to the washstand. "I have left you that bar of soap," Houston said, "for a governor should have clean hands. Mine are, sir." Clark appeared too stunned to respond, and, grinning, Sam Houston left the Capitol.

The men who complained that their wives did nothing all day but natter sat outside the barbershop next to the post office doing what they did best: gossip and pontificate on matters of importance.

"Crockett," one said. "That's who we need. Davy. Why he'd lick the Yanks."

"I'd sure enough fit alongside Davy," said

another. "More'n I'd join up to serve under Johnston."

"Johnston's all right," said the third, "but I like Ben McCulloch. Why, once the Yanks found out Jeff Davis had put McCulloch in charge here in Texas, they skedaddled like the yellow dogs they are."

"Who's McCulloch?" asked the fourth.

"Shhhhh," the first whispered. "Here comes ol' Sam Jacinto hisself, the traitor."

Ignoring the chin wags, Houston posted a letter to Sam Junior, now attending Colonel Robert P.T. Allen's Military Institute in Bastrop, and continued on for home. The know-it-alls were talking as soon as he passed the haberdasher.

"How old you reckon he is now?" asked the first.

"Right behind Methuselah," answered the second.

"Sixty," said the third.

"Eighty," guessed the fourth.

"I wonder what got into him, turnin' down the governor's job and all," said the third.

"All 'em years in Washington City," the second said. "They got to him, the Yanks did."

"Shoot," said the first, "if he had any backbone, Davy Crockett'd still be with us. Travis and Bowie, too. He was marchin' to the Alamo, Houston was, but drug his feet. Didn't see no hurry, he did. Ask me, he's to blame."

33

"Well," said the fourth, "but wasn't for him and San Jacinto, we might not be here."

"Maybe," said the third, "but, still, he weren't no Crockett."

When war finally reached Texas, Houston figured, those windbags would still be in front of the barbershop, their mouths filled with tobacco and lungs filled with hot air. They'd be sitting there when the war ended, as well.

In the dining room, he ate only half a sandwich, but drank all the tea, before handing the copies of Homer, as well as the rest of his dinner, to Lewis, the oldest slave he owned. Exhausted from the walk to the Capitol and post office and back, though refusing to admit it, he climbed the stairs and sank into his rocking chair.

Maggie checked on him again. So did Mary Willie, his ten-year-old daughter. So did the slaves—Aunt Martha, Joshua, old Lewis. He wanted the damned door shut, to be alone, but he lacked the strength to stand up and close it.

He felt older than his sixty-eight years. He had a wife, beautiful Margaret Moffette Lea Houston, who would turn forty-two next month. They had eight children, the youngest, Temple Lea, born right here in this governor's mansion less than a year ago. Looking up, Houston caught his reflection in the mirror. Silently, he had mocked Governor Clark's bald pate, yet Houston's own hair had thinned so much, he no longer could find much to comb over. What remained glowed stark white, yet still as unruly as his temper and, he had to concede, his own ego. He ran his fingers through his sideburns, and then rested the cleft in his chin against his right hand.

Down the hall, Temple Lea began to cry, and footsteps immediately sounded on the stairs. He stared through the open door, too tired even to see to his youngest son as he watched a black woman hurry to change the diaper or whatever Temple Lea demanded right now. Houston pushed himself out of the rocker, removed his coat and vest, and then his shirt. He pulled off his undershirt, and walked to the wash basin.

"Are your wounds bothering you again, Sam?"

Margaret stood on the threshold. Before he could answer, she moved to his side, dipped a washcloth in the soapy water, and brought it to his right arm. She grimaced, but refused to let the clear fluid bother her. Most women, even most men, would be sickened by the sight, but not Margaret.

The bullet had struck him forty-seven years ago, and for forty-seven years that wound had refused to heal completely. Just like another bullet wound in the shoulder, as well as one from a Creek arrow in his groin—three unhealed scars from the same damned battle. "They annoy me when my Ebenezer is up," he often complained, but the wounds troubled him even during good moods. His dander rose again for he did not want Margaret to clean the other wound.

"I can do this," he said. "Or get Jeff to dress it."

"I know you can," Margaret said. "But so can I."

Defeated again, he sighed. "How is Temple?"

"Dry." Her grin proved infectious.

"Why," he asked, "are you with a leaky, mouthy old reprobate like me?"

"Sam Houston," she said, "I was smitten when I first laid eyes on you." She dipped the cloth in the basin and began to wring out the water. Her voice, always musical, turned dreamy as she reflected. "The Reverend and Missus McLean said that we must go to the docks for the great hero of the Texas rebellion was being brought to New Orleans, and that we should be there to cheer on such a leader." The cold compress returned to his arm.

He had heard this story a million times before. He could hear it a million more.

"Why there must have been a thousand people on the docks that day, waving flags and ribbons and flowers. And we went, and we waited, and they told us that the *Flora* had been delayed by storm. And thus I said my chance at seeing a hero was gone. But the next day, our chaperones insisted that we return. So off we went, the reverend, his wife, and a bunch of schoolgirls from the Pleasant Valley Academy. And on this day, maybe five thousand people massed together on the waterfront. Bells from the cathedral pealing, bands playing, everyone clapping. They knew, for we had been told, that this time, the *Flora* had arrived . . . what a decrepit ship she was. Not fitting, I thought, to be transporting a grand hero, and this time you limped out on crutches. I had read about heroes, in *Ivanhoe* and *The Last of the Mohicans*. But you were the first I saw."

Houston's big head bobbed. "The surgeon said that I would be carted out on a stretcher, but when I heard the cheers, I refused. I walked. Somehow, I walked."

"And talked," she reminded him. "After we made the bands stop their infernal racket."

"Briefly," he said. "I spoke but few words."

"And fainted." She returned the cloth to the basin.

"I prefer not to remember it that way," he said.

"It proved most effective." Margaret twisted the cloth in her hands and let the water splash and then drip into the basin. "I feared you dead, that I had witnessed the great Sam Houston die in New Orleans. But then you roused yourself, and Grace McMillan said . . . 'It is like Lazarus.' And the Reverend McLean said . . . 'Blessed be the Lord.' And I said . . . 'Blessed be Sam Houston.' That night, I went to bed dreaming that one day I would meet and marry the great Sam Houston."

His head shook as Margaret wiped the wounds in his arm and shoulder once more, wrapped them with linen, and then led him back to the rocker.

"It was the Lord's hand," she said.

He looked up into her beautiful eyes.

"Who else," Margaret whispered, "could have brought a seventeen-year-old student on a trip from Marion, Alabama, to New Orleans?"

A servant called out for her from downstairs.

"The Lord works in mysterious ways," he told her.

"So does Sam Houston." She left to instruct the Negro on what needed to be packed, and what would remain in Austin.

CHAPTER THREE

For as long as Houston could remember, the Cherokees called him *Co-lo-neh*. It meant The Raven. Some years later, they also called him *Oo-tse-tee Ar-dee-tah-skee*, which meant The Big Drunk. He spied a pitcher of water, but studied the bottles and jugs on the table in his library. The urge came to him—as it so often did. Rye, bourbon, Scotch, gin, sour mash, brandy, port, scuppernong, and Madeira, plus a homemade concoction that used to be his drink of choice—bitters and orange peel, which he had vowed to be no more spirituous than Margaret's sweet tea. That had worked, until he slurred his words and stumbled over the settee. And since he and Margaret had become betrothed, he had been sober. Mostly.

He had slipped more than once. That time in Huntsville, when Margaret had gone to Alabama, when he had demanded that Joshua—a slave owned by Margaret who had become one of Houston's manservants—chop off the bedpost because it spoiled his view. Or in Liberty, when he had fallen into the bushes and probably would be there yet had not Lee Bailey heard his curses and found him, pulled him to his feet, and deposited him inside his law office on Main Street to let him sleep it off. And he might have been inclined to go on another bender had Margaret not threatened to leave him.

Such a statement from a hard-shell Baptist from Alabama proved enough. "Let me try," he had begged her, and she had let him.

Years now, without one single drop. His Cherokee friends would not have believed it. Hell, he had trouble believing it himself. Margaret gave much of the credit to the Reverend Rufus C. Burleson, the tough-nut Baptist who had dunked Houston's head into the freezing waters of Rock Creek on a November day more than six years ago.

"God gives you only as much as you can handle," the reverend liked to say.

So God had given them a blue norther that sent the temperatures plummeting on the day Sam Houston was baptized. But, by Jehovah, he thought he would either drown or catch his death from the cold when Burleson held him under. When they came out of the creek, the spectators whispered that the pair might freeze solid before they could get them near a stove.

Houston, who had been a Presbyterian and red heathen, an agnostic and a questioner, a Catholic and a drunkard, had found that the Baptist faith suited him. Well, it suited Margaret.

"It's your own fault," Margaret had chided

him. "You could have been baptized inside the church."

"Not after those raucous tricksters filled the baptismal pool with mud and sticks," he had reminded her.

"The Reverend Rufus and I guessed you had bribed those boys to do that," she had said. "To delay the inevitable."

They had laughed, and hugged, and she had whispered in his ear: "I dreamed of this all my life, Sam Houston, and when you stopped drinking, I thought it could never be better than this. Until this day. God bless you, my husband."

A man could not go back on his promise now. Not to a fine woman like Margaret.

But, damn, he could taste whiskey on his tongue, feel the warmth as it glided down his throat. He would enjoy the power it gave him. He could forget. Forget everything. By thunder, how he wanted a drink. Just one, even if one turned into twenty. Even if it left him vomiting all over his clothes and wetting his britches. Whiskey. Glorious whiskey. God help him, he loved it so.

Margaret, he thought to himself. The urge did not die in him, but he stoppered it . . . for now.

Picking up the glass, Houston turned back toward his desk. "What's your pleasure, George?"

George Henry Giddings kept pounding away on his deerskin britches with his battered old slouch hat, sending dust into the air. A rough beard hid much of his face, bronzed from years in the wind and sun, and his dark hair resembled an eagle's nest. Houston found it hard to believe that the man standing in front of him hailed from Pennsylvania, or that he had not reached his fortieth year. Houston supposed that working with mules, mails, stagecoaches, not to mention the federal government, sure aged a fellow.

"Sorry, General." Giddings frantically fanned away the cascading dust with his floppy hat.

Houston gestured at the empty bookcase on the wall near him, and then to the crates and boxes that filled the library, or, as it was better known, "the Green Room", after the God-awful green paint on the walls.

"Let Governor Clark's servants worry about cleaning, George."

"Well, sir," Giddings said, "I apologize again for calling at such a late hour, but I just reached town."

"Nonsense. We have not yet taken our supper." He nodded at boxes filled and empty. "Packing." He held up the empty glass.

"Bourbon, General, if it's handy." Giddings sat down on a crate filled with books.

Bourbon. Houston grinned. *You can take a boy out of Pennsylvania but . . .*

After filling the glass, he corked the bottle and brought the liquor to Giddings, his boots sounding loud on the hardwood floor since the slaves, Pearl and Nash, had rolled up the rug. After settling into the swivel chair at his desk, Houston turned around to face Giddings.

"Did you get your money back?" Houston asked.

Giddings shook his head, took a sip of bourbon, wiped his mouth with his shirt sleeve, also deerskin, and set the glass on the crate to his right.

Giddings had been contracted to run the San Antonio-San Diego Mail line, better known as the "Jackass Mail," but Comanches, Apaches, economics, and politicians had fought against the enterprise. John Butterfield's Overland Mail had not helped, either, and now, even after Butterfield's line had been moved north, out of Texas, out of the South, Giddings's mail line remained in dire straits. Giddings had been in Washington City to plead his case for the promises Congress had made to reimburse him and his partners for their financial losses.

"You know what it takes to get anything done in that town, General."

"A miracle or a war." Houston frowned bitterly at his poorly timed answer.

"Beggin' your pardon, Master," the slave Lewis said from the open doorway, "but Missus Houston wants to know if your guest will be stayin' for supper?"

Houston looked at Giddings, who shook his

head and lifted his glass. "Supper enough for me, General. And I asked Charley to hold the stage to San Antone for me. He's waiting."

"Very good, sir." Lewis started to walk away, but Giddings nodded at the door.

"Lewis," Houston said.

The old man turned.

"Close the door for me, if you'd be so kind."

"Yes, sir."

When the door shut, George Giddings drained his glass and rose. As he crossed the room, he withdrew a crumpled, folded, and well-traveled envelope from the pocket of his britches. Wordlessly, he held the letter to Houston.

Taking the envelope, Houston smoothed it out and saw the address: *To Governor Houston.*

That was all.

Quickly, he looked on the desk for an opener. Seeing nothing, he frowned, but George Giddings had already pulled out a pocket knife and opened the blade, offering the knife, handle first, to Houston.

Letter opened and knife returned, Houston read just a few lines before looking up at the mail carrier. "Do you know what this says?" he asked.

Giddings nodded. "I didn't read it, mind you."

"He gave this to you, personally?"

"Yes, sir. Montgomery Blair, the new post-master general, used to be my attorney. After

I met with him about the contract and all those debts, Blair said someone wanted to meet me."

Houston folded the letter and rose.

"General?"

Houston's eyes locked on Giddings, who did not look away.

"I also ran into General Longstreet back East." Giddings wet his lips. "He resigned his commission."

Houston knew James Longstreet by reputation only, and the Army officer's reputation was outstanding. That Longstreet, a Southerner, had left the U.S. Army could come as no surprise. Just last month, Robert E. Lee had departed Fort Mason, northwest of Austin, to return to his home state of Virginia.

"General Longstreet was a big help to me out in west Texas, General, and he has been a good friend," Giddings said. "He spoke a lot about the South, the cause, and how Texas will need a lot of help to keep any Yankees coming in from Mexico. He made a lot of sense to me, General."

"You are a Yankee, George," Houston said. "And a Unionist."

Giddings shook his head. "I'm a Texan. If I might be so bold . . . so are you, sir."

Houston waved the letter toward Giddings, smiling in an attempt to bring some levity to the library.

"Did he have horns, cloven feet, and a pointy tail, George?"

The buckskin-clad figure laughed. "Just not as big as yours, General."

Houston roared so hard he thought tears might begin flowing down his cheeks. When he stopped laughing, though, the sadness struck him, and he felt weak. He returned the letter to the envelope, which he shoved in his coat pocket, then held out his hand. After the handshake, Giddings turned for the door but stopped when Houston called out his name.

"Could I impose upon you to do me a favor?"

"Name it, General."

"Before you take that stage south . . . and I know you will have to wake most of them . . . would you ask Jim Throckmorton, George Paschal . . ." He paused to think, dismissing some names, before adding: "Ben Epperson and Dave Culberson to meet me here in . . . two hours." Luckily, the clock had not been packed away.

"I'll find them, General. And, sir . . ."

Houston waited.

"I was sworn to secrecy, General. You don't have to fear that I'll go blabbing to Clark, or anybody. I gave my word to him, General, and I'm giving it to you, too."

"I know that, George. And, George . . . whatever happens to Texas, to the Union, to me, I wish you Godspeed."

When the door to the library closed behind Giddings, a powerful thirst seized Houston again, but he refused to look at the whiskeys. He stoked the fire, just to do something, and cursed. Epperson, Culberson, Throckmorton, and old Paschal would not be here for some time—if they came at all—and he had no appetite. Returning to his desk, he retrieved the letter from his pocket.

Jeff, his personal slave, appeared at the doorway, and cleared his throat.

Without looking up, Houston said: "Jeff, ask Margaret and the children to forgive me, but I sha'n't join them for supper. Tell Aunt Liza to leave a plate and some milk at my place, but not to worry about heating it up. And please bring some coffee and five cups here before you take your own supper, Jeff. Lastly, tell Margaret not to wait up for me."

The young man turned away, but Houston stopped him, and called him back into the Green Room. He held out the letter.

"Jeff," he said, "I want you to hold this."

With a shaking right hand, the slave took the letter. Uncertainty filled his eyes. "You want me to read this, Master Sam?"

Many Texans hated Houston for teaching his slaves to read and write. Houston did not give a damn what they thought.

"That, I cannot allow," he told Jeff. "I just want you to hold it. One day, Jeff, you can tell your

47

children and grandchildren that you once held a letter written by a great, great man."

The slave glanced at the envelope. He smiled. "Yes, sir. You writ' this letter to yourself, Master Sam?"

Laughing, Houston took the envelope back. "No, Jeff." The laughter died and his eyes turned sober. "See to your chores, Jeff. Good night."

When Jeff left, Houston removed the letter from the envelope and finished reading it before dropping it to the floor, clenching his fists. He whispered bitterly: "Too late . . . too late . . . too late. . . ."

CHAPTER FOUR

7 March '61

Dear Governor Houston:

Although we never met personally during my previous—and short—service in Washington City, I have long admired you from afar, even before your outstanding work during the Compromise of 1850. I opposed, as might you remember, the war against Mexico, and I oppose what will come to our nation, too, if we follow the current path. But I must fight for our nation, else I might as well spit on Adams, Washington, Jefferson—and our glorious Constitution.

As the proverb goes, "When two tigers fight, one will certainly get hurt." Sir, we must stop both tigers from sustaining serious, perhaps fatal, injuries.

Another proverb comes to mind as I think about you, Governor, and that one goes, "When one man is ready to risk his life, ten thousand men cannot defeat him."

You have the grit of a bulldog, sir, as you have proved in countless battles. The Union needs Texas, sir, and we need you. I hereby, with approval from the Secretary of War and other close associates, authorize you to recruit an army of 100,000 men, if such can be found, and save Texas for the Union. I promise you support from another 50,000 troops in our Army and Navy, which can land at Indianola.

Governor, you will be commissioned as a major general.

My knowledge of war is so inferior to yours, sir, that I hate to bring it up, as my battles during the late Black Hawk War came mostly against mosquitoes, although I did lose a pretty good horse. That said, Kellogg's Grove, though far, far from Horseshoe Bend or San Jacinto taught me one thing: *Dulce bellum inexpertis*!

Please, Governor, help us prevent seeing our country torn asunder.

My God bless you and our States. I anxiously await your answer.

Your humble servant,
Abraham Lincoln

Having read the letter aloud to the four men in the Green Room, Houston folded the letter. He happened to glance at the life-size oil-on-canvas that hung on the wall next to the fireplace. John Gadsby Chapman's portrait of David Crockett had been in the Capitol before Margaret, lover of heroes, asked that it be moved to their residence. It had never been Houston's favorite painting, but something struck him now that he had never noticed before. Crockett waved his hat as though bidding farewell. His eyes affixed on Sam Houston.

Quickly, Houston shifted his attention to the portrait hanging over the fireplace, the one of Andrew Jackson, a painting he liked.

"By God, Sam!" James Throckmorton thundered. "That's . . . that's . . . that's . . ." Throckmorton downed his whiskey, shook his head, and spoke again. "I oppose Secession as much as anyone here, but . . . by God!"

"There you have it, gentlemen." Turning away from the painting, Houston studied the men Giddings had delivered, the men who had crawled out of bed, dressed, and hurried to the governor's mansion at—he glanced at the clock—one o'clock in the morning. "I have asked you here for your counsel. Since I favor military rule . . . and by this I mean to listen to views, not battle . . . I want to hear from the youngest man present first. That means you, Epp."

Ben Epperson had arrived in Texas after statehood. A lawyer, he had tried and failed at politics, which turned out to be a blessing because he had succeeded at everything else. Houston always said, when the Baptists were out of earshot, that Ben Epperson was richer than

God. But the young man was lame in one leg. Now, he limped away from the liquor, saying: "Yes, damn it. Yes. When the President asks you to do something, by thunder, you do it." He quickly downed the whiskey. "Under your leadership, General, we could keep the Stars and Stripes flying over Texas."

That surprised Houston. Epperson had been born in Mississippi.

Houston turned to David Culberson, a lawyer from Alabama and a newcomer to Texas, having lived here for roughly five years.

The big man with fat cheeks, wild dark hair, and a mustache and goatee rose from the corner chair and grinned. "Not that you ever make a mistake, Governor, but I do believe I am younger than the honorable, and passionate, Mister Epperson." You could almost smell molasses and Georgia peaches when Culberson spoke.

Houston bowed. "Math was never my strongest suit, sir."

"That's all right, Governor. Mother always told me I was wiser than my years." The laughter left his eyes. "But Latin, sir, was never my strong suit. Those words President Lincoln wrote toward the end of that plea. What do they mean?"

"*Dulce bellum inexpertis*," Houston repeated. "War is sweet for those who have not experienced it."

The fire crackled as old George Paschal stoked the burning cedar in the fireplace. Culberson finished his drink and shook his head.

"We cannot prevent Secession, sir," Culberson said. "I certainly learned that . . . the hard way."

Newly elected to the Texas House of Representatives, Culberson had opposed Secession with such fervor that when Upshur County voted in its favor by more than ninety percent, he had immediately resigned his seat.

"But . . . ," began Epperson.

Houston's raised hand silenced Epp. David Culberson had the floor.

Culberson filled his huge lungs with air, and, exhaling slowly, shook his head. "Our neighbors have joined the Confederacy. Texas would be cut off from the rest of the Union. And, I think, despite Mister Lincoln's boasts of assistance, we are too far from the North to expect help." He raised his finger. "And as such, likewise we are too far away to see much blood shed on our native soil." He turned to refill his glass. "But . . ."—he paused to sip, before turning back to the men—"were we to accept the President's proposition, fire and sword would destroy our state, ourselves. Much horror would we witness. I respect Mister Epperson and his opinion, but I cannot, in good conscience, agree. The people of Texas have spoken, and quite loudly. I must stand with her, and with my neighbors."

"The people of Texas always speak loudly," Dr. James Throckmorton said without waiting to be called upon. "We wouldn't be Texans if we didn't."

Usually, such a statement would bring about a few chuckles, but no one laughed this night.

"I don't know if the United States can survive Civil War," Throckmorton continued. "But I know Texas cannot." His head shook sadly. "I treated enough wounded men in the Mexican War. I've seen enough men die in battle. I have to side with young Mister Culberson, Governor. Besides, you saw the numbers . . . how many Texans voted for Secession. We can't put together an army of a hundred thousand. I'm not sure we could put together an army of a thousand."

"Thanks, Doc." Houston walked to the fireplace, where George Washington Paschal continued jabbing the poker against the burning logs.

Paschal was maybe twenty years younger than Houston, but they had lived similar lives—Southern born (Paschal in Georgia; Houston in Virginia), teaching school, lawyering, and living with the Cherokees. Like Houston, Paschal had married a Cherokee woman, and like Houston, Paschal and Sarah had divorced. Sarah Paschal had followed the white man's law about divorce. Sam Houston and Tiana, however, had divorced the Indian way.

The stately-looking gentleman, with dark hair thinning on top but a full white beard covering his angular face, did not turn around, just stoked the fire as he said: "You can't do it, Sam." He removed the poker from the fireplace and set it in the stand. "You just can't do it." Then he turned, folded his arms across his chest, and looked at the others.

Eventually, all eyes fell on Sam Houston.

"I remember," he said, "back in January when I was doing my speechifying from the balcony of the new Shady Villa Hotel in Salado. Naturally, I'm preaching about the travesty of Secession and the carnage such an act might bring to Texas. It was not what I would consider a popular sentiment in Salado. And one old boy, he cups his hands and hollers . . . 'General Sam, we can whip them Yankees with cornstalks!' And I say to him . . . 'That may be true, but they have not agreed to fight with cornstalks.' "

The chuckles, he remembered, had spread like fire on that chilly day in Salado. In the library this night, he found only polite smiles.

Houston raised the letter to read again, but stopped. His head shook and he murmured once more: "Too late." He drew in a breath, and began crossing the room toward the paintings of Crockett and Jackson and the fireplace. Paschal stepped aside and found the Scotch.

"Gentlemen," Houston said, "I had resolved to act in this matter on your advice." With a sigh and a final glance, he tossed the letter into the flames. Watching it burn, he said, almost bitterly: "But were I ten years younger, I would not."

In the quiet house, Houston knew sleep would not come for him. He found the crate of books in the library, and fished out Virgil's *The Aeneid*. After settling into one of the chairs by the fireplace, he opened the book, and turned immediately to the passage, and read:

> The gates of hell are open night and day;
> Smooth the descent, and easy is the way:
> But to return, and view the cheerful skies,
> In this the task and mighty labor lies.

Exhaustion at last overtook him, but he doubted if he could make it upstairs and crawl into bed. Besides, as wound up as he felt, he would toss underneath the covers, disturbing Margaret's sleep. He thought about the letter he had just burned, and the advice he had heard. Glancing at the portrait of Andrew Jackson, and Chapman's painting of Crockett, he remembered those old fools at the barbershop. Should he have accepted Lincoln's offer? He tried to envision Major General Sam Houston leading men into battle. Would his men love him, or think him a coward as many had . . . before, and even after, San Jacinto.

Being an old man in these times was a hell of a thing.

He sighed. He cursed. He considered. He slept.

CHAPTER FIVE

Crockett

"Sam, Sam, Sam . . ."

The whisper startles Houston, who lifts his head to find a man in buckskin britches, moccasins, and a tailored green coat over a calico shirt turning away from the portrait of Crockett.

Houston blinks. Blood drains from his face. He gasps in terror.

It *is* Crockett.

The smiling figure hooks a thumb back at the painting. "When that ol' spiller of paint stuck his dandified dog in the corner yonder, I give up all hope of him makin' a picture that was worth lookin' at. I don't think it really captures me, but you must like it." The accent is as pure as Tennessee sour mash.

Houston cannot speak. He wants to run out of the Green Room but cannot rise from his chair.

Crockett turns back to the painting, shakes his head, and says: "All 'em artists got stuck on this one notion. You put a fellow in buckskins and that's all you need to do to make Davy Crockett a dashin' figure. Ask me, Chapman made me look like a circuit-ridin' sky pilot." Laughing, he moves to the ardent spirits, finds the jug, and splashes corn liquor into a glass. "If Chapman had any sense at all, he would have had me aimin' Ol' Betsy and shootin' that stupid, uppity pup of his."

Facing Houston again, Crockett steps toward the fireplace, and raises his glass at the other portrait.

"Now, this fellow here. He knowed what he was paintin'. This one, well, I look at Jackson and I say to myself, I say . . . 'Now this son-of-a-bitch here . . . he was somethin'. Somebody. He was a man.' Even when I hated his hard-rock heart, I admired the cocksure bastard. Here's to you, Andy, you ol' bastard."

He drinks, spies Houston, and laughs. "Oh, now I done hurt your feelin's, Sam. I spoke ill of Ol' Hickory, forgettin' how you was always lickin' his boots. Don't mind me none, ol' hoss. I'm just David Crockett, speakin' his mind." Crockett settles into the other chair facing the fireplace.

"Never figured I'd see the day when a cat got Sam Houston's tongue." Crockett drinks more of the clear, biting fluid without flinching.

Houston thinks: *I must be dead!*

Crockett shakes his head. "I know why you'd put up a likeness of Andy. You worshipped Ol' Hickory like Foster McIntosh loved 'em peach pies Missus Cassady baked ever' September in Lawrenceburg. But why a paintin' of me? Guilt?"

Houston drops the book onto the table. *No, I am not dead. I'm dreaming. I must be dreaming. A nightmare.* He squeezes his eyelids shut, hoping to wake to nothing but darkness, but, instead, Crockett's intense blue eyes bore through him.

A dream, Houston tells himself again. *Do not scare yourself witless. Soon enough, you will wake up. Soon cannot come soon enough.*

"Guilt?" Houston finally manages.

"Well . . ." Crockett sets the empty glass atop *The Aeneid.* "You did leave Bowie and me and all 'em others there to get chopped to pieces by lances, cannonballs, and Mexican lead." His head shakes. " 'Tweren't pretty, ol' hoss."

That bit of nonsense has followed Houston far too long. Now Houston's eyes flash and he leans forward, balling his fists. "I told . . . I ordered Bowie to blow up that mission. I told him it would be impossible to hold such a station with volunteers."

Crockett's laugh stops him. "And I bet Jim's final thought, if he had one, coughin' his lungs out as he was doin', was that he sure wished he had listened to Gen'ral Sam. Come to think on it, I was wishin' the same thing when 'em Mexicans boarded our vessel like Blackbeard's pirates."

Houston shakes his head. "You would tell a lie if the truth suited you better."

Rough hands clapping together like a thunderbolt, Crockett rocks back, laughing mightily. "I

60

am a professional liar, hoss." Straightening, the smile vanishes, and his voice drops to a whisper. "But I ain't lyin' now. Be glad Jim didn't blow up that station, as you call it. Be glad you dragged your feet tryin' to . . . ahem . . . rescue us avowed patriots. Be even gladder that you wasn't there with us."

Now Houston rises. "We were at Washington-on-the-Brazos, when a courier told us that Santa Anna had you trapped. And what did Robert Potter do? That idiot made a motion that the entire convention should march to San Antonio de Béxar."

Crockett's head shakes. "Now, hoss, might you have a wee bit of bias against ol' Potter? Since he didn't want you to get that job of major general of our new Texian army."

"What army? What I had did not even pass for raw recruits. Madness. Pure folly. Marching to Béxar would have destroyed everything we were working for."

Crockett grins again. "So, you let 'em Mexicans destroy us. And so you done what Sam Houston would always do, followin' the ol' advice I always give you and anybody else who'd even pretend to listen . . . be always sure you're right, then go ahead."

"I was right. Had I met Santa Anna at that time, the revolution would have ended. I had to plan. I made the right one."

"And we made the sacrifice. All hundred and eighty of us, includin' your friends." He's staring up at Houston, still smiling.

"I did what I had to do," Houston whispers, "for the future of Texas."

Crockett's next words caused Houston to sit down and sigh.

"And you done what Sam Houston done better'n anybody I ever knowed. You got drunk."

Such truth he cannot deny. Even in a nightmare. Certainly not to a ghost. Houston remembers that march. Five days after leaving Washington-on-the-Brazos, word reached Houston and his men that the Alamo had fallen, that Crockett, Travis, Bowie, Bonham . . . all those brave lads . . . had perished by the sword of Santa Anna.

From the corner of his eye Houston watches Crockett pick up the glass and head back for the liquor. When Crockett returns, he holds two glasses, one of which he extends toward Houston.

Though desperately needing whiskey, Houston shakes his head.

"That wife of yourn sure took the starch out of you, Sam." Crockett does not lower his offering.

"What would you know about it?" Houston says angrily. "You left yours in Tennessee."

Crockett sips from his own glass. "I would've come back to my honey-pie, hoss. 'Tweren't no permanent departure, you understand. But I seem to recall you leavin' one in Tennessee, too. And another in Indian Territory. C'mon, Sam. This is David Crockett talkin' to you. I've seen you throw up in people's front yards."

He cannot stop his hand from accepting the glass, and he lifts it with a shaking hand. He sniffs, then sends a curious look at Crockett.

"Ice water," Crockett says, and polishes off his liquor. "*Sans* the ice. Reckon it melted."

Houston drinks the water in two gulps, stifles a cough, and shakes his head. "I have made mistakes. Many that I would gladly cut off my arm to go back in time and do what's right."

"Not that arm, Sam."

Crockett nods, and Houston sees the ring on his pinky, the one his mother had given him so many lifetimes ago. His head raises and he studies Crockett.

"Am I right now, David?"

Crockett shrugs. "Who can say? Will anybody recollect and write about what we done at the Alamo? Maybe. Maybe not."

Houston recalls passing the old mission on his last trip to San Antonio. The sight numbed him: crumbling ruins, home to rats, wild pigs, trash, and decrepit old wagons and boxes.

"Will anybody remember what Sam Houston done?" Crockett continues. "What all he lost . . . ? Was it worth it, hoss, to you?"

Houston draws in a breath, exhales, and

63

says: " 'I would rather be politically dead than hypocritically immortalized.' "

"Sound words. Yourn?"

"David Crockett's."

"That's a good one. I wonder if I really said that. Here's another, hoss . . . 'Fame is like a shaved pig with a greased tail, and it is only after it has slipped through the hands of some thousands, that some fellow, by mere chance, holds onto it!' You'll hold on to it, my friend."

A silence fills the room, and Houston shivers from the cold. The fire is burning out, and he wants to rise, put another log on the fire, but again he cannot move. Fearing that he is dying, he looks at the specter in front of him, swallows down his fear, and asks: "Is it hard, David? Dying?"

Crockett gathers the glasses and returns to the liquor. "I wouldn't know, Sam." Liquid splashes into one of the glasses, and Crockett steps back. "But this I do know, hoss. Us gettin' killed, and Fannin's boys gettin' shot down like dogs at Goliad, well, we helped you latch onto that greased pig. Because us dyin', well, that give your boys somethin' worth fightin' for. Otherwise, you wouldn't have been able to whip Antonio López de Santa Anna along Buffalo Bayou." He sips, shakes his head, and laughs. " 'Course, you was a mite lucky, too, catchin' Santa Anna with his pants down and his pecker preoccupied."

Still drinking the corn liquor, Crockett stares up at the portrait painted by John Gadsby Chapman. "I don't know. Maybe it does look like me. At least I ain't wearin' one of them god-awful skunky-smellin' caps. 'Be always sure you are right, then go ahead.' You might've said that first, Sam. I might have stole it from you. Wouldn't surprise me none."

Houston feels the pressure lifted off his chest and shoulders, and he relaxes in the presence of this ghost, this dream, this . . . Crockett. "What surprises me, David," he says, "is that you somehow did not talk your way out of the Alamo."

Crockett turns only his head, and that beam in his eye causes Houston to relax even more. "Sort of surprises me, too," he says.

A silence fills the library, and Houston shivers. He wets his dry lips, draws a deep breath, and, after exhaling, says: "In all these nigh thirty years, David, many a night I have gone to bed feeling as though I let you, my friend, down. You were . . ." Words fail him. All he can think of to say is: "Unlucky."

Crockett shakes his head, and those always bright eyes of his turn serious. "Sam, Sam, Sam," he begins. "I did not live to see ever'thin' I fit for crumble into ruins. It be you, ol' hoss, who's unlucky."

CHAPTER SIX

March 19, 1861

"Sam, Sam, Sam . . ."

Houston looked at the specter standing over the table of liquor. When the phantom turned around, Houston blinked. It was not Crockett.

Margaret glared at him, and Houston frantically scanned the library, searching for David Crockett. Houston's eyes stopped at the first window. It was daylight. His heart raced, his hands felt clammy as though he were about to fight a battle. His throat turned drier than a limeburner's hat. He started to push himself up. *Where the hell is Crockett?*

"Well?" Margaret demanded.

The Aeneid lay on the floor, a circled stain from where Crockett had set his glass on the leather cover during the night. Confusion racked his mind, and he wet his lips.

"Well!" Margaret spoke sternly.

He sank back into the chair, and sighed. What did he expect to find? The ghost of David Crockett. Maybe Jim Bowie. Hell, why not Hamlet's father standing in front of one of the empty bookcases? Margaret walked to him, and he croaked like a parched frog: "I did not drink."

At least, he thought, *I don't think I did.*

He examined *The Aeneid* again. Doubt crept into his mind.

"I'm not accusing you of no longer being on the water cart, Sam." She held the glasses. He counted them—four. Four. Epp, Doc, Jim, Dave. He located the fifth, his, on the stand by his chair. Crockett's? There was no other glass, just the ghostly stain on the cover of the book by Virgil.

"Why did you not come to bed?" Margaret stood over him. "Too much coffee?"

He glanced at the pot and the cups—all clean— that had been brought into the library by Jeff long before his guests, real and possibly one imagined, had arrived after midnight.

"Too many memories." He sighed. "Troubles. Decisions. I feared I would waken you."

"Sam." She leaned against the chair where Crockett had sat last night. Her voice softened to one of concern. "Are you all right, my husband?"

He could barely nod.

"You are no longer governor," Margaret told him. "You are a civilian, and a civilian should not trouble himself with the troubles of the state, or our nation, be it South or North."

"The troubles of Texas will always be my concern," he said, his voice no longer trembling, but far from strong. Now he had to tell himself over and over again that it had only been a dream,

67

only a dream, but still he searched the Green Room for some sign of Crockett.

Ghosts. He tried to reason with himself. A sane man did not believe in ghosts. Only a lunatic would think a dream real. There was no David Crockett. Yet the Cherokees believed in visions, in spirits. As a child, his mother had told him ghost stories. And he remembered telling Deaf Smith that he had seen the fields of San Jacinto in his mind, clearly, and knew it would be the place in which Santa Anna would be crushed. He remembered Smith's reply: *Hell, Sam, I always knowed you was a mystic.*

Margaret placed the back of her hand on his forehead. "You are certain you feel all right?"

"Dreams," he told her. "Strange dreams and a tiring night."

She bent over and kissed the top of his head. "Wash your face and hands, go to the kitchen, and eat the breakfast Aunt Liza has made you. Clean your plate, Sam Houston. Then upstairs and take a nap. You are too old to be sleeping in a chair."

As she walked toward the door, he called her name. When she turned, he pointed toward Chapman's portrait of Crockett.

"We should have this returned to the Capitol," he said. "I mean, it cannot go to Cedar Point with us."

She glanced at the painting and shrugged. "Do you not think Clark would want it?"

"David Crockett would not waste his time with that dunderhead."

With wounds cleaned and wrapped, face shaved, Sam Houston stood in the entryway by the staircase, leaning on the crutch and directing his daughter Maggie and the slave Pearl as they lowered the oil landscape off the wall and to the blanket on the floor. Half-heartedly, he wished the girls might drop the painting in such a way that it would catch the corner of the table and rip the canvas.

They didn't.

"That's good work, girls," he told them. "Now . . ."

Someone pounded on the door. Houston stopped the curse on his lips. Pearl looked at the door, and then down the hall, hoping Joshua, Jeff, or Lewis might show up to take charge, but Houston started hobbling. "I will see to this," he said.

After opening the door, Houston gawked at Noah Smithwick, armed for bear.

At least, Smithwick came alone. Even better, no one passed down the street. In Austin, however, on a Tuesday afternoon, Colorado Street would not remain empty. Quickly Houston let Smithwick enter, and slammed the door shut.

"By God, man, what are you doing with . . . ?" Houston stopped himself. Pearl and Maggie gawked. Margaret, holding the hems of her skirt, came down the stairs, but paused on the landing. Her mouth fell open.

The lean man, with a face bronzed by years in the sun and eyes set too close together, held a rifle in his right hand, a shotgun in his left. He carried a Bowie knife sheathed on his left hip, two Paterson Colts tucked inside his waistband, and a Walker Colt—a revolver most people carried in a saddle pommel—holstered on his right hip.

"I got a hundred men waitin'," Smithwick thundered. "You give us the word, Sam, and, damn it all to hell, we'll get the Capitol back for you."

"Noah," Houston said. When the warrior took a moment to shift the tobacco from one cheek to another, Houston pointed to the open door to the library. "In there."

The wiry man moved like a catamount into the room, speaking as he walked. "Damn right. We'll shoot down Clark and anybody else who gets in our way. This ain't right, Sam. You know it. I know it. All of us know it. You just say the word, Sam. We'll make them sons-of-bitches pay the piper. I was with you in 'Thirty-Six, and I'm with you right now. So, you tell me what you want us to do and who you want me to shoot dead first."

"My word . . . ," Pearl whispered.

Houston did not know whether he should laugh or cry. He looked up the stairs at his wife, shrugged, and started after Smithwick. He stopped at the doorway, however, suddenly embarrassed by the crutch he used. So he held it out, and Maggie instinctively took it. Gathering his composure, Houston went into the Green Room, closing the door behind him.

First, he held out his hands and accepted the Mississippi Rifle, which he examined, approved with a nod, and rested against the cold fireplace. A good lawyer had to think fast on his feet. So did senators and governors and even presidents of republics. Even retired old legends.

"Noah," he said, "you tell the boys that I appreciate them. All of them. And I sure appreciate you, old friend."

"What they done was wrong, Sam," Smithwick said. "You know it. I know it. Law-breakin' sons-of-bitches."

"Yes, Noah, but . . . any man who would overthrow the law shall not learn that lesson from me."

Smithwick blinked his narrow eyes, and again shifted the tobacco in his mouth from one cheek to the other.

"That's from a speech I thought about giving the other day, at the Capitol," Houston told him. "But I decided to keep my damned mouth shut. I was going to tell those sons-of-bitches what they could do with their oath to this farce called the Confederate States of America. But I couldn't. We're too old for war, old hoss." *Old hoss?* He glanced at the portrait of Crockett, moved closer to Smithwick, and put an arm over the lean man's shoulder. "We're Texans. We are all Texans."

He remembered how he had stayed up the night before the Confederate leaders had shouted his name in the Capitol.

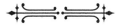

He had prayed. He had walked around this very room, and up and down the halls, door to door, pacing across the long rug—now rolled up against the wall beneath the painting in the entry hall—in his stocking feet. Back and forth. Back and forth. Thinking. Praying. Cursing. Plotting. And then that fateful morning, before heading to the office for what he knew would be his last day as governor, he had seen Margaret waiting for him at the foot of the stairs.

"Margaret," he had told her, "I can never do it."

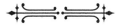

"Noah," he now said, "I can never do it. In 'Forty-Six, I went back into the Union with the people of Texas. Now I go with them, out of the Union. We stand by Texas, my friend."

Now, he wondered why he had even asked George Giddings to fetch those other men from a good night's sleep. He could not take up arms against fellow Texans.

"You ain't . . . ?"

Houston looked deeply into the old war horse's face.

"You ain't." Smithwick sought a place to spit, but the cuspidors had been removed. He did not swallow the juice, nor did he spit it onto the floor. "You ain't wantin' nobody to fi't with?"

"Gloom's before us, Noah," Houston said. "But Texas has spoken. Go home, Noah. Enough blood will be spilled directly. Let's not start it here."

He picked up the rifle, and walked to the library door, which he held open for Noah Smithwick. The warrior took the weapon, shook his head, and stepped into the entryway, now abandoned. Even Margaret had retreated upstairs.

Houston opened the front door, made sure the street remained empty, and walked outside. Smithwick followed, and quickly spit into the bushes. The battle-hardened Texan began whispering to himself as he descended the stairs and then turned back around.

"Bad days, Gen'ral," Smithwick said. "You sure you don't wants us to fi't with you?"

"Maybe later, Noah. But not now. Let's see how this all plays out."

"Hell," the fighter said. "Things ain't like they used to was, Gen'ral."

Houston wished Smithwick would get to his buckboard and disappear before someone— a reporter or, even worse, a member of the Confederate congress—saw him and his arsenal. Houston held his breath until Smithwick pitched both long guns into the back of the wagon, and climbed into the driver's box.

A phaeton passed him. A couple walked on the other side of the street, arm in arm. A horseman trotted down toward the Capitol. None paid any attention to Noah Smithwick as he released the brake and drove away. None paid attention to Sam Houston, soon to be exiled governor, standing on the front porch of the tall mansion.

CHAPTER SEVEN

March 31, 1861

" 'Hell is empty,' " he whispered to Margaret, " 'and all the devils are here.' "

"Hush." She took his arm in hers before leading him down the steps. "You should not swear on the Sabbath. You should not swear on any day."

"I was not swearing," he told her, "but quoting Shakespeare." Yet inwardly he cursed as he led his wife toward the caravan of wagons—some overloaded and listing so much, a strong gust might send them toppling over. Across the street waited the gawkers, staring, whispering, and a few shouting.

"Be gone, traitors!"

"Ignore them," Margaret pleaded.

He said nothing, though his insides blazed with fury.

Twelve slaves and the children waited by the wagons. Houston walked his wife to the yellow coach. He had ordered it back in 1843 from New Orleans—a double barouche with four seats and a double harness. The yellow paint was chipping, the doors squeaked when they were opened, and the damned thing never did much at keeping out dust, wind, heat, or cold. He had been ashamed when he had first seen it after the wagon arrived in Galveston, for he had expected a fine wagon that befitted a woman like Margaret, who had been chauffeured across Alabama in expensive, beautiful conveyances.

"I should get a new carriage," he told her.

"It is still 'tolerably genteel,'" she told him, using his words from so many years ago.

Lewis opened the door, and the slave and Houston helped Margaret inside.

"We goin' now Master Sam?" the old slave asked as he stepped away from the carriage.

"We're going." Staring off toward the Capitol's flagpole, Houston sighed. No Stars and Stripes flew this day, just that plain blue flag with the star in the center flapping in the wind. As he walked toward his own coach, the gatherers lining the sidewalk hissed.

Voices of young men in song grabbed his attention, and he stopped to find a group of men in mismatched uniforms marching down the sidewalk.

Then hoe it down and scratch your gravel,
To Dixie's Land I'm bound to travel.
Look away! Look away!
Look away! Dixie Land.

They shouldered muskets, fowling pieces, and even one hoe, but the man marching alongside them knew what he was doing, and wore an old uniform from the war against Mexico.

"Here comes your firin' squad, Sam Jacinto!" someone from the crowd barked.

Laughter rocked the line.

He stood, observing but not commenting. Ordered to halt, the young, pockmarked one with a Pennsylvania rifle that was taller than he was tripped over his brogans, knocking the kid in front of him off the curb while he dropped to his patched knees. Both quickly jumped back into line and stood in something that might have resembled attention. Their commander barked.

The people on the sidewalks turned their attention to the raw, young Texas militia.

Finally, the drillmaster, James W. Throckmorton, removed his Hardee hat with the purple ostrich plume, and grinned at Houston.

"General," Throckmorton said.

"Doc," Houston said.

They shook hands.

Houston pointed at the crowd. "They think you've come to shoot me."

After donning his hat, Throckmorton whispered: "They couldn't hit a barn door ten feet away."

"So you have joined the cause," Houston said.

The doctor shrugged. "My state," he said, "right or wrong."

Houston wondered if his face looked as gray as he felt.

"Cedar Point?" Throckmorton asked.

"Eventually," Houston said. "Margaret desires to see her mother, so we shall journey to Independence after stopping at Bastrop to see Sam Junior on our way there." Looking at the young Texas boys Doc Throckmorton would try to mold into soldiers, Houston saw his oldest son's face in all of them.

"I hope to see you in better days, General," Throckmorton said.

"Better days." Houston again shook hands with his old friend, and walked down the street to find Jeff waiting by his black top buggy.

The militia resumed marching, Throckmorton barked more orders, and the lads sang again, joined by the crowd.

I wish I was in Dixie, Hooray! Hooray!
In Dixie's Land I'll take my stand,
to live and die in Dixie.

The exiled governor's cortege began.

Two blocks later, Houston ordered Jeff to stop.

"Nash," he called out to the slave driving the wagon immediately behind him, "continue on!" He waved the first wagon past, and when the yellow barouche stopped alongside Houston's buggy, Margaret opened the door.

"We'll catch up," Houston told her.

She gave him a questioning look. Margaret had worn her best dress this morning, although she had shunned a hoop underneath her skirt for the comfort of the ride east. Her hair remained parted in the middle, with finger curls flowing from tucking combs of silver. She held a handkerchief in her left hand.

"Don't let Nash get in a hurry," Houston said, more to Lewis than Margaret. Asthma plagued his wife, and this March appeared to be going out like a lion instead of a lamb. To his wife he tried a reassuring smile. "I desire to show Jeff something," he explained. "We sha'n't be long. Likely we shall rejoin you before you have reached Bastrop."

"Very well, Sam." She closed the door.

After the other wagons passed, Houston pointed at the next street.

"Since we're both out of the office, Jeff," Houston said, "we have time on our hands. Turn there. I'll give you directions."

"Where we goin', Master Sam?"

"The Treaty Oak," Houston answered.

The cluster of oaks shaded Baylor Street near the Colorado River, and when Jeff stopped the buggy, Houston stepped down. He gripped the side of the wagon with his left hand and raised the cane Jeff had placed in the wagon with his right.

"The old capitol stood west of here," Houston said, "back when Texas was a republic. You see that tree yonder?"

"Yes, sir, Master Sam. Can't miss that one. Must be fifty feet high."

"Nearer sixty. That, Jeff, is the Treaty Oak."

The leaves rustled in the wind as Houston walked to the tree. Sensing that Houston wanted some time alone, Jeff stayed in the buggy. Houston entered the shade long before he came to the trunk, and, on a whim, paced off the distance of the diameter of the live oak's canopy.

"A hundred and thirty feet," he said, marvelling and breathing in deeply, trying to savor the fragrance of oak leaves in the spring. He circled the tree, stopping once to lean against it, then walked around it again before staring at a limb that had fallen during some recent storm. Groaning, his joints popping, he sat on the limb and leaned back, resting against the massive trunk. In the years before Houston arrived in Texas, folks said, Stephen F. Austin had met with Indians here to negotiate a treaty with the Tonkawas and Lipans. Reaching down, Houston began plucking leaves from the fallen branch.

He had heard that during a full moon Indians would gather leaves from this tree to brew a tea that would protect the warriors in battle. He let the wind carry the leaves toward the river.

Tilting his head, he looked at the limbs and leaves, and thought about John James Audubon.

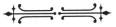

Back in the early spring of 1837, the naturalist and his twenty-five-year-old son had arrived at Galveston Bay aboard a revenue cutter, and Samuel Rhoads Fisher, then the Republic's secretary of the Navy, had brought the artist and his son to see Sam Houston. Naturally, as president of a republic barely one year old, old Sam Jacinto had left Houston City and escorted the Audubons across Texas.

He had watched the elder Audubon shoot many a bird, and Houston had felled a few, too. The artist proved such a marksman that Houston had quipped: "We could have used you at San Jacinto, sir." Old Audubon had proved quite a humorist, as well, for he had quipped back: "But had I shot Santa Anna dead, Mister President, where would you and Texas be today?"

Mostly, however, Houston had marveled at how deftly the artist could look at the birds he had killed and quickly sketch their likenesses—teals and ducks, herons and stilts, woodpeckers and sandpipers, spoonbills and buntings.

Houston had brought the Audubons here.

"How old do you think this live oak is, sir?" Houston had asked.

The naturalist had whispered: "Five hundred? Four? It should live hundreds more. It should never die."

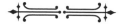

A blue jay began squawking from somewhere high, hidden by the green leaves and stout branches. Houston tried to stand.

"Hell's fires." He tried again. Then, sighing and cursing and thanking the Lord that Margaret was not here to hear his blasphemy, he waved Jeff over.

After the slave had helped Houston to his feet, Houston pointed the cane at the tree. "Jeff," he lied, "this is why I brought you over here. I wanted you to see the Treaty Oak."

The slave stared up at the massive oak in wonder.

"For hundreds of years, Indians have been coming here. For war councils and war dances. Weddings, I imagine. I've often wondered how many peace pipes have been smoked under its shade." He leaned against the cane. "It must be looked upon by those Indians as a holy tree."

"I reckon you's right, Master Sam. I seen me a lot of big trees in my life and all, but I ain't never seen nothin' as big as this one. How old you reckon it is?"

"A great naturalist I once knew guessed five hundred," Houston answered. "But I think it is as old as Eden."

They caught up with the caravan a few miles east of Austin, and followed the road that paralleled the Colorado River. Post oak, loblolly pines, and junipers replaced the buildings and civilization that was, or at least had once been, Austin. By the time they reached Bastrop County, they saw no one, which Houston had expected. For as long as he could remember, the only town in Bastrop County was Bastrop.

Over the past three decades, trees had been thinned out, mainly to help build Austin. Yet a man could still get lost in the thickets and hills, or drowned in the river. It remained a dangerous place.

Back in Texas's early years, Indians had kept settlers out of this promised land. Santa Anna's soldiers had been just as ruthless. After the Runaway Scrape, settlers had returned to the town of Bastrop to find nothing but ashes and charred ruins.

"You'll do no battle in Bastrop, Sam," Margaret told him as he helped her out of the yellow carriage. "Promise me."

"Battle whom?" Houston asked. Night had fallen, and the town slept.

"The citizens," she answered.

He laughed. "Bastrop was one of the few counties to oppose Secession, my darling. Yet you have my promise. I will battle no resident of this fine little town. Now, let us find our room in this hotel and sleep. It has been an arduous journey, and we have miles yet to go."

Only after Margaret had entered the hotel did Houston bite his lip.

No, he told himself, *no citizen will I fight here. But my son?*

CHAPTER EIGHT

April 1, 1861

Memories flooded him that morning, with neither rhyme nor reason, but firing out as random as rain.

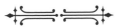

Sleeping with the baby beside him, while Aunt Liza tended to the infant's exhausted mother. Fathers knew nothing about handling babies, but his son had fallen asleep, and so had Houston. Now he woke up, and prayed to the Almighty that when he glanced at his son, the baby's eyes would remain closed. Seconds later, he found himself staring into the startling blue and wide-awake eyes of a newborn. *Lord,* he remembered saying, *you must sit on your throne and think how funny you are. But you ain't. . . .*

Exhausted again, but this time from the traveling on steamboats up the Mississippi, Ohio, and Cumberland Rivers, and arriving in Nashville to hear the terrible news that Death hovered over Andrew Jackson. "Go," Margaret told him, and Houston took Sam Junior with him, urging the buggy driver on with curses as they raced to the Hermitage— only to meet Old Hickory's doctor as he returned to town, and hearing the stunning news: "He was called to Glory an hour ago." Soberly, they continued to the Hermitage, to be greeted by a weeping Negress. Gripping his son's hand, he led the two-year-old down the hallway to the bedroom and opened the door. His son shivered from fright at the rare sight of seeing tears cascade down his father's cheeks. Houston lifted the toddler up and gestured at the white-haired corpse. "My son," Houston told the boy, "try to remember that you have looked upon the face of Andrew Jackson."

Reading the letter in Washington City and imagining the scene his wife described of Sam Junior's governess bringing the boy into the nursery in Huntsville to see his sister for the first time. "You swore I was getting a brother," Sam Junior told Margaret. "You promised." His mother and the hired teacher and helper laughed and shook their heads. "We thought the way she kicked and gave me fits," Margaret tried to explain, "she would be Andrew Jackson Houston." "Well," the almost-seven-year-old boy replied, "she ain't no boy." "No, she's Mary William Houston, but we, I think, shall call her Mary Willie." The boy pouted. "Still ain't no boy." Then, Miss O'Neal, the governess, asked Sam Junior: "Sam Junior, do you desire for us to send her back and exchange Mary Willie for something different?" And Sam shuffled his feet, frowned, and at length leaned forward to take a closer look. "I reckon," he said at last, "she'll do."

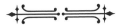

"A hearty brat," he remembered bragging about his first child, his first son, "robust and hearty as a Brookshire pig." Margaret always referred to him as "my baby."

Yet Sam Houston Junior could no longer be called a baby.

Leaning on his walking cane while standing on the porch of a recitation hall, Houston watched the boys—no, men—of the Bastrop Military Institute.

"Company, right . . . face! By file left . . . march!"

These cadets did not resemble the rag-tag lot commanded by Doc Throckmorton back in Austin. They looked, acted, and marched like soldiers—but Houston tried to tell himself:

Isn't that why I wrote a check for $230? Or was it because of the Latin, Greek, geography, mathematics, and other courses they forced these young men to study?

On the other hand, the Bastrop Military Institute did not look impressive—barracks, recitation halls, a parade ground, and a flagpole. Houston saw only Texas's state flag hanging limply; at least Colonel Allen had not raised that Bonnie Blue flag.

"Company, halt!"

They stopped with precision.

"Front."

They moved in unison to face Houston.

"General, what do you think?" Colonel Allen stepped onto the porch, and looked at young men in gray coats, blue pants, and black shakos. Bayonets affixed to muskets, and brass pinned on the uniforms gleamed in the morning sun.

"They march fine, Colonel," Houston answered, studying the young men. "But can they debate with erudition on the merits of Chaucer?"

"Sergeant?" Colonel Allen called out.

The baby-faced leader of the group needed no further prompt. Wheeling around, he barked: "Can any one of you ripstavers give General Houston a good talk about *The Canterbury Tales*?"

From the ranks came a hearty reply: "As quickly as Absolon can kiss Alisoun's ass."

Without grinning, Houston turned toward the commandant. "My compliments, Colonel."

"Thank you, sir. Would the general care to inspect the cadets?"

He did not want to move off the porch, but pride commanded him. "Indeed, I would, Colonel." He moved down the steps gingerly, pretending that he savored this chance to walk down the lines of young men. As he examined each musket, he complimented those cadets who kept their weapons spotless as well as those who did not. He did the same with his son, showing no favoritism, and after returning the musket to the last student, he returned to the welcomed shade of the roof.

"You have trained them well, Colonel," Houston said.

Allen's boot heels clicked and he bowed. "It is an honor to have you here, General."

"Might I have a few words with one of your cadets?"

"By all means, sir. Which one interests you?"

He scanned the boys, kept his eyes on the big one with the bent nose who knew Chaucer's "The Miller's Tale" and waited for the kid to crack a grin. Once that happened, Houston, feeling victorious, pointed to the strapping lad standing two cadets down. "That one looks like he should do."

"Cadet Houston," the sergeant barked. "Fall out."

• • •

The floorboards squeaked inside the recitation hall as Houston settled into a chair he pulled away from a desk. Shifting the cane from his right hand to his left, he nodded at his son.

That tall cadet looked sharp in his uniform. He remained at attention.

With a sigh, Houston shook his head. "If you don't want to sit, you can at least stand at ease."

Sam Houston Junior barked out—"Yes, sir."—and fell at ease.

Houston glared, and the young man quickly found a seat opposite his father. Now the old man grinned. "You always were fairly smart at some things," he said. Pain shot through his joints, but Houston refused to grimace in front of his oldest son, yet he shifted in the hard-bottomed chair and tried to find a position that did not rack his body with pain. He nodded at the window that faced the parade grounds. "Not as many students here this morning," he said. "Sick call?"

"The call to arms," Sam Junior replied. "Many have left. They say war is coming."

Houston sighed. "Yes," he answered, "I suppose it is."

"Sir," his son said, his voice cracking, "I would like to enlist, too."

Well, you knew this was coming, and you are prepared, Houston thought. His head shook.

"Now is the seed time of life," he said, "and the harvest must follow. If the seed is well planted, the harvest will be in proportion to it. You enjoy the classics they teach here, I pray."

The boy shrugged.

Houston sighed. "If only I had enjoyed an education of one year, I would have been happy."

The boy said: "In May, I will be eighteen years old."

"And three years later, you will be old enough to vote," Houston said sharply.

"I can enlist at age eighteen," his son reminded him.

Houston frowned. "With my permission." He waited a moment, letting his anger—no, it was fear—subside, and tried another approach. "When it is proper, Sam, you shall go to war . . . but only if such is in your heart. It is every man's duty to defend his country, but when the school session ends, your job, Son, will be dropping seeds of corn. We are not wanted, or needed, outside of Texas, yet soon we may be wanted, and needed, in Texas."

Tears welled in the boy's eyes, but he fought them down.

"Son," Houston said, "you will find that the Houston name is not well thought of in this Confederacy."

The silence turned chilly.

Change the subject, Houston told himself.

"Your mother trusts you will be home after the term ends."

"There is talk," his son said after a long while, "that Doctor Smith will form a company . . . to defend Texas."

Houston sagged at this news about Old Ashbel Smith, North Carolina-born patriot who had settled in Texas during the spring of 1837. Houston had bunked with the doctor, who had become surgeon general of the Republic's army, but Smith had been more than just some sawbones. Houston had sent him to negotiate with the French and the British. He had even sent him to work out a treaty with the Comanches. Houston trusted few men more than he trusted Doc Smith. Now Smith had also joined the Confederate cause.

"All I wish for you to do," Houston said, his voice soft now, "is to love and revere the Union. This is my injunction not just to you, but to all my boys. Mingle it in your heart with filial love."

"Yes, sir."

Houston shifted his cane and pushed himself to his feet. At best, he had fought his son to a tactical draw. At worst . . . ? "You should return to your studies," he said. "It is good to see you, Son. Your mother sends her love, and desires to see you as soon as the term ends."

"Sir?"

Houston stopped. The boy, now standing,

reached inside his blouse, and withdrew a folded piece of paper.

"Mary Willie's birthday is next week," Sam Junior said, and held out the paper.

Houston frowned. He had forgotten his daughter's birthday.

"Would you give this to her and send her my love?" The boy began rebuttoning his blouse.

Houston opened the card. *Margaret could draw beautiful pictures, and that was fine for a woman,* he thought. *But for a boy, and a student at Colonel Allen's academy, drawing seemed silly. To laze around and sketch scenes . . . Idle hands. Idle minds.* Yet he had to concede that Sam Junior inherited his mother's gift. As long as Houston could remember, his oldest son had drawn this and that—once on the wall of the foyer at their home in Independence. He admired what the boy had sketched: their old plantation home in Huntsville, Raven Hill, and a young girl—Mary Willie—in front of the gazebo.

This, Sam Junior had done from memory, and he had written a sentiment and birthday greetings below, which Houston did not read.

Folding the card, Houston sought out a pocket to keep it safe.

"Indeed. You have . . ." Try as he might, he just could not find any words of praise for a drawing. "You have a good day, Son. We will see you at Cedar Point in two months."

"Yes, sir." The cadet snapped to attention, nodded his farewell, and strode out of the log cabin.

For the longest while, Houston stood in front of the chair, looking out the open doorway at the parade ground. Those boys, cadets, young men, finished their morning drill and marched off to their various instructors to learn Greek, Latin, mathematics, geography, surveying, engineering.

Houston felt completely and totally alone.

CHAPTER NINE

Elizabeth

He has fallen asleep in the rocking chair by the upstairs window in their next roadside inn, *The Iliad*, Alexander Pope's translation, cradled across his chest. Stirring, and suddenly cold, he remembers the last verse he read before weariness and age had finally forced him to close his eyes:

> A barren island boasts his glorious birth;
> His fame for wisdom fills the spacious earth.

Someone spits, and he smells snuff. Margaret frowns upon all tobacco use, and Houston realizes he is being visited . . . again.

Margaret sleeps under the covers, turned away from him. The woman sits at the foot of the bed. She is just as Houston always remembers her.

Silver-streaked, coarse hair curled up in a bun, rail thin, hollow-faced, gripping the spit jar in rough, long-fingered hands. Her face is weathered, but her eyes burn full of starch. She wears a dress of blue calico, faded, frayed, and patched after so many years of washing, of working in the fields, of trying to bring up a

95

brood of kids with a husband long dead, gone and buried in Virginia. She wears scuffed brogans.

She lowers the jar. "Off your feed, Sam?"

"Ma." His voice cracks, and he loses sight of her from the tears, which roll down his cheeks as he blinks rapidly, fearing that this specter, this illusion, this dream will be gone when he can see again.

Elizabeth Paxton Houston still sits on the inn's bed. He sighs with relief. His wife does not stir.

"Never could hold you down, Son. You had your own mind. Your own ambition. What troubles you now?"

"My oldest boy," he tells her, as if in a normal conversation with a woman now dead for decades. But this, he tells himself again, is another dream, and he is not as frightened as he had been when Crockett came calling.

Elizabeth's face brightens. "My oldest never give me no troubles at all." Her grin reveals the mischievous thoughts of a younger girl. "Come to think on it, the next three wasn't no trouble, neither. The spit jar raises; she deposits more juice. "The fifth one, now, he sure was a handful."

He leans forward, listens. The spirit of Crockett had frightened him, but this illusion or dream, he prays, will go on for all of eternity.

"Couldn't get no work done out of him," Elizabeth Houston says. "Not in Virginy, and certainly not oncet we moved down to Tennessee. You tol' your boy this morn' that he needs to be droppin' seed, but I don't recollect you ever doin' much in the fields. So we put you in the store, and that proved even worser. Couldn't live with a roof over your head, it 'peared to us, but you couldn't live with no hoe in your hand, neither. I tried scoldin' you. I tried tannin' your hide with a willow switch. I even tried reasonin' with you, but you had your mind set. Often I wondered where you got 'em notions. Wasn't like me. Wasn't like your pa. You was your ownself. And it come to me, after this longest while, that that's what you needed to be."

Her head shakes; her smile widens.

" 'Course, it took some time for the Lord to help me see that." She spits again, wipes her mouth with the threadbare sleeve, and sighs. "Sure wished I'd learnt that sooner, because you sure aged me."

The wind blows through the open window. Outside, a hound howls.

Elizabeth continues: "First, you taken off fishin', then a-huntin'. You never cottoned to no schoolin' till you started teachin' chil'ren yourself. And that must've shocked all of Tennessee. Sure staggered me and your siblin's. You sure was a handful, Sam." She bursts out in laughter, then spits into the jar. "Handful? Bosh. That don't describe the half of it. You taken up with the Injuns. Just run off. Didn't ask me, didn't tell nobody, just up and tromped to the woods. I had to send your brothers after you, and you tol' 'em that you's just fine. We figured you'd get a-tired of livin' with the Cherokees, but they must have given you somethin' we sure couldn't."

What they gave him, he remembers in silence, was a father. And independence. And an understanding. Yet he knows to mention that would break his mother's heart. And he did that plenty in his early years.

"You gots a good boy, Sam. Make a fine man. Wished I'd been alive to hold 'im in my arms."

"I do, too." His mother died on Baker's Creek in 1831. He cannot remember the date. You tend to forget those things. Most people recollect the birthdays of their parents, but even Elizabeth always told her children that she didn't know, that she had been too young to recall or even consider the importance of such a date back when she had been born. The year? That she knew. "I was born in 1757," she would announce, "in Rockbridge County." Then she would wink and add: "Or so my folks claimed."

"You was livin' on your own when you was younger than your son is now, Sam. You was bored on the farm. Even more bored when we put you to clerkin'. Don't you recollect?"

Sitting back, he frowns. "But things are

different now, Ma," he tells her. "We live in trying times."

"Balderdash," she says. "It ain't no different bein' no parent today than it was sixty years ago or six hundred. And it won't be no different sixty years from now or six hundred. A ma worries herself sick over her chil'ren." She tilts her head toward the sleeping Margaret. "Your wife, she cried herself to sleep this night. Because she fears all the harm that might befall her oldest child. I done the same. I feared for all my children. Even you, 'specially you."

His head falls. "I must've been a burden."

"You'd come home," she reminds him. "Clothes odorous and full of holes. You'd return to pay your respects to your hard-workin' ma, and, Lord help me, I'd get you all fitted up so you could tromp back into 'em woods and live with 'em heathen savages. Till you come back to get yourself all duded up some more." She laughs. "You always wanted to be stylish, and Lord knows how many hats you gone through. That boy, he likes hisself a mighty fine hat, too. He's a lot like you, Sam. Not as tall. Nowhere nigh as big. And, thank Jesus and your wife, he don't look that much like you, neither."

She slaps her thigh, almost spilling the tobacco juice onto the rug, and laughs.

He smiles, too.

"Well, I'll give 'em red devils credit for one

thing. They taught you somethin'. On account, one day you come home, and I should tell myself that you ain't no little boy no more, that you's a man. Those Cherokees, they taught you responsibility. You says you're gonna pay off your debts, even get that job teachin' school."

"It didn't last," he tells her. He never could hold onto a dollar for very long.

"You remember that day, don't you?" she asks, and he shivers. He cannot forget.

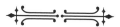

March of 1813. He's just twenty years old, no longer teaching school and in debt once again, and walking into Maryville with his friend, Bobby McEwen, when those soldiers of the 7th Infantry Regiment came marching—to the music of fife and drum—to the courthouse.

"His Majesty is stirring up the Indians and assaulting our citizens on the oceans," a fine-looking officer announces, "and we are at war with England again." He slaps a handful of coins on the top of an oaken keg. "A dollar bounty for new recruits." Then the soldier goes on to talk about all the foul things England is doing to these new United States, but it's the dollar that brings Bobby McEwen closer. It's the thrill that makes Sam Houston follow.

When Houston picks up a silver coin and starts to sign his name, Mr. Worth Lewallen snaps at Houston: "Has living with the Cherokees dulled your memory, boy?" Houston stops and stares at the big, balding man who lowers his corncob pipe. "Your father was Major Houston, and you're named after him. I served with honor under him in Morgan's Rifle Brigade."

Luther Chapman chimes in. "You're Major Houston's son, boy. You can't be no common soldier in the ranks."

Houston fires back: "And what have your craven souls to say about the ranks?" They blink. Mr. Lewallen drops his pipe. Mr. Chapman opens his mouth, but finds no words. "Go to, with your stuff. I would much sooner honor the ranks than disgrace an appointment."

"Who is that uppity lad?" Roscoe Fountain whispers just loud enough for Houston to hear.

"You don't know me now," Houston says as he dips his quill in the inkwell, "but you shall hear of me."

He signs his name with a flourish, and the captain of the 7th Infantry says: "And how old are you . . ."—he stops to read the name—"Samuel Houston?"

101

"Twenty," he answers, and the captain sighs.

Which is what brings him to his mother.

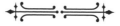

When he looks at the ghost sitting on the inn's bed, Elizabeth Houston picks up the story.

"You got tears in your eyes when you come ups to me that afternoon, sayin' that you can't fi't no British redcoats nor no Red Stick Injuns lessen I sign this paper that says I grants you permission to run off and fi't for your country and maybe get yourself killed. That's a hard thing to ask a mama to do, Sam. A hard, hard thing."

His heart is almost breaking as it did that March afternoon so many, many years ago.

"You didn't show it," he says.

She stares into the spit jar as though it's the form of consent she had signed all those decades ago.

"Wasn't no holdin' you back, Son," she says. "Never was. Twenty years old . . . no matter what the law, what the Army had to say, you was a growed man. Reckon you'd always been growed up. And, well, I was proud of you. But then, well, I was always proud of all my boys."

"Robert enlisted, too," he reminds her, remembering his older brother, who had fought against the British, too, though not in Sam's regiment. The Robert Houston who returned from war, however, would never be the same man. In 1820, Robert had put a pistol ball in his brain. The church in New Providence had denied a request to bury him in the cemetery, so poor Robert had been laid to rest along the road.

"I was proud of you both," Elizabeth says. "I reckon it was meant to be. Your pa fi't ag'in' the English. You was a lot like that man, and I loved him dearly. So when you come with that paper in your hand and 'em tears in your big eyes, that wasn't nothin' for me to do. Nothin' I could do."

She leans forward to say: "So I point to that Lancaster rifle that was over the door, and I tells you, I says . . . 'You take that musket, and don't you never disgrace it.' I says . . . 'You jus' remember that I had rather all my sons should fill one honorable grave than that one of 'em should turn his back to save his life.' And you gets up offen your knees and you goes to that door and you fetches that rifle. And so I tells you, I says . . . 'Go, and you remembers that while the door of my cottage is open to brave men, it be eternally shut against cowards.'" Her head bobs, and she dribbles more juice from the snuff into the jar. "I was puttin' up a strong wall, Sam."

Again, she dabs her eyes with the sleeves of her dress.

He stares at the slim band of gold on his pinky.

"That," he says in an unsteady voice, "is not all you gave me that day."

"No," Elizabeth says, "it ain't. An ol' long gun. It ain't important at all. You ain't got that musket no longer has you?"

His head shakes sadly. "No," he tries to say, but can only mouth the word.

"Don't matter. I tol' y'all that it was your Pa's musket, but that ain't altogether honest. I mean, I didn't tell no falsehood or nothin'. It was your Pa's, but it ain't like he carted that off ag'in' the redcoats. Your pa won that rifle from Ray Allen Howard. They'd bet on some horse race. Least, that's how your pa said he gots it." She raises a bony, ancient finger at her son's hand that grips the arm of the rocking chair.

"That ring yonder," she says. "That be the most important thing."

"It is," he whispers.

"Don't you never forget what it means," she tells him, as she had told him on that blustery March afternoon back in Tennessee.

"I won't," he tells her. "I haven't."

She straightens. "I'd say you up and tried to forgets it a time or two or thirty."

He only partly succeeds at smiling. "I reckon so," he tells her.

"It's all right, Son. You remembered, for the most part. I'm still proud of you. You done good. And you've brung up a slew of good children. You just remember, Sam. God has his hand on you. God's always had his hand on you."

He lifts his head, sniffles, and releases the tight grip on the rocking chair's arms.

"You know what that day was?" Elizabeth asks.

Uncomprehending, he merely stares at his mother.

"That day? Back when you come to me with that paper I had to sign to let you go off and fi't and win all that glory and fame and honor and make a name for yourself?"

He can only guess. "The Ides of March?"

Her laugh sounds, as it always did, like a braying donkey, and she again almost topples the spit jar's contents, this time on the quilt.

"You and all 'em books you was always readin'. No, this ain't about Julius Caesar. It's about you. It's about me." She reflects, and, as tears fill her eyes again, she looks at her brogans. "'Bout ever' mama and papa that ever lived, I reckon."

A long while passes.

"It was the hardest day of my life," she tells him.

He lets this sink in, and another eternity passes before he can find the words to speak.

"You did not show it," he tells her.

"Like as not, you won't show it, neither, when it's your turn." She looks over her shoulder and stares at the sleeping Margaret. "Or hers. But it's somethin' ever' parent gots to do. You and her won't like it none. No one ever does. I sure didn't.

105

But there comes a time when you just gots to . . . let go. You gots to tell yourself that your young 'uns, well, they've all growed up on you. They've become a man, their own man, or a woman, full-growed. Gots their own thoughts, their own ideas, their own roads to travel. And you gots to lets 'em go. Live their own lives. Hope and pray that they turn out better'n you. And you gots to tells yourself that you done your best."

The rockers squeak as he leans forward and studies his mother.

"Sam'll be a good boy," she tells him. "No, that ain't right. He was a good boy. He's a good man now. But you gots to let him be his own man."

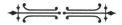

His eyes close, and he sees his son drawing stick figures on the foyer wall, and hears his own voice as he explodes and threatens to tear the hide off the boy's buttocks until Aunt Liza and Margaret rescue the boy and Lewis begins a desperate attempt to clean the wall. And then he sees the image of Sam Junior, maybe five years old, finding a cigar left burning in his father's ash tray and puffing away, his face turning green but refusing to remove the cigar. And again Houston is roaring, demanding that he will make the boy finish the damned cigar no matter how sick he gets. Until Margaret is telling him: "It's your own fault, Sam. He sees you smoking and he wants to be just like you." That staggers him, and he calmly takes the cigar from Sam Junior's trembling hands, and lets Margaret take the now gagging boy into her arms.

"Well," he tells his wife, and their son, "he will never see me smoke another."

And Sam Junior did not.

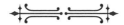

When his eyes open, Elizabeth Paxton Houston no longer sits on the bed. He bolts out of the chair, turning to the door, still closed, back to the bed, where Margaret remains asleep. He races to the window, as though this ghost, this dream, this hallucination has taken off toward the street and that he might catch one final glimpse of his mother, dead nigh thirty years.

She has vanished, and Houston chokes out a sob.

He gathers himself, and moves to the bed, setting *The Iliad* on the nightstand, and pulls back the quilt, blanket, and sheet. After blowing out the lantern, he crawls under the covers.

This night, he slides closer to Margaret, and puts his left arm over her shoulder. Then, as his wife had done earlier in the evening, Sam Houston cries himself to sleep.

CHAPTER TEN

April 3, 1861

As the train of wagons crawled through the woods road—moving slowly to keep the dust to a minimum and protect Margaret from an asthma attack—Houston asked suddenly: "Jeff, do you know what dreams mean?"

The slave, holding the lines expertly, shot his master a confused glance. "How's that, Master Sam?"

"You people," Houston answered irritably, "know about such things better than we do."

"You people, Master?" The young black man looked troubled.

"Negroes," Houston explained. His mood had been foul all day, and as they approached the town of Brenham, that feeling turned even sourer. He knew what awaited him in Brenham. Last night, he had burned the note left for him at the inn.

Talk yer treaSon in Brenham, huston,
& youll nevR talk nomore

"I dream, Master Sam," Jeff said. "Don't know what they all mean sometimes. Sometimes,

I'm happy with 'em. Sometimes, they scares me somethin' awful. Sometimes I don't dream nothin'. You havin' bad dreams, sir?"

"I know of dreams," Houston said. "I know of visions. I saw the plains at San Jacinto clearly, long before I ever led my troops there into battle."

Yet seeing San Jacinto was one thing. Having dead-of-night conversations with Crockett and his mother? That could land a man in an asylum. "But lately . . ." He had not told Margaret about these visits from the past. He wasn't certain he desired Jeff to know.

"You must not run off and tell my wife what I am to tell you," Houston barked. "You tell her or Aunt Liza or Aunt Martha . . . you even let on to Lewis or Joshua or anybody . . . and I'll lay welts on your back that will take a month of Sundays to heal."

"Yes, sir, Master Sam." Jeff trembled.

Houston sucked in a deep breath, and slowly exhaled. Turning away from Jeff, he stared at the passing trees.

"I did not mean that, Jeff," he said at last. "It's just . . ." The wagon hit a hole, forcing Houston to grab a tight hold to keep from tumbling about. He shifted to a spot in the seat slightly more comfortable and let out another heavy sigh. "The dead have visited me," he said.

"That don't seem like no good dream, Master Sam. Sounds more like a nightmare."

"No," Houston said. "Not a nightmare. Not a bad dream. Maybe not even a dream at all."

"How that, sir?"

"A visit." He stared into Jeff's face, trying to read it, but the slave revealed little.

"A visit?"

"David Crockett, some weeks back," Houston said. "Last night . . . my long-departed mother."

"You mean like a haint?" Jeff asked.

Houston shrugged. "Hobgoblin. Specter. Ghost. Apparition. Spirit." He managed a smile. "Or maybe the visions of a raving madman."

Jeff kept his eyes on the team pulling the carriage. "My mammie once told me how she saw this wraith right after my baby sister died of the fever. Said it was that little girl, and she was smilin', but that was a good thing. Not scaresome or nothin'. That Mister Crockett or your mama. Was they somethin' like one of 'em wraiths?"

"I don't know, Jeff." Irritable again. "Forget I mentioned it."

"You might go an' asks Aunt Liza. She knows more 'bout such things than me."

"Forget it," he barked again. They reached the outskirts of Brenham, and he had more important matters to consider than wraiths and lunacy.

As the slaves carried the luggage into the hotel, Houston crossed Alamo Street and stepped onto the town square. A crowd had gathered around the

110

new depot to marvel at the 4-4-0 locomotive—the Washington County Railroad's lone engine, black smoke puffing out of that upside-down-bell-shaped stack. The Washington County Railroad—all twenty-plus miles of track—had finally reached Brenham. Yet Houston had seen his share of trains in Washington City. What he stared at now was the flagpole.

Someone had chopped it down.

Sighing, he looked up at the courthouse and saw a blue flag hanging down from the rafters. Another flag flew from a pole nailed to the façade of Jack Gibbs's Grocery.

"You gonna speak today, Gov'nor, ain't you?"

Houston turned to find old Chic Gaddy standing with a string of seven or eight catfish in his left hand. Grinning at a familiar face, Houston shifted his cane to his left hand and held out his right.

"Fish fry, Chic?"

The old man shrugged, shaking Houston's hand.

"Where are they biting?" Houston asked.

"Got these at Hog Branch."

Houston admired the catch. "That's a nice one there. Must weigh eight, nine pounds."

Gaddy shrugged. "Would've weighed even more," he said, " 'cept she laid her eggs, my guess, a couple days back."

Houston grinned, but Gaddy persisted: "You

got to talk today, Gov'nor, let 'em all know where you stand, what you done."

"I'm retired, Chic," Houston said. "Perhaps I can drown a worm with you sometime soon."

After shaking hands with the old fisherman again, Houston returned to the hotel, using his cane, stopping at the edge of the square. Men had gathered on the boardwalk in front of the hotel. Houston brought the cane up, holding it as one might for defensive purposes, waited for a buckboard to pass, and crossed Alamo Street, prepared to do battle. He stopped just a few feet from the wall of men.

"You ain't speakin' here, you damned traitor," one of the men said.

"Yes," he said, "I am." Still stubborn, or foolish enough to let a bunch of b'hoys force him to make a stand. "I shall make my position clear from atop the stump that once was a flagpole." He fished the watch from his pocket. "In an hour and ten minutes." Sliding the watch back into his coat, he plowed ahead. The sea of men parted, and Houston entered the hotel.

He did not tell Margaret what had happened, and she knew better than to ask. Instead, he sat at the desk in the room and wrote a letter to his son.

I enjoyed the chance to visit with you and trust you are well. Your card for Mary

Willie I keep to present to her on the Eighth, and I know she will be delighted and will praise you in her own words, in her own hand.

You will have a veritable list of chores when you return to Cedar Point, and I know you shall do a wonderful job as overseer. Be industrious, Sam. Keep the hoes in the corn, and keep them down. See to the goats and our other stock. If it becomes too wet to work the corn, then put up a new pen for our cows . . . and one for the goats. Keep the hands busy.

He stopped, frowned, and dipped the pen in the well.

Or better yet, my beloved first child and oldest son: Do what you think best. I intend to be satisfied with whatever you may do.
Your devoted father,
Sam Houston

After sealing the envelope with wax, he told his wife that he had a meeting to attend, and moved to the trunk. He donned his leopard skin vest, and found a rakish hat to wear.

"What do you think, Margaret?"

She looked, smiled a forced smile, and said: "You will knock spots off them."

He grinned, walked up to her, and kissed her firmly on the lips. "Your reassurance will do me good, Missus Houston." He stepped out of the room, closed the door, withdrew the Navy Colt from his coat pocket, checked the caps, and slipped the revolver into his waistband at the small of his back. Readjusting his coat, he began the descent.

He had expected a turnout—the reason he had given the fine citizens of Brenham more than an hour to gather—and slid between saddled horses tethered to the hitching rail to get onto Alamo Street. As he crossed the street, he heard the hisses and curses.

"You try your damnyankee talk and you'll never speak again," someone said.

A tomato splattered in front of his boots.

He saw the stump of the flagpole, but then it vanished. This time, the sea of armed men would not part.

So, he stopped and waited.

"Put him out!" a voice roared. Several burly men hoisted a rough-cut tie from the new railroad.

Well, he thought, *men have tried to run me out on a rail before.*

"Don't let him speak!" cried another.

A gun popped, and he caught the odor of gun-smoke.

"Kill him!"

A man brushed against him, and Houston stiffened, but did not reach for the .36. To do so, he feared, would lead to bloodshed, and there were many more of them than there were of him. Still, he was Sam Houston, and refused to cower. "I am here to have my say," he said.

"We're part of the Confederacy now, Houston," another man said, "and you ain't got nothin' to say to us."

That man suddenly flew forward, landing against the big cuss who had fired his heavy single-shot pistol just moments early. A man stepped into the small patch of grass not covered with men. That man held a Walker Colt in his hand, the hammer at full cock, and his index finger touching the trigger. He wore a long gray frock coat, ribbon tie, and straw hat. Houston knew the planter from just outside of Brenham. Hugh McIntyre was no friend of Sam Houston.

"Listen up!" McIntyre bellowed. "I and a hundred other friends of Governor Houston have invited him to address us!" That was a lie. Houston did not have a hundred friends in Brenham anymore, and the planter had never been among Houston's allies. "You know me, boys, and you know where I stand, and it's not with Sam Houston. Ask me, I say the governor ought to have taken that oath to the Confederacy and accepted the situation. But he didn't. He thought otherwise, and that's his right as a Texan."

Hearing the creak of leather, the lean planter whirled and aimed the massive .44 into the crowd. A mustached face paled, and the man slowly raised his hands away from his waistband.

McIntyre went on. "This is Sam Houston. Governor. Senator. President of the Republic. There is no other man alive who has more right to be heard by the people of Texas."

He stepped in front of Houston and said— "Follow me, Governor."—and this time the sea of homespun, wool, and duck parted, and Sam Houston soon stood on the stump, with McIntyre, still brandishing the Walker Colt, at his side.

"Now my fellow citizens," McIntyre said, "give the governor your close attention." He waved the .44 at the more rowdy element. "And you ruffians, keep quiet, or I will kill you."

With that introduction, Hugh McIntyre stepped aside. He lowered the revolver, but not the hammer.

Clearing his throat, Houston began: "We hear the Latin maxim a lot these days. *Vox populi, vox dei.* The voice of the people is the voice of God. The Whigs used that back in the early Seventeen Hundreds. The archbishop of Canterbury used it centuries before. Sam Houston has heard the voice of the people of Texas." He spoke of himself in third person, which he had learned

116

from Cherokees. Indians, of course, spoke in third person out of politeness, which never had been among Houston's talents. "But the *vox populi* is not always the voice of God, for when demagogues and selfish political leaders succeed in arousing public prejudice and stilling the voice of reason, then on every hand can be heard the popular cry of 'Crucify him, crucify him.' " He studied the faces of the nearest men. "Then," he said, "the *vox populi* becomes the voice of the devil, and the hiss of mobs warns all patriots that peace and good government are in peril."

No one spoke, not even in a whisper.

"Civil war is inevitable." He shook his head with a mirthless laugh. "Gentlemen, there is nothing civil about any war. Especially the coming one. When the tug of war comes, it will indeed be the Greek meeting the Greek. Fellow Texans, this fearful conflict will fill our fair land with untold suffering, misfortune, and disaster. It will be stubborn and of long duration, and the soil of our beloved South will drink deep the precious blood of our sons, our brethren."

They did not believe him. He could read that in most of their faces. He shook his head. Soon, they would know he spoke the truth here tonight.

"You should know that Sam Houston cannot," he said, "nor will Sam Houston, ever close his eyes against the light and voice of reason. But the die has been cast by your Secession leaders, whom you have permitted to sow and broadcast the seeds of Secession, and you must ere long reap the fearful harvest of conspiracy and revolution."

It felt strange as he stepped away from the stump and made his way through the silent crowd, leaving the courthouse and crossing the grass on the town square. Once, this had been his country, but no longer. What had become of his people and his friends? Just a few months ago they had been driven by Providence's hand; now fear and hatred ruled their emotions. Having seen specters of patriots and family long deceased, Houston worried that he might be losing his mind—but these men, these Texas planters and merchants and industrialists, they were the ones truly mad.

Chapter Eleven

May 10, 1861

Independence became strange to Houston, too. As in Brenham, men had taken a hatchet to the flagpole, but the citizens here had failed to remove the pole, or the Stars and Stripes, which now lay trampled, half-buried under leaves, mud, and weathered chewing tobacco.

He longed for the old days.

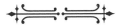

For that day in the fall of 1853 when he had led Margaret, the children, the slaves, and his wife's mother, Nancy Lea, to Independence. Having been re-elected to the U.S. Senate, he had bought a house in town—to allow Sam Junior a better education at Baylor's school—and rented their home in Huntsville. . . . Watching Sam and Nannie walk down the oak-lined avenue to school, and sending one of the slaves with pails to the children for lunch. . . . That June day in 1854 when, although Houston had been in Washington City working on behalf of those New England preachers who protested the

Kansas-Nebraska Act, Andrew Jackson Houston came into the world. . . . The day Houston had been baptized and how lovely Margaret had looked. . . . And those evenings when Margaret and he would walk over to her mother's house, to sip coffee and converse lightly until Nancy Lea would bring up her impending death, and then show off the metal coffin she had ordered from New Orleans.

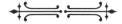

He walked with Margaret across the Baylor University campus. Anson Jones had been president of the Republic back in 1845, so Jones garnered the glory of signing the act that established the Baptist college. Yet Houston had donated $5,000 to start that ball. Back in 1855, school officials had separated the university into Baylor University for men and Baylor Female College for women. Now, those two schools feuded so much that Rufus Burleson, the preacher who had baptized Houston and now headed the men's college, and Professor Horace Clark, in charge of the women's school, threatened to tear the institution asunder. Rumor had it that Burleson would take the men's university to Waco.

Another Civil War, Houston thought.

They had passed the Baylor Female College,

perched atop a small hill four blocks away, in the yellow carriage. Young girls in hoop dresses moved outside the commanding building that stood three stories high, made of yellow limestone, and with a cupola atop—alive, vibrant, and young—and no Bonnie Blue flag waving in the sky. But here at the men's school, Houston saw few boys, just balding, white-haired Rufus Burleson making his way from the brick building toward Houston and Margaret.

"It is good to see you both," the preacher said after shaking Houston's hand and kissing Margaret's.

"Where are all your students?" Houston asked. "Studying, I hope."

Burleson's head shook. "What few we have left, perhaps. Yet most of the boys have gone home. To volunteer for a militia or whatever they are forming in these small towns across Texas." He let out a sigh. "They fear their chance of glory, of seeing the elephant, that the war itself will be over before Independence raises a company of patriots."

Houston's home here had sat deep off the street, with a fine apple orchard and a cool spring, but they no longer owned the log cabin, so they stayed with Nancy Lea.

Who never liked Sam Houston one whit.

Yet Houston did have to thank his mother-in-law for one thing. If not for Nancy Lea, he likely never would have met Margaret. His memories carried him back to that May day in 1839.

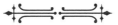

On a visit to Nashville, after finishing his first term as president of the Republic of Texas, he stopped in Mobile, Alabama, and found his way into a tavern. Over a lot of rum, he befriended Martin A. Lea, who suggested that his mother, a widow, might be interested in investing in property in the new republic.

"And who oversees her investments?" Houston asked.

His new friend almost coughed rum out of his nose. "You will find Mother can handle her own affairs, Mister President."

At a strawberry festival, this striking girl in a beautiful green dress caught his attention while he sipped a cordial and admired the brilliantly colored flower garden. The girl brought a pair of glasses that hung around her neck up to her face, briefly studied her admirer, and then, laughing at something a redhead said, took the trail through the flowers.

"When I sold the Cane Break, I learned that real estate is the best investment anyone can make," said the Widow Lea, interrupting Houston's thoughts, and he forced himself to turn away from the beautiful girl disappearing in the flower garden. He smiled at the widow. "But that is in Alabama. Tell me of this Texas."

He piled praises upon his republic. She stopped him when he mentioned cotton.

"The market for cotton is fickle. Like a whiskey drinker's whims."

"In Alabama, perhaps," Houston said. "But in Texas, cotton is gold."

When they finished talking, Houston walked to the garden and waited with Martin Lea. At length, Margaret reappeared with her red-headed friend, and Houston allowed Martin to introduce him to his sister. Martin had the decency to escort the redhead—Houston couldn't remember her name, or even what she looked like beyond that carrot-colored hair—for punch and sugar cookies, and Houston had been bold enough to take Miss Margaret Lea on a stroll through the garden.

Before they reached the gardenias, he had fallen in love.

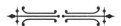

That evening in Brenham, he walked back to the flagpole to give yet another speech. The crowd of men, and quite a few women, gathered on the square, but he saw no guns among them. In fact, most appeared to be a handful of Baylor students and old men. No need for fire and brimstone. Living in a Baptist town, the people of Independence got enough of that at Sunday sermons. He told them that Sam Houston—using the third person again—held no ill will to those who had kicked him out of Austin, and whether or not Sam Houston had been treated unjustly no longer mattered. He told the few young men that differences must be set aside, and he told them that if, indeed, they did fight, then they must follow orders.

"I have been a soldier," he said with a smile, moving to a more conversational tone with the lads. The boys grinned back. "I know a few things, such as the value of subordination and discipline."

He paused, for the Reverend Burleson hurried across the street, his coat over one shoulder, and a piece of yellow paper flapping between his fingers in his left hand.

The crowd turned to see what commanded Houston's attention, and he stepped across the fallen flagpole, careful still not to step on the already desecrated American flag. The old preacher stopped running, his chest heaving and his face peppered with beads of sweat, and walked the final few rods.

"God have mercy on us all," the Baptist minister said. "They have fired upon Fort Sumter in South Carolina." Several of the gatherers gasped. "War," Burleson said, "has begun."

"When did it happen?" someone asked.

Houston took the paper from the old man's hands and began reading it.

"Last month," Burleson answered.

How many times can a man of my years endure a breaking heart? Houston thought, returning the telegram to the reverend.

"What do we do now, General?" a blond-headed boy said.

"Follow your heart," Houston answered. "The time has come when a man's section is his country. I stand by mine."

That evening, for the umpteenth time, he drank coffee with Nancy Lea and Margaret, listening to the former babble and watching the latter work her needlepoint, until Nancy Lea suggested they take a walk.

As always, she led them down the same path, taking the well-worn trail behind her house, across the street, and into the churchyard. Nothing could be called fancy about Independence's Baptist church. There was no steeple. In fact, inside you would not even find a stove. Which did not matter because Nancy Lea never led them into the church. She stopped in front of the limestone-plastered tomb, and pulled open the iron door.

"I'll be here before you know it," she said. "In my metal coffin. It wears on a body, getting old, but it's comforting knowing where you'll pass eternity till the Lord calls my name on Judgment Day."

Houston nodded, as he always did, without sincerity.

"Varilla and Antoinette and you, child . . ."— she nodded at Margaret—"you'll be here, too. It's big enough. I spent enough money so we'll all have a place of rest."

And, repeating the ritual she performed every week or so, she closed the door and stared at Houston.

"There's room enough for me and my daughters," she told him. "But nary a husband."

When they entered their bedroom, Houston leaned his cane in the corner, and sank onto the bed. Margaret removed the tucking combs in her hair, and her eyes looked at him through the reflection of the mirror.

He had been thinking about this for days, but knew not how to say it. So she said it for him.

"You would like to return to Ben Lomond."

When they had settled at Cedar Point on Trinity Bay twenty years ago as newlyweds, Margaret, ever the romantic and lover of heroes, renamed the cabin from a line in one of Sir Walter Scott's poems.

"Your mother will throw a conniption," he told her.

"Which sha'n't be her first." Margaret turned. "Nor her last."

He began to tug off his boots, still grinning, and his wife turned back to the mirror.

"Of course"—she removed her necklace—"we could always take her with us."

Seeing his reaction, Margaret laughed.

CHAPTER TWELVE

May 12, 1861

He did not leave immediately for the coast.

Margaret wanted to register the girls—Nannie, Maggie, Mary Willie, and Nettie—at Baylor Female College. It was a fine school, and, having her granddaughters around would also ease Nancy Lea's anger at being abandoned again.

That morning, Houston asked Jeff to drive him over to Washington-on-the-Brazos. It lay along the La Bahía Road, high on the bluff overlooking the confluence of the Brazos and Navasota rivers, which ran high this day. The air smelled of fresh rain and wet grass. Houston had not been here in four or five years, back when the town boomed. But the residents had rejected the chance to get a railroad. He recalled the editor of the Washington *American* editorializing: "We are a river town, and we shall and must support our steamboat brethren." Fools had reaped what they had sown. Today, Washington-on-the-Brazos looked like it had during the Runaway Scrape—abandoned.

"Over there." Raising his cane, Houston frowned as Jeff guided the carriage toward the crumbling, weathered building—almost hidden

128

by an overgrowth of trees, brambles, and brush. Yet they were not alone, for Houston detected a mule-drawn buckboard close to the building, and a bearded man in a muslin shirt, sleeves rolled up on his massive arms, slops over his pants and shirtfront.

When Jeff set the brake, Houston handed him his cane and commanded: "Wait here."

Boards lay in the back of the wagon, and the man knelt on the ground, struggling with a hammer to remove another plank from the old building. The stranger looked up, keeping the hammer ready as a weapon.

" 'Morning," Houston greeted.

The man spit tobacco juice and nodded.

"What are you doing?" Houston asked.

"This your property?" the stranger asked.

Houston's head shook. "No. I always thought maybe it belonged to the people of Texas."

"Well." The big man went back to work on the stubborn lumber. "I happen to be a people of Texas, and the winds knocked the roof offen my cabin. Ain't seen nobody on this here property in a coon's age, so I figure it rightly belongs to anyone in need." The end of the wood finally gave way, splitting a bit, and Houston caught the scent of turpentine. He would not want such a tinderbox as his roof, but he smiled.

"I suppose you're right," he said. "Let me help

you." He moved to the other end of the wood, and felt the dampness of the dew on his knees as he tugged on the siding.

"You sure you up to this, old-timer?" The stranger rose and moved toward Houston.

No, Houston thought, and grunted.

"Why don't you get your boy yonder to help?" Houston lifted his head as the big man pointed his hammer at Jeff, who was sipping from a canteen while sitting in the wagon seat.

"Work never hurt a healthy man," Houston growled, wiggled the wood, tugged harder, and felt splinters dig into his palms.

"You need this here hammer," the big man said.

"No." Strength came from deep inside Houston—maybe bottled up from all the rage—and the siding came off, almost knocking Houston onto his buttocks.

"Criminy," the stranger said. "You strong for an old coot."

Houston laughed, and helped carry the wood, sliding the three pieces, including the one Houston had helped remove, into the wagon bed.

"That ought to do it." After tossing the hammer onto the wood he had stolen, the stranger offered his hand. "I'm much obliged, stranger."

Houston liked the hard grip. The man pulled out a plug of tobacco from his stained overalls. "Chaw?"

"Thanks." Houston tore off a mouthful and

worked the apple-cured tobacco. "The name's Houston," he said.

Which meant nothing to the wood-thief.

"McCutcheon." The stranger slipped the quid back into the pocket of his slops. His head tilted toward the river. "Brother Leo and me got us a cabin 'bout a mile 'cross the ferry. He's doin' the plowin'. My name's Wilbur. Leo and me come from Alabama 'bout five months ago."

"Call me Sam." Still no recognition. "Welcome to Texas," Houston said, but McCutcheon had already turned away to climb into the wagon.

Houston did not watch him go. He went to the dilapidated building, peering first through the small window. No glass panes, only a dusty homespun curtain, which he pushed aside, catching the scent of dust and mold. Frowning, he went up the steps, pushed open the door, and stepped inside.

Sunlight showed him where floorboards had rotted away. Any furniture inside had long been removed, and he caught the musky odor of a skunk. He went no farther. With the sun on his back, he could see all he needed to see. And he could hear: *Now is the day, and now is the hour, when Texas expects every man to do his duty. Let us show ourselves worthy to be free and we shall be free.*

If he closed his eyes, he knew he could picture Henry Smith as fiery and as independent as he had been back during those long days early in 1836 when convention delegates had gathered inside this building.

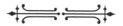

Governor Henry Smith. Houston's head shook at the memory. His back straight as a ramrod, unbendable, Smith knew no compromise. If someone said Houston's eyes were bloodshot—and undoubtedly they were back then—Smith would counter: "By damned if they are. His eyes are rubicund." Smith had tried to dissolve the council; in turn, the council tried to impeach Smith.

"It'll be a miracle," Houston had whispered to Willis Faris, "if we agree on anything before Judgment Day."

The town's organizers had offered this monstrosity they called an "assembly hall", then unfinished, to the delegates. It felt warm today. Twenty-five years ago, Houston thought he might freeze to death as men hemmed and hawed over picayune matters.

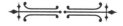

Moving to where he had sat, he pictured that young Sam Houston, a delegate from Refugio— only because those citizens had elected him after

132

the town where he lived, Nacogdoches, had not. Strapping enough that he needed no cane. Thick, brown hair, not thin and white. And, yes, hung over.

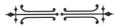

March 2, 1836, his birthday, and Houston had signed his name on this declaration of independence with typical flourish. He recalled feeling as though he had waited hours before the quill was in his finger, the paper flattened before him, held by secretary H.S. Kimble and Richard Ellis, the convention's president.

He had hoped his hand would not shake, and thought of the weight this signature would have. It was enough to sober a man.

The memory of Samuel Maverick's grumbling made him smile.

"Hell's fire, Houston. Don't read the damned thing. Get with the signing so the rest of us can put our names on our own death warrants."

Five copies had been made, given to riders to carry to Bexar, to Brazoria, to Goliad, and to Nacogdoches—and one more to San Felipe, where the printer would be ordered to make a thousand copies as handbills.

A great day. He was forty-three years old.

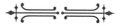

The convention, of course, had just started.

He looked at the place where James Collinsworth usually sat or stood. Shifty-eyed, with a high forehead, but a good man, and an even better supplier of whiskey. It had been Collinsworth, a fellow Tennessean, who—two days after the declaration had been signed—had nominated Houston to be commander in chief of the army of this newly created Republic of Texas.

Houston turned, smiling as he remembered the faces of David Burnet and Robert Potter as Houston's nomination, after some bickering, was confirmed.

He could see the dark-skinned but continuously cheery, boyish face of Manuel Lorenzo Justiniano de Zavala y Sáenz. The best of the entire lot, Houston believed, a true diplomat, hard to rile, but firm in his convictions. After San Jacinto, Zavala had escorted Santa Anna back to Mexico to force the Mexican government to recognize Texas's independence. Houston frowned. That had wrecked cherubic Zavala's health, and he had been fishing in Buffalo Bayou that November when the boat capsized. Zavala had died of pneumonia a short while later.

Which brought back another sad memory.

Turning again, and frowning, Houston thought about Collinsworth, his old drinking buddy.

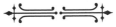

"No man holds his liquor better than the two of us," Collinsworth had told him here, after the convention had recessed for the evening, and they had started drinking until late in the night.

"Must be the Tennessee in us," Houston had said.

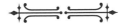

Only, Collinsworth was no Sam Houston when it came to whiskey. Two years later, in 1838, Houston had felt with all certainty that Collinsworth would be elected president of the Republic of Texas, and there could have been no better successor to Sam Houston than Collinsworth. This was the man who had served as Houston's aide-de-camp and had shown his bravery at San Jacinto. He had served in the Texas Senate and later as chief justice. A man like him certainly could beat Mirabeau B. Lamar, who wanted to put the capital in the hills of Austin, or Peter W. Grayson. Yet Collinsworth did what he did too often.

He got drunk. Again.

One summer night, he drowned in Galveston Bay. Some say he had slipped off the boat. A few fools even suggested he had been pushed. But Houston knew Collinsworth too well, and understood that he had leaped off.

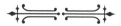

"You're a good man, Jim," Houston remembered telling him during the convention of 1836.

"No. I'm a good drunk. It's all I'm really good at, Sam. It's all I'll ever be good at."

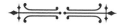

They called it an accidental drowning, but Houston would always believe that poor Collinsworth had taken his own life, unable to bear the responsibilities of serving as the republic's president, unable to follow Sam Houston's footsteps.

Deep in thought, Houston lost track of time until something flashed in the corner of his eye. A rat moved among the dust and leaves, stopped near Houston's boots, glanced at him, wiggled its whiskers, and leaped into a hole in the floor.

"Yes," Houston said, "it is time to leave."

He did not bother closing the door as he left the old assembly hall.

Jeff waited for him, holding the cane.

"You all right, Master Sam?" the young man asked.

"I am fine, Jeff." He accepted the cane.

"Ain't much to this buildin', is there, sir?" the slave asked.

"I guess not." He shook his head.

"Was there some treaties signed here, too?" Houston looked at the Negro. "I mean. Like that big ol' tree you showed me back in Austin. Was this here place somethin' like that?"

"Something like that, Jeff. Let's get back to Independence."

"Yes, sir. You must be doin' a lot of remem-berin'."

Houston nodded. "A lot." He started to laugh, only to realize there was not a damned thing funny about what he had to say. "But, Jeff, when you reach the years I have accumulated, and the miles I have traveled, and you accept that they have put you out to pasture, there is not much for a doddering old fool to do. Except remember."

CHAPTER THIRTEEN

June 3, 1861

The salt air revitalized Houston, as it often did. So did the oysters. He spent his mornings walking along the beach with Margaret—and, sometimes, did not even need his cane—as she gathered a few seashells. When she had first arrived at Cedar Point, she had decorated the cabin christened Ben Lomond with shells. Shells were harder to find after all these years, but Margaret had a keen eye.

Sam Junior had returned home from Bastrop, and Houston put him to work overseeing the slaves as they chopped firewood to be sold in Galveston or Houston City. Money had become scarce, and Houston's credit could only buy so much. His name, these days, bought even less.

Yet with new-found energy and a new purpose, he retired to his office to work on a plan, one that could save his family, his legacy, and if not all of Texas, at least a good part of it.

As he pored over the maps, Lewis the slave appeared at the doorway, and cleared his throat. Irritated, Houston looked up and scowled.

"Beggin' your pardon, Master," the old Negro said, "but you got visitors. A Mister McCulloch and Capt'n Ford, sir."

A beaming smile replaced the hard look, and Houston straightened over the desk. "By all means, Lewis, show them in. Show them in. Then fetch us fresh coffee and brandy for our visitors."

Few men loved a fight better than Ben McCulloch and John "Rip" Ford, or were better at it.

McCulloch wore the tailored uniform of a general. Standing a couple of inches under six feet, his brown hair had begun to thin on top, but his beard seemed thicker. Yet from all his years on the Texas frontier—fighting Indians with the Rangers and John Coffee Hays, scouting for Zachary Taylor during the war with Mexico, and serving as United States marshal in the Eastern District of Texas, he remained fair-skinned. Houston remembered him at San Jacinto, where McCulloch commanded one of the army's "Twin Sisters", the two six-pounders that inaugurated the battle and helped win Houston's greatest victory.

He knew something else about McCulloch. The man absolutely despised Mexicans.

McCulloch hailed from North Carolina. The other man in the library came from the other Carolina.

John Salmon "Rip" Ford had served as doctor, congressman, Indian fighter, soldier, and newspaper editor. Tall, thin, Ford's blue eyes appeared almost opaque, and his Roman nose revealed that he knew fists well.

Ford sipped coffee. McCulloch had already drained his first brandy.

Beckoning them to the map, Houston pointed. "Gentlemen," he said, "ere long, there will be stirring times on the Río Grande." They looked up. "Reclamation," he said.

He laid out his plan.

It was not his alone. Representatives from England had first broached him even before he had been kicked out of the governor's chair and exiled from Austin. Houston had already reached out to friends he knew he could still trust, Edward Burleson of Texas, Henry L. Kinney in Nicaragua, and Lewis Cass in Washington City. He had formed a secret society that he called The Order of the Lone Star of the West.

"We make reclamation upon Mexico," Houston said. "For all her wrongs. We form a new republic."

McCulloch did not even blink. Rip Ford, however, set his coffee cup on the nearby table.

"We shall be a buffer," Houston explained. "England still has access to cotton."

"England will have access to Texas cotton," McCulloch shot out, adding a respectful, "begging the general's pardon."

"Do you not think the Navy will blockade us, General McCulloch?" Houston fired back. "By

Jehovah, General, the ships are already gathering, and the Confederate navy will be no match for Union guns, sir."

McCulloch frowned.

Ford spoke in a soft, Southern drawl. "You call this *reclamation,* General. But what you're really saying is *invasion,* or am I mistaken, sir?"

He did not answer Ford's question. "Ten thousand troops," he said. "We can, we will, fill that muster in thirty days. Captain Burleson is already south of the Nueces, where he is secretly enlisting six loyal *Tejanos* who will serve as guides in this glorious endeavor. You gentlemen know Burleson. He has lived in Mexico, speaks the language fluently. He knows the country. He knows the people." Houston laughed. "Burleson's raring to go. I'm having trouble keeping him from starting the war right now."

McCulloch moved to the liquor and refreshed his drink. "General Houston," he began, then sipped for a moment. "You wouldn't need ten thousand Texians to whip the Mexicans, for a more indolent, stupid, and worthless race does not exist. But armies cost money. You footing the bill, sir?"

Houston laughed. "I am still waiting to receive the salary owed me as governor of Texas, gentlemen. But we have backers across the Atlantic, my friends." He did not have to say England.

Actually, the British agents had proposed

raising an army of twelve thousand, but Houston thought ten thousand would do the job. Nor did he tell the British operatives that representatives from France had visited him, too, with a similar offer. What he knew was this: he had made both the French and English agree to it, in writing. Should he fall in battle, Margaret need not worry about money. She would be paid a generous sum *per annum* until her own passing.

"A lot of boys, sir, have already enlisted in militia, companies, whatever you want to call them, sir." Ford's melodic voice always made Houston relax. "And maybe you haven't heard, sir, though I expect you have, but General McCulloch and I already have jobs."

Ford now commanded the 2nd Texas Cavalry along the Río Grande. Jefferson Davis, president of the so-called Confederate States of America, had commissioned McCulloch a brigadier general and assigned him to Indian Territory, to build something called the Army of the West.

Houston stared hard at the two men. "Texans," he said, "comprise the bulk of your command." He brought the coffee cup to his lips, and grinned.

"Mexico." McCulloch drained the glass again, and set it down. "Sir, to do this will be the crowning act of your life."

Houston straightened. Pride, power shined in his eyes. "Yes," he said with as much modesty as he could find. "I warrant you are correct."

"I know what the Confederacy has promised to pay me," McCulloch said. "But what is your offer?"

"We can negotiate your spoils, General, to terms I am certain you will find agreeable."

Staring at the map, McCulloch grinned in triumph. Ford, however, remained more reserved.

"Let's say you get your ten thousand men, sir. You got to feed them. And you have to arm them. Some of the boys I have down along the border, by Jacks, they have muskets that'll likely blow up in their faces. I see more shotguns than rifles. More than a few don't even have a long gun."

"My contacts have promised two thousand percussion rifles," Houston said, "one thousand new Sharps rifles, and three thousand Colt's revolving pistols." He grinned. "Immediately. Once we are ready to march."

"A fellow in Charleston, years back," Ford drawled, "once promised me the most beautiful ruby in the world . . . if I could fix him up without taking off his right arm. Took some doing, but he not only kept his arm, he had full use of it, too." Ford's head shook. "That was more than thirty years ago, and I'm still waiting for that ruby."

"You should have broached this idea with General Lee, sir," McCulloch said, "whilst he remained at Fort Mason."

I did, Houston thought bitterly. *While I remained governor.* He said he was a servant to the President—at that time—and to his superiors, not to Texas.

"But I have seen you fight, General McCulloch." Houston appealed to the man's vanity. "And you, Captain, remain wise beyond your years."

Ford checked his timepiece, and McCulloch moved to the rack to gather his hat.

"You will let us know when you are ready, sir?" McCulloch asked.

"Indeed, General."

"I eagerly await your command, sir, and I thank the general for the libation and conversation, yet I must catch the train in Houston City. Colonel Ford." After bowing, McCulloch walked out of the house.

Rip Ford wound his watch stem, and eventually slipped the timepiece into a trousers pocket.

"Rip?" Houston asked at last.

Looking up, Ford shook his head. "You remember back when John Floyd gave you all that grief when you suggested that you bring in a bunch of Cherokees to help us win the fight against Santa Anna?" he asked.

"I do," Houston said.

"What was that you called the Indians? I mean, what you said they'd be."

"Auxiliaries."

"Yeah. That's it."

Houston waited.

"I never cared for that word, at least the way you used it, General. No offense, sir. It just struck me that auxiliary meant a backup, that those Cherokees . . . and they were your friends, sir, for you lived among them for I don't know how long . . . were just folks to fall back on. To use. To get killed. Save some of our boys from dying, I guess."

Houston frowned. "I did not mean it that way. I meant that they would support us."

"And die for us. Reclamation or invasion, no matter what you call it, people are going to die."

"And when war comes to Texas, when Lincoln's armies reach our borders . . ."— Houston frowned—"our men will die then, too, Rip. This you know as well as I do."

"Yes, sir. But they'll die defending our state, sir. We won't be the invaders." He found his hat, held it against his trousers, and shook his head.

"I can lead my boys against an army attacking us, General Houston. But I won't lead them as invaders. You understand that, sir?"

Rip Ford had rejected him. Well, so had Robert E. Lee. Yet Houston had piqued McCulloch's interest—for the right price—so Houston persisted. He could put Edward Burleson, the Reverend Rufus Burleson's cousin, in charge, ask him to raise more than just Mexican scouts and interpreters. He worked through the afternoon until Margaret entered the study, and even then, she had to call his name twice before he looked up.

"Sam Houston." Margaret placed both hands on her hips. "Lewis has twice called you to supper, and twice you told him you were coming. It is growing cold, sir, and the family awaits."

Houston frowned. He did not even remember the slave coming into the library.

Excitement, however, bubbled over him, and he called her to the desk. Standing, he moved to the maps, and pointed. "I have it all figured out, Margaret," he said with the enthusiasm he remembered having as a boy hunting and fishing in the Tennessee hills. "A new country!" He tapped the map with one of his scarred, massive fingers.

"New." Margaret shook her head. "That's Mexico, darling."

"But not after we reclaim it."

She looked up, concern etched in her features. "Reclaim?"

"It will save us, at least part of Texas, from the civil war that shall consume us," he explained. "A new republic. Ben McCulloch says it will be my crowning moment, and, by Jehovah, he is right."

She backed up a few steps, her mouth hanging open, and studied him. He sang out a few of his ideas until she stamped her foot on the floor, silencing him.

"You . . ." She had to shake her head, gather her thoughts. "You go to war . . . to prevent a war?"

"Yes, damn it!" he roared, thinking she mocked him.

"And what shall we name this new republic?" Margaret asked.

He had not thought of a name. The Order of the Lone Star of the West sounded far too lengthy.

Margaret suggested: "Houstonia?"

He blinked. He stared. He watched her walk out of the library. The door slammed so hard, the map toppled off its perch and dropped to the floor.

Timidly, he entered the bedchambers late that evening. His stomach growled, for his supper had gone uneaten while he dashed off letters to Rip Ford, Ben McCulloch, Edward Burleson, and foreigners—one French, one English—staying in hotels in Nacogdoches and Austin.

Margaret sat on her side of the bed, the candle fluttering as she read the Bible.

She did not speak as Houston undressed and put on his nightshirt. He picked up his own Bible, laid it on the bedside table, then took his candle and walked over to Margaret, where he used the flame in Margaret's candle to light his own. There, he waited for her to look up. When she did not, he started talking anyway.

"My foible has been vainglory. A worse

147

weakness than whiskey, I fear. It can consume me." His head shook and he let out a chuckle that had no mirth. "You won't believe me, but I actually thought I could save Sam Junior from war by leading him into war." He sighed, and she lifted her gaze toward his blue eyes. "You have always brought my flaws to my attention," he continued, "and you have saved me countless times from my own imperfections, decisions, ideas, things that would have ruined me. Ruined us. I am sorry."

"You would have reasoned everything out eventually." She closed her Bible. "Eventually. You are an honorable man, Samuel Houston. Now come to bed."

Relieved, he crossed the room, set the candle down, and slipped underneath the covers. She extinguished her candle. He sat up and opened the Bible.

Through the open window, he smelled salt air as he read Matthew, finding the verse he knew he wanted to close on: *And ye shall hear of wars and rumors of wars: see that ye be not troubled: for all these things must come to pass, but the end is not yet.*

Bible returned to the nightstand, he settled into the bed after blowing out his candle.

"I have not seen you so furious," he said in the darkness, "since the night you caught me dancing."

He heard her shift, rise, and then felt her above his face.

"That was because," Margaret said, "you were not dancing with me."

Her lips found his.

CHAPTER FOURTEEN

July 4, 1861

That morning, Jeff rode with him to Houston City. Over protests from the slave, Margaret, and Sam Junior, Houston insisted on riding his gray stallion, and not "in that damned carriage." When in one of those moods, they knew better than to argue too much, so they let him go, with Jeff accompanying him on a sorrel gelding.

"Now you see why I made us ride horses," Houston said with a smirk when they entered his namesake city.

Rains had flooded the Texas coast for several days, turning the city's streets into swampy bogs. Wagons along Main Street had sunk to their beds, and muddy tracks hid even the cobblestones of the few paved streets.

As they dismounted in front of a hitching rail, a skinny soldier in a coat of butternut and tan trousers stained with mud called out: "Sir, I must see your passes."

Houston finished tethering the stallion before he stared at the teen.

"I beg your pardon," Houston said.

"Your passes, sir. The city is under martial law. You cannot travel without a pass."

Face reddening, Houston stepped around the rail and onto the warped boardwalk, stretching out his frame until he towered over the slight soldier. He leaned forward, scowled, and his voice made the youngster shiver.

"Go to San Jacinto, and there learn my right to travel in Texas."

The kid practically dropped his fowling piece.

"At ease, soldier," a voice called from a mercantile doorway. "Let General Houston pass."

Holding a parcel wrapped in brown paper and tied with string, Dr. Ashbel Smith stepped onto the boardwalk. His hair was graying, thinning on top, and his mustache and goatee had already lost all of their brown, but his eyes sparkled with humor. He wore a neat shell jacket with French braid on the sleeves, gray trousers, tall boots, and, rather than carrying a doctor's satchel, he wore a holstered revolver and sheathed saber.

Once he shifted the package, he offered his hand, which Houston gladly accepted.

"I have a hankering for some of Murdoch Lind's chicory and a lemon tart," the doctor said. "Would you care to join me, sir?"

"A pleasure."

As they walked, Jeff following behind them, Houston asked: "A pass? Martial law?"

"The Yankees have begun their blockade," Smith explained.

Yes, but Houston had seen no signs of a Yankee

151

invasion. *And you declare martial law . . . so soon?*

"Our foolish governor fears invasion," Smith said. "But that's Governor Clark for us. The Union ships will not stop our runners. They have not enough ships."

For now, Houston thought. *Bales of cotton almost reached the roof of a warehouse. Had rains delayed those being loaded onto ships for export, or were Federal ships responsible?*

They waited for a woman to cross the plank laid across a street, bowed politely, before Smith changed the subject. "What brings you to town, Sam?"

Houston said: "Do not you know what day it is, Doctor?"

Smith laughed. "But of course, Sam. It is Thursday."

The doctor stopped as a man staggered in front of him and through the doors of a saloon. He pointed across the street. "There is your Independence Day celebration, Sam."

Houston watched another man weaving in front of a gambling hall, waving a bottle in one hand and yelling: "Hurrah! Hurrah for Jeff Davis. Down with all the Yanks. Damn all the Yanks!"

"Jeff Davis is as ambitious as Lucifer and as cold as a lizard," Houston said.

With a chuckle, Smith resumed his walk, but Houston had stopped, staring at a board nailed onto the wall of a saloon. Smith returned to join Houston and Jeff for a closer look.

The whitewashed board, about eighteen by twenty-four inches, appeared to be some type of chart. Houston turned his head, trying to make sense of it.

	Mon	Tue	Wed	Thu	Fri	Sat	Sun	Total
Houston	0	0	1	0				1
Hempstead	0	1	0	1				~~1~~ 2
Richmond	0	2	1	0				~~2~~ 3

"Too wet to race horses," Smith explained. "And not everybody plays cards." The doctor tapped the board with his index finger. "So, they've been betting on shootings. Well, actually, killings. You can bet on the day, but most prefer to wager on the weekly total."

Houston frowned. "I am distressed to find my namesake city unable to compete with Hempstead and Richmond."

He said it as a joke, and Smith grinned, but Sam Houston did not know what to think about a city named after him, being known for blasphemers, gamesters, drunkards, liars, and slanderers. Then again, perhaps men of such ilk fit Houston City better than anyone else.

Jeff waited on the bench outside of Lind's coffee shop as Houston and Smith sipped New Orleans brew and reminisced.

James Pinckney Henderson had talked Smith into leaving North Carolina back in 1837, and Houston could not count the number of lives the doctor had saved, from yellow fever, from cholera, from gunshots. The uniform he wore now, though, made Houston frown.

"Are all your soldiers as sound as the young man who demanded to see my passport, Doctor?"

"The Bayland Guards will be a credit to Texas, and to the Confederacy, Sam." He gestured in the direction of the Gulf of Mexico. "The Yankees do not know it, but the blockade will fire up the young men in our area. I may have more than a company in a few weeks, Sam. I may command a full regiment."

Houston frowned. He thought of Sam Junior.

" 'We are not enemies, but friends,' " Houston said. " 'We must not be enemies.' "

Smith stirred milk into his coffee. "Sound words. Yours, or Andy Jackson's?"

"Abraham Lincoln's," Houston said. "From his inaugural address."

"Ah." Smith sighed. "Alas, it is too late for that."

"Yes," Houston lamented. "Fort Sumter has . . ."

"No." Houston saw the gravity in the surgeon's face. "Not Fort Sumner, Sam." The doctor pushed his coffee cup across the table. "I have heard reports of some small skirmishes . . . artillery . . . gunboats . . . along the Virginia coast, but nothing definite. Yet a courier brought word last week of an engagement in Missouri."

"Missouri?" Virginia, Houston could understand. Yet to hear of fighting already beginning this far west chilled Houston. Besides, from what Houston had read, the state of Missouri was attempting to stay out of the war—more or less—refusing to join the Confederacy, yet also not quite adopting the cause of the Union.

"The courier made the engagement seem like Waterloo," Smith said, "but you know how these reports are. After he calmed down, I determined that it was no . . . well . . . a far cry from San Jacinto." He tilted his head toward the street. "Likely, Hempstead, Richmond, and our fair city will see more casualties by Sunday than whatever actually happened at Boonville." He forced a smile, lifted his cup, and drank. "The war will be over in six months, Sam."

"No," Houston said. "It won't, Doctor. It won't be over for a damned long time."

He did not return to Cedar Point directly, but rode east with Jeff, following the narrow path along Buffalo Bayou until the sun began setting. Jeff let out a horrified yelp when Houston spurred the gray stallion into the water, and crossed the flooding marsh.

"Master Sam!" Jeff called. "Master Sam!"

Paying no attention, Houston rode on. Jeff

said a prayer before he eased the sorrel into the murky, stinking water. He could not swim, and he closed his eyes and did not open them until he felt the horse coming out of the water. Then he kicked the gelding into a trot to catch up with Houston.

Insects swarmed in the fading light, and the trees turned ghost-like. Houston paid no attention but charged forward with unannounced purpose. He rode, not speaking, but looking this way and that. Jeff trembled. He did not know this country, but he feared it. To the young slave, this place felt like a graveyard.

Bull bats began feasting on the insects as the night darkened, and, eventually, Houston reined in the gray, and swung out of the saddle, handing the reins to Jeff.

Jeff could just make out a big oak tree and watched Houston cross the wet ground. The tree was big, but certainly not like the Treaty Oak back in Austin. Yet again, Houston walked around it. After a few circles, he sat underneath the tree, bracing his back against the trunk. He sat there until the moon rose.

By then, Jeff feared his master dead, so he swallowed, dismounted, and led the two horses to the oak. Houston lifted his head, and Jeff thanked God that the big man had not died.

"Do you know where we are, Jeff?" Houston asked.

"No, sir."

"San Jacinto," Houston said.

"Where you whupped Santa Anna?"

"Yes." He raised his right arm. "Under this very tree I lay wounded, my ankle a bloody mess. Under this tree they brought Santa Anna to me. My boys wanted me to execute him, and if any man deserved the sentence of death, it was that . . ."—he laughed—"Napoleon of the West. I told them that living, Santa Anna would be of incalculable benefit to Texas, but that dead, he would be just another dead Mexican."

Jeff's head bobbed.

"There were enough dead Mexicans here by then, Jeff."

Jeff's heart pounded.

"Hundreds of dead," Houston said. "We butchered them like hogs in the fall. 'Remember the Alamo,' my boys cried. 'Remember Goliad.' Oh, how well they remembered. We could not stop the slaughter. The bloodlust could not be slaked." He pointed toward the water. "Some tried to swim, only to be shot down. Some cried . . . 'Me no Alamo. Me no Goliad.' They were murdered, too. It was a brutal day, Jeff. War does that to men. We tell our young men to kill, that they must kill, and then it can become damned impossible to stop them from killing."

"Shouldn't we be goin', Master Sam?" Jeff pleaded.

Houston grinned.

"Whilst I lay here after that battle, I noticed that at dark, when the moon rose, just about midnight . . ." Frowning, he stopped. He had planned on playing a joke on the young slave, telling him about the ghosts of dead Mexican soldiers coming toward him, the spirits howling at him. He had envisioned himself laughing at Jeff's expense, but now he felt ashamed. To play a joke on a young slave wasn't funny. And Sam Houston had seen enough ghosts recently.

"Help me up, Jeff," he said. "There is a ferry we can use to cross. We cannot make it back home tonight, but we can be far from here at the least."

So, they crossed Burnet Bay on a ramshackle ferry, leaving the ghosts of Mexican soldiers behind. They camped that night along Cedar Bayou.

Once Jeff had fallen asleep, tossing and turning, Houston jumped at the croaks of frogs, the jumping of fish. Coming through San Jacinto had been a tactical error. Ghosts. Another ghost was sure to visit him, and this one would be a Mexican soldier murdered at San Jacinto.

It was not.

CHAPTER FIFTEEN

Jackson

"I asked you to get Texas for me. You went and got it for yourself."

Houston throws off his blanket and sits up, finding Andrew Jackson squatting by the coals of the campfire, stirring them with a stick in his right hand. His left arm is bent across his thigh. A bullet fired by one of the Benton brothers had always troubled that arm, even after the lead had finally been cut out twenty years after the injury. Old Hickory, his face bathed by moonlight, stops toying with the fire and stares at Houston. "By the eternal, it shall serve you right to see you lose it, too."

The false teeth give Jackson no impediment this evening.

Moonlight, quickly closing in on a new moon, and dying coals provide the only light this evening, yet Houston sees Jackson as clearly as though at Horseshoe Bend . . . the Hermitage outside of Nashville in the summer . . . in Washington City. Six-feet-one but hauntingly thin, the gray hair unruly, blue eyes as cold as steel. A Tennessean by way of South Carolina, a backwoodsman like Houston himself, Jackson is dressed in resplendent fashion—or what would have been thirty years ago: a double-breasted redingote, calf-length, of green wool with black velvet trim, with matching, double-breasted waistcoat with a rolled shawl collar; black trousers that cover all but the polished patent leather of his boots; and a black Dollman hat at his side, crown down, but not flattened, resting next to his walking cane.

"I would not expect you to visit me . . . here," Houston tells him.

After spitting onto the coals, Jackson watches the sizzle. The glow reflects in his brutal eyes, like some wild animal's in the dead of night.

"You would not be in Texas, my boy, were it not for me. Remember?"

Houston frowns. Andrew Jackson had been more of a father to him than Major Houston had, but death had robbed the major of that chance, and, well, there had been four sons born to the Houston home before Sam came along. Yet, Jackson had never been the father that *Oo-loo-te-ka* had been, either.

"I groomed you to be President, Sam. You were governor of Tennessee, married to this pretty young thing. Who absolutely despised your guts. She broke your heart, and you ran off. Left Tennessee. Moved in with those heathen friends of yours. Turned your back on your own kind. By the eternal, you always were more Indian than white."

Houston frowns. "I found them to be more honorable than white men," he says.

"What the hell would you know of honor, son? You remember what they called you in those days? The Big Drunk. The Cherokees called you that. I did not. Ever. Even when you were."

"I remember."

"Then you come back to Washington City. Dressed as a damned savage. Arguing for your new family . . . which was like you slapping me in the face. But I risked my reputation, my legacy, and my presidency by inviting you to the White House. I sent you to a tailor and I paid for your new clothes."

"I paid you back," Houston says softly.

Jackson tosses the stick into the coals. "Paid me back. *Bah!* You gave my son's wife an engagement ring. The very same ring you gave that hussy you married. . . ."

"You will not slander Eliza's name, sir!" Houston stands, pointing the cane at his surrogate father. "No one will say anything vile about her. Even you, sir." His voice falters. He whispers: "Even you."

Jackson's eyes burn, but the venom fades. He does not apologize. Old Hickory can never say *I Am Sorry*. He merely moves on.

"You and Crockett both despised me for

161

sending the Indians away, but that was land white men and women needed."

"Justice Marshall thought otherwise," Houston counters.

"And as I told him . . . 'Enforce it,' " Jackson says, his eyes deepening with anger. Then he roars: "Do you think Georgia would have let the Cherokees stay? In a land where there was gold? Sending them away from civilization saved their lives."

"Saved the lives," Houston says, "of those who did not die on *Nu na hi du na tlo hi lu i*." The Trail Where They Cried.

"Now you sound like Crockett, that back-stabbing fiend. My boy, I was not dealing just with John Marshall, Georgians, and Cherokees like John Ross and Major Ridge. You don't remember John C. Calhoun and those damned nullifiers? I was saving our country. You were not in Washington City. You were not in Nashville. You, who I took under my wing, who I made into what you should have become, you who embarrassed me, who abandoned me . . . and not just me, but your entire race. You turned Injun . . . again."

There is nothing he can say.

Jackson has found his cane, and uses it to push himself up. Leaning on the hickory stick, he raises his free hand and points that long, rugged finger at Houston.

"But I forgave you, as I always did. When you

162

came back, after you sobered up for the time being and must've realized that living in the wilds wasn't quite as profitable as being governor of Tennessee, whose sponsor happens to be President of these United States, I helped you get back on your feet. I gave you a commission from the War Department. I sent you to Texas with a mission. To procure her. For our United States."

Houston smiles. "Or, as you have already stated . . . 'to get Texas for me.' "

" 'The finest country to its extent upon the globe.' That is how you described her when you had crossed the Red River. Remember?"

He will never forget. All too well he recalls those first sights of Texas, when, as that emissary of President Andrew Jackson, he came to Texas, allegedly to negotiate treaties with the Comanches, but with something else in mind. Something secret.

"Damn you, Sam. I was willing to pay Mexico five million dollars for this patch of cactus and grass and rocks. I trusted you."

Houston's head shakes. "You trusted Anthony Butler even more, though." His eyes match Jackson's fury, and he mocks the phantom. "Remember?"

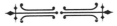

In 1829, Jackson has appointed Butler, a scamp and double-dealing son-of-a-bitch, United States chargé d'affaires in Mexico City. Butler wants Mexico for the United States, as does Jackson. Of course, by 1832, Jackson has sent Houston to Texas, to work on getting all that land for the United States. Yet when Mexican diplomats in Washington suspect some secret agenda by Butler, or perhaps Houston, the American President, Houston's patriarch and loyal backer, plays his hand with Anthony Butler. He disavows Houston.

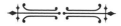

"You chose Butler, sir," Houston says. "You abandoned me."

"Politics, my boy. It's all politics. I had no choice. Even if Butler was a louse, even if he eventually failed me, too."

"I told you," Houston reminds him, "that Butler might destroy a country, but would never gain one."

"And you said . . ."—Jackson closes his eyes, remembering, making sure he got the words right—"you said . . . 'It is probable that I may make Texas my abiding place.'" His brilliant eyes open, and Jackson gazes into horizon. "Abiding place. I do not see now why I would want this as part of my legacy."

"It became my legacy," Houston tells him.

Jackson shuffles the coals with his stick. "Your legacy . . . but only after San Jacinto. My boy, did you know that I predicted your victory there?"

His voice has changed, and Houston raises his head to see a mellowed man. Jackson even smiles.

"In Washington City, in my office, we had learned of your retreat. The Runaway Scrape. The Alamo had fallen. Crockett was dead. Santa Anna had put the prisoners at Goliad to the sword. The rebellion that we had desired in Washington City was about to become another Thessalonica."

Houston listens intently. He has never heard this story.

"Lewis Cass told Mahlon Dickerson and Van Buren that you were retreating desperately to reach Louisiana and American soil. John Forsyth prayed to the Almighty that you would be delivered." Jackson snorts. "But I know you. I made you. You can fool an ignorant Mexican like Santa Anna, and you can fool Van Buren and my cabinet, but you cannot pull the wool over the eyes of Old Hickory. I walked to the map." Now Jackson moves past the dying fire, and approaches Houston until he towers over him. He uses the cane to draw an outline. "I find the map of Texas. I study it. I trace it, knowing where you are. Because I can see you. As well as you can see me this night. And I know you. I know you."

The cane moves like Jackson's finger across a map. "I find the place, and I told those men in my office. 'He will turn and fight. Sam Houston will fight the Mexican army.' " The cane slams into the earth. "There."

Only Jackson has turned now, and is pointing west, across the bay, toward Buffalo Bayou. Toward San Jacinto.

"Is this what you came to tell me?" Houston asks.

"No. I came to tell you that war breaks hearts. That your heart will be broken. But that broken hearts heal."

CHAPTER SIXTEEN

July 5–August 23, 1861

Houston trembled, suddenly cold, and drew in a deep breath. The ghost of Jackson had disappeared, if it had even actually existed. He tossed off the blanket, and moved gingerly to the fire, adding twigs and dead grass to it, watching the kindling smolder, then ignite into flames.

Jeff raised his head.

"It mornin' now, Master Sam?" the slave asked in a sleepy voice.

"In an hour," Houston answered. "I thought we should get an early start."

"That suit me, sir. Let me help you, Master Sam."

"There is coffee and salt pork in the saddlebags, Jeff. Fetch that and the skillet. We did not eat last night, and you must be starving."

"I can eat, sir. I surely can eat."

The slave departed for the tethered horses and tack, while Houston added a few small twigs to the fire. The heat warmed him quickly, but this was Texas, on the coast, in July. He thought of Andrew Jackson, and he remembered a newspaper journalist asking him about the late President, and all that Jackson had accomplished.

Now Houston repeated the words to the spirit of Jackson, or to himself.

" 'Whether his policy was right or wrong, he built up the glory of the nation.' "

"What that you say, Master Sam?" Jeff asked.

"Nothing, Jeff." He added larger sticks to the fire, and stopped, staring.

One of those sticks, twisted and gnarled but long, would have made a fine walking stick. It appeared to be a piece of hickory.

He grumbled as they returned from church, complaining about the preacher's sermon, the stares he had received from those Christians who despised him and his beliefs. And the church choir? "I could sing better than them." Houston's face soured. "They cannot carry a tune in a bucket."

"You are in one of your moods." Margaret tried to change his mood. "But smell that. Aunt Liza has a Sunday feast for us."

He said: "The pastor's interpretation of Isaiah was ridiculous."

The door swung open, and Sam Junior stepped outside.

Margaret gasped. Houston forgot all about Baptist preachers and congregations. He started to tear his son's head off, but stopped himself. Hell, he should not be surprised. He had sent Sam Junior to Houston City on Friday to see to business. The boy had not returned before Sunday services, and, now, Houston understood why.

The slaves rushed inside, taking the young children with them. Margaret paused for just a moment. Her lips quivered, and, as tears welled in her eyes, she pushed through the open doorway, with no words for her oldest boy. She'd leave that to her husband.

When Houston stood in front of his son, he gently touched the badge pinned to the lapel of Sam Junior's coat. In Houston City . . . in Galveston . . . everywhere he had traveled along the South Texas coast, Houston had seen many such rosettes and cockades. This one had a blue ribbon—most sported red ribbons—descending from a bronze five-point star. The Texas star. Gold letters on the ribbon read:

The
South
Forever

"A Confederate rosette, I believe," Houston said, after lowering his hand.

"Yes, Father," Sam Junior said.

After a curt nod, Houston said, just for spite: "Son, that is not the proper place for a Confederate rosette. Those should be worn not on the lapel of your coat, but on the tail."

The boy stiffened. Houston had not been altogether joking, but now he turned serious.

"I have seen many such emblems of triumph floating across our state. In due time, I will see them replaced by badges of sorrow." He wet his lips, and leaned on the cane for support. Once he had done this, he asked, unable to hide the hopefulness in his voice: "Ashbel Smith?"

"Yes, Father," his son replied. "I enlisted in the Bayland Guards. I trained with them yesterday."

"Asclepius is transformed to Mars." Yet Houston felt some hope. Ashbel Smith might be commanding a militia, but he would always be a doctor and, as Houston's friend, would do all in his power to protect Sam Houston's oldest child.

"I can forbid you to go," Houston told him. "You are just eighteen years old."

The boy did not blink. Houston realized how tall his son had grown, now just a couple of inches short of Houston's towering height. Quite handsome, with firm features, and eyes that showed no fear.

"Yes, sir," the young man said, "but my heart pleads that you know that this is something that I must do. That I have to do."

What would he have done had his mother refused to sign the release paper back in 1813? His answer came quickly. Even younger, he had run away from home to live with the Cherokees.

His mother must have known that he would have run away again, found another town, another recruiter, and lied about his age.

"I told you that it is every man's duty to defend this country," he said, "and that I do wish my sons would do so . . . at the proper time."

"This is the proper time, Father. Word reached Galveston a few days ago of a great battle in Virginia. The Yankees are in full retreat back to Washington City."

He had seen the story in the Galveston *Civilian*:

MANASSAS WON.
10,000 FEDERALS KILLED.
CONFEDERATE LOSS 3,000.
FEDERALS ROUTED.
SIX BATTERIES CAPTURED.

Sam Junior must have read only the headlines. Houston remembered the sickening report of *great slaughter on both sides.*

Still, he understood. "I cannot give you my blessing, Son, nor can I deny you. Best go to your mother now, Sam, and mend the heart you have broken." His son saluted, sharply, and turned to head into the cabin. Houston stood there, feeling the heat of the summer sun, and feeling his own heart, as Andrew Jackson's spirit had warned, crumble into a thousand pieces.

Margaret did not speak to him that day, nor much of the following day. Sam Junior had left that evening, after supper, vowing that he would write his mother every day—even if his destination for the time was no farther than Galveston—and that he hoped and prayed that he would spend the duration of the war in Texas, close to home and family.

Houston knew better. A boy Sam's age needed to see the elephant. Besides, the Confederates had won a victory at Manassas, Virginia, and followed that with another victory, closer to Texas, at Wilson's Creek in Missouri. He remembered that favorite saying of Robert Walpole, an English prime minister: "Let sleeping dogs lie." Abraham Lincoln and the Union Army would not be easily defeated.

He busied himself over the next week, riding into Houston City, putting the slaves to work at chopping more cordwood to be sold in Galveston, and penning a letter to Senator Williamson Simpson Oldham.

Politicians did many things necessary for democracy that were hard to stomach. Fathers did, too. Houston despised Oldham, but now he pleaded with the louse.

Oldham had feuded with Houston all during the campaign of 1857, calling Houston an idiot, a Yankee-lover, and a traitor to the Texas cause.

Now, Houston blew on the ink and lifted the paper closer.

> My son has spent two sessions at Colonel Allen's military school in Bastrop. He is a fine scholar, with habits that are good, and he remains ardently devoted to the cause in which he is engaged, as well as to the life of a soldier.
> If you might procure him a commission as a lieutenant, or any promotion which you might deem proper, you will confer upon me an enduring obligation.
> I trust, and firmly believe, that he will never disgrace his patron.
>
> Your obt servant,
Sam Houston

"No!" the voice screamed outside his office. "No! No! No! No!"

Placing the letter on his desk, Houston pushed himself to his feet, and moved to the door.

Margaret stood, tears pouring down her cheeks, her face red like a beet. Aunt Martha and Aunt Liza hurried toward her, but Houston stepped out and held up his hand. The women stopped, and Houston walked toward his son, who sat in the corner, a wooden saber in his hands, his head bowed, sniffling.

"Andrew Jackson Houston," Houston demanded.

The youngster raised his head, wiped his nose, and managed a "Yes, Pa."

"Come with me, Son."

When they entered the library, Houston said: "Have a seat, Andrew."

The boy blinked. "But that's your chair."

"You're big enough for it, I reckon."

The boy hurried and climbed into it, bouncing on the cowhide seat. He grinned until Houston said: "You have angered your mother."

"Ma didn't call it 'angered,'" Andrew corrected. "She said I was agger . . . um . . ."

"Aggravating?" Houston guessed.

"Yes, sir. That's it. Aggravating."

Houston's right hand reached out for the saber the boy held in his hand. Two or three years ago, Houston had carved it as a present for the boy. The youngster sniffed, staring at the toy, then reluctantly handed it to his father.

"How did you aggravate your mother?" Houston already knew the answer.

"I just told her that I want to join up, too. With Doctor Smith's soldiers. Sam . . . he told me that war's glory. I don't know what glory is, exactly, but I think I'd like some of it, too. Sam shouldn't get it all, I mean."

"Glory," Houston repeated.

"That's what Sam told me."

Houston sighed.

"I mean . . . Sam joined up," Andrew said. "Why can't I?"

"Sam is eighteen years old," Houston said. "You are but five."

"That ain't so," the boy snapped. "I'm seven."

"You're . . ." Realizing that Andrew was right, Houston shook his head, wondering how two years had passed without his noticing.

"Can't I be with Sam in the army, Pa?" The tears started again. "Can't I?"

Houston said: "Then who would defend us?"

"Huh?"

"Come with me, Andrew." Houston helped the seven-year-old out of the chair. Hand in hand they walked out of the library, down the open hallway between the two cabins of Ben Lomond and to the beach, where Houston pointed across the bay.

"What do you see, Andrew?" Houston asked.

The boy shielded his eyes from the sun. "Gulls. Some boats. They's casting nets. There's a pelican!"

"Over yonder," Houston said, "is Galveston. Where your brother drills with his fellow soldiers. And beyond that, the Gulf of Mexico. And out there are ships. Warships . . . of . . ." The next words came tougher than he had imagined. "Of . . . our . . . enemy."

"Really?"

Houston nodded.

"They's that close?"

"Yes." He sighed. "Sam, of course, will not be in Galveston forever. Soon he will be marched to wherever the Confederacy needs him. That will leave no one to protect us from the Yankees, Andrew. That is why we ask that you stay with us."

"Golly."

"Yes, golly, indeed."

He stared at the shimmering water. A fish jumped. A gull dived.

"Can we fish, Pa?" Andrew asked.

"I would like that very much, but we left the poles and buckets at the house."

"I can get them, Pa. Is that all right?"

He smiled. "Yes, but you must promise me not to aggravate your mother any more. And do not tell her that you stay here to fight the enemy when they arrive. This we must keep to ourselves, to keep the citizens from panic. Do you understand?"

The boy shook his head. "No, sir."

Laughter felt good, a wonderful release, and Houston pointed at the trail that led to the cabin. "Don't worry. Just be gentle with your mother. It is harder being a mother, Son, than it is being a father. Remember that."

"I'll try." He thrust out the little saber that Houston had given back to him when they left the house. "Here. Hold this. I'll fetch the poles and bait."

Houston took the toy he had carved, and watched his son hurry off the beach and dash for the house. How small the saber looked in Houston's hand. He remembered holding a larger one, a real one.

CHAPTER SEVENTEEN

Horseshoe Bend, March 1814

The Indians called this place *To-ho-pe-ka*, a bend in the Tallapoosa River that had created a hundred-acre peninsula filled with briars, brambles, gullies, snakes, mosquitoes and—now—hundreds of Red Stick warriors.

Houston fished out a rag to mop sweat off his face. March was supposed to be spring, but there was no spring in Alabama. Just hell.

The Cherokee named Gunter, one of General Coffee's scouts, ran in a crouch, water dripping from his buckskins and his black, braided queue. Houston had known Gunter, of the Long Hair Clan, for years, as far back as when Houston ran away to live with the Cherokees. The Indian stopped, gestured toward the Tallapoosa, and spoke in Cherokee.

"The canoes of our enemy," Gunter said, "are gone. They cannot escape."

Houston thanked his old friend. "I will see you later," he said.

"It is my strongest wish. That means you will not be dead."

"Nor will you," Houston said.

"That . . ."—the Cherokee grinned—"is my

strongest wish. I was mistaken. Seeing you alive at the end of this day is my second wish."

He wanted to laugh, but Houston could not bring himself even to smile. Fear had taken root, and he had never known fear—at least not this kind of fear. What if he showed yellow, turned and ran? What if he just didn't do anything . . . important? After muttering a Cherokee blessing, he left the edge of the river.

A full year had passed since he had joined the Army. He touched the ring on his pinky finger, and stopped to wipe the sweat from the palms of his hands. The damned hands would not stop sweating. So much had happened, and so quickly.

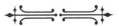

He had enlisted as a private. By the end of the first day, he had been made a sergeant. He had enlisted in the 7th Infantry, but that had been merged into the 39th Infantry, and Lieutenant Colonel Thomas Hart Benton had taken notice of him, and promoted him to ensign. Now, Houston held the rank of third lieutenant. Also, he joined to fight the British, but soon would engage in battle against the Creek Indians. A short while ago, he thought no one could command an army better than Colonel Benton. Now he worshipped Major General Andrew Jackson.

Tecumseh of the Ohio region had been stirring up trouble, and had brought that trouble to the South, persuading the Creeks to join with the British and kill Americans. Back in August, the Creeks had burned women and children alive in a massacre at Fort Mims. Jackson had been put in charge to make the Red Sticks pay, but his command was made up of a bunch of backwoods volunteers who knew nothing about discipline or taking orders. So Jackson had requested real troops to assist him, and the 39th had been ordered to Fort Strother.

Houston would never forget his first sight of General Jackson, that wild growth of untangled hair, the lean face, and the ferocity of his eyes. The general had been holding a burning match over a cannon's fuse, and the cannon had been aimed at his own men.

"You're hungry. I'm hungry!" the lean man with a demon's eyes had roared. "But I will share with you what I have." The left hand had reached into a pocket in his jacket, and had brought out a handful of what looked like acorns. "But you want mutiny, and this is what you shall reap." The hand holding the match had lowered closer to the fuse. "What shall it be?

Do we fight the savages and avenge the loved ones you have lost? Or do we fight amongst ourselves?"

A moment later, the rag-tag group of militia, in calico, hunting frocks, and battered caps, had dispersed back to their tents and fires, and General Jackson had raised his match and blew it out.

"That took gumption," Houston had whispered to Lieutenant Newell Graham.

"He's tough, Sam," Graham had whispered back. "Tough as a piece of ol' hickory."

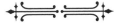

Now Houston found the general and saluted. Jackson stared coldly.

"The Cherokee scouts have removed the canoes to the far bank, sir," Houston reported.

Jackson nodded and turned to another Indian scout whose spear had been adorned with a long white handkerchief.

"Take a message to their chief," Jackson said. "Tell him to send his women, children, and old men across the Tallapoosa. Tell him he has one hour. Then we shall commence the attack."

The Indian's head bobbed, and he disappeared.

Houston stared ahead. It had taken the army ten days to cut through the brush and cover the distance between Fort Strother and the bend.

During that time, the Creeks had built long, wooden breastworks. Back along the riverbank, Gunter had told Houston that he estimated between eight hundred and a thousand Creeks waited for Jackson's army.

Houston tried to control his breathing, his racing heart.

"Prepare the cannon for the assault," Jackson told one of his officers.

"Cannon will do no good, General." Houston didn't even realize he had spoken until he saw Jackson's cold eyes boring through him.

"Explain yourself!" the general barked.

Somehow, Houston found enough saliva in his mouth to answer. "Those are green logs, sir. Likely, the balls will just bounce off them. Like the British balls did at Fort Moultrie in Charleston during the Revolution."

"You are a student of war, Mister . . . ?"

"Houston, General, Sam Houston. No, I'm no student . . ." He found himself grinning for some damned reason. "Of war or anything much. But I've read a mite."

"If our cannon fail, then the savages shall taste the steel of your saber, Lieutenant. To your post, Mister Houston. You have an hour to pray."

Cannons roared. His ears rang. Smoke burned his eyes, his lungs.

"Is that the redoubt burnin'?" someone in the ranks asked.

"Be quiet!" growled Major Montgomery, standing to Houston's left.

"No, fool," came another comment. "It's like Gen'ral Jackson tol' us earlier. We'll have to put the redskins under with ball and bayonet."

"I said, silence!" the major shouted.

Beside Houston, his good friend from Maryville, Henry Morris, whispered: "You scared, Sam?"

He could only nod. There wasn't enough spit in his throat to allow him to speak.

The smoke, Houston knew, did not come from the redoubt, but beyond that. The Cherokees had fired many of the Creek huts. Bullets sang through the forest, and arrows whistled beneath the high limbs of the pines. Enemy marksmen kept the artillery crews hugging the ground, and, as Houston had expected, the leaden balls merely bounced off the logs of the formidable breastworks. He started sweating again, and not just his hands. He ran a coarse tongue over cracked lips.

Major Montgomery raised his saber. To his surprise, Houston found that he had enough strength to lift his own. The drummers began tapping.

"Charge!" Colonel Williams bellowed.

To his right, General Doherty shouted the same orders to his Tennessee boys.

Houston didn't know if he had actually yelled, or just opened his mouth, but he was moving toward the log barrier, flinching as bullets zipped past him, then no longer reacting, no longer even afraid.

The breastworks came into view, disappeared behind clouds of white smoke. Lead balls tore off his hat, clipped his coattail, grazed his side. He smelled sulfur. Or was it the doors to hell? No longer did he hear the musketry behind him, the screams of men, the drums, his own voice.

Creeks appeared, firing arrows from bows, bullets from muskets. Others charged out of the breastworks with tomahawks. He thrust his saber, realized that he had just gutted an Indian warrior, then kept walking, then standing at the wall of logs.

After dropping his saber, Major Montgomery pulled himself to the top of the palisade. Drawing a pistol, he aimed beyond the logs and fired. He slipped, came back up, and turned, waving the empty pistol over his head. "Follow me, boys! Fol- . . . !"

Then he fell backward, landing in the pillow of leaves and pine straw. Houston blinked. "Major?"

Lemuel Montgomery did not respond, simply stared up in Houston's direction, his eyes unblinking. A moment later, Houston realized that the top of the major's head was missing.

Shock snapped him out of whatever had been controlling him. He screamed: "Follow me, men!" He climbed over the logs, dropped below into an angry sea. The saber slashed. A warrior tumbled past him. He heard the oaths he swore, the screams of men, the clangs of tomahawk against musket, sword against spear.

Henry Morris rammed the barrel of his musket into a port hole, pulled the trigger, withdrew the musket, swung it like a club as a Creek came at him. Houston turned, brought the saber up, saw another Indian run into it. Closing his eyes, he held his breath, and felt the rotten breath of the Creek in his face. His eyes opened to find the Indian just inches from his face, blood leaking from the corners of the man's lips. Houston backed up, ripping the saber from the man's breast. The dead Red Stick tumbled onto a pile of dead men, white and red.

Rage controlled him. Again, he raised the blood-stained saber. Henry Morris climbed over the logs. "Give them hell!" Houston shouted, and suddenly grunted. The saber left his hand, clanging as it fell onto a musket near a dead warrior. Houston tried to step toward the musket, but his leg would not move. Looking down, he found an arrow sticking out of his groin, on the right side. He gripped the shaft, tugged. The arrow did not budge, but an intense pain shot through him, and he laid back, staring up at the tops of the trees, a smoke-filled sky.

The dead served as his bedroll and pillow. He tried to sit up, but the pain rocked him to his back. His throat begged for water. Maybe he begged for death. His head turned, and he saw Henry Morris.

"Henry," he managed to whisper. "Help get this damned arrow out of me."

Morris did not answer. A spear stuck out of his friend's chest.

A warrior came at him. Houston reached for the saber, but couldn't find it. He gripped something, tossed it. A damned pine cone bounced off the brave's thigh, before a crimson geyser erupted from the charging Creek's throat, and he slammed against the wooden barrier.

Sitting up, looking around, then seeing the flintlock pistol in Morris's waistband, Houston reached over and jerked it out. The pistol bucked in his hand, and he tossed it aside, made himself stand. He searched for a weapon, and, finding nothing, he pulled the lance from Morris's dead body, and drove it into a charging warrior. The Indian fell back against the log wall, now slick with blood, and slid down into a heap, resting against dead soldiers, dead Creeks.

"Damnation, Sam!" Lieutenant Newell Graham knelt beside him, his face blackened by powder and grime. Graham's big hands gripped the shaft of the arrow. His eyes showed fright. "Does that hurt, Sam?"

"Hell, yes, it hurts." Houston spit out both words and phlegm. "Get it out."

Graham had turned away. "Injuns are runnin'. Got 'em on the run."

"Pull that damned arrow out!" Houston realized his left hand gripped the saber. Somehow, he had found it, but he did not remember when. "Pull it out, Newell!"

Newell Graham suddenly sprang to his feet, and he snapped a salute as a lean man with wild hair and an iron face reined in a horse the color of midnight. Part of the breastworks had been torn down, and soldiers were pouring in through the opening.

"General Jackson," Graham said, "the Creeks have fled." Graham moved his arm. "Taken up in that redoubt over yonder in the woods."

"Finish them, Lieutenant," Jackson ordered, but then he paused as he stared down at Houston. The general's eyes, which had reminded Houston of a buzzard's, softened. "Your day is done, Mister Houston. Get back to the surgeons. That is an order."

Houston watched the black stallion carry Jackson away.

"Sam," Graham whispered when Jackson had disappeared, "I got to go. Can you get to 'em sawbones?"

The word sawbones sickened him, petrified him. Houston raised the saber. "Just pull that damned arrow out, Newell, before I chop your fool head off."

Newell Graham tugged again, and Houston cried out, blinked back tears, and ordered his friend: "Again . . . again . . . get it . . ."

The barbed arrow ripped out flesh, and blood gushed as Houston sank back against the logs.

"Oh, hell!" Graham yelled, and Houston slipped into a world of blackness.

Awake, he bit his lip, and dug fingernails into his palms, anything to stop himself from passing out again. He desperately sought Newell Graham, but found only rows and rows of writhing, bleeding soldiers. A shadow crossed Houston's eyes, and he recognized the bearded, bespectacled face of Major Carroll Player, regimental surgeon.

Player packed the hole in Houston's groin with wads of cotton soaked in turpentine and rum. The surgeon might well have filled Houston's leg with fire. Finally, the doctor wrapped a silk rag around the wound, tying it off on the inside of Houston's right thigh.

"That's all I can do for . . . ," Player began, but Houston did not let him finish. He pushed himself to his feet, used the saber as a crutch, and moved toward the sound of the guns.

"Confound it, Lieutenant!" the doctor thundered. "You shall bleed to death!"

Cannon had been rolled toward the river, and now blazed at a Creek fort, with a roof of logs and walls seven feet high. These balls bounced off the wooden fortress as they had against the breastworks.

Houston watched from underneath a tree, much of its bark shot away during the battle. Newell Graham brought him a ladle of water, and Houston drank greedily. Sweat soaked Houston's uniform.

Exhausted soldiers knelt, sat, lay on backs, stomachs, or curled up like infants. At length, the cannon fell silent, and General Jackson walked up and down the lines.

"We have asked the damned savages to surrender, and they have replied with nothing but scorn. Night will be falling soon, and we have not marched this far to watch the murderers of your mothers and sisters and aunts and nieces slip away in the darkness. Who will volunteer to lead the charge? Who desires the glory of this day? Who amongst you is a man?"

He wanted to just sit there, yet he heard not Jackson's words, but his own, boasting to Maryville's village men: *"You don't know me now, but you shall hear of me."*

Pride, not bravery, not even the challenge from

General Jackson, caused Houston to push himself to his feet with his saber. The frog-sticker slipped from his grasp, and landed on the ground. If he tried to get it, he would fall back down, and would not be able to rise again. Newell Graham watched, his face in wonder and shock. Houston turned away and limped past the men who barely glanced at him. Stopping at one soldier he did not know, Houston held out his arms.

"Your musket," he pleaded in a cracked voice. "Please."

Without a word, the soldier handed the musket to Houston. Taking it, Houston walked on, stopping only for a minute to study the redoubt that was smoking from some of the cannon shots. He knew there were Creek Indians moving behind the walls.

Cocking the musket, he yelled: "Follow me! Give them hell!" Then he stumbled down the incline toward the fortress.

The Red Sticks let him come. Within musket range, Houston fired. Unable to reload, he some-how found enough strength to raise the long gun over his head. He staggered on. Then a blow to his right shoulder dropped him to his knees, and almost simultaneously his right arm seemed to shatter. Gasping, he turned back and yelled: "Charge, boys! Charge!"

Another bullet clipped a lock of his hair, and he blinked, suddenly understanding.

He had led the charge . . . but no one had followed.

An arrow zipped between his legs, and he rose. Staggering back up the ravine, dragging his throbbing, bleeding body, watching his fellow soldiers stare at him with open mouths and hollow eyes. Newell Graham and General Jackson's orderly rushed down the last twenty yards, each grabbing one of his arms. Then Houston closed his eyes and fell once more into that bottomless void.

When he woke in the gloaming, smoke burned his eyes. He lay in a tent, men all around him groaning, some praying, some begging, a few screaming, many dying.

Bile rose in his throat as he made himself look at the sheets covering his body. A heavy sigh of relief escaped when he saw that he still had both legs. His right arm and shoulder throbbed. But nothing had been amputated . . . yet. He might die whole.

Doc Player, his face even more haggard, set a black satchel on Houston's bed, opened the case, and reached inside.

"Your groin is a bloody mess. We managed to take the ball out of your arm, but the one in your shoulder refuses to budge," the major said. He withdrew a pewter flask. "If you live through the night, they will take you to Fort Williams. If you survive those sixty miles, you will at least find comfort at the fort. I will send word to your mother in case she wants to bring your remains to Maryville." He offered the flask. Houston just blinked. "Whiskey will ease some of the pain. But not all," Player explained as he leaned the flask against Houston's side.

"You understand that you will die, Mister Houston?"

Houston shook his head. "You don't know me at all, do you, Major?"

Suddenly, life reappeared in the surgeon's eyes, and his face warmed.

"I might enjoy getting to know you, Lieutenant Houston." He snapped the black satchel shut, picked it up, and moved toward the next patient.

"Major?" Houston said.

Major Player turned. Bile again crawled up Houston's throat, but this came from a terrible stench. "What stinks so much?" Houston asked.

The surgeon's face again hardened. "The damned Red Sticks refused to surrender, so General Jackson ordered the redoubt torched. They are burning alive, Lieutenant."

Color drained from Houston's face, and now he fumbled to open the flask. "Dear . . . God," he whispered hoarsely.

Player shook his head. "You forget, Mister Houston, what those bloodthirsty devils did at Fort Mims."

The whiskey burned his throat, dulled some of the pain, but could not lessen the foulness of burning flesh embedded in his nostrils, his hair, his clothes, the sheet, the very air itself.

"But . . ." He coughed, took another pull from the flask. "The Red Sticks are the savages. We are supposed to be . . ." He could not finish.

"In war, Lieutenant," the major said as he walked away, "all are savages."

Chapter Eighteen

March 15, 1862

"You comfortable, Master Sam?"

Houston's eyes opened, and he gave Jeff a warm nod as the slave worked the sail of the skiff.

"Jeff," he said, "if they had let me travel this way, after the slaughter at Horseshoe Bend, I might have no need of this cane."

His head sank back against the pillow, and he let the motion of the boat, the rocking of the water, and the warm sun on his face soothe his joints. The groin and shoulder had leaked again that morning, but Jeff had bathed and wrapped the wounds, and he began thinking again of Horseshoe Bend.

In war, Lieutenant, Dr. Carroll Player's words rang in his ears, *all are savages.*

Indeed. Some eight hundred Creek Indians had been killed at Horseshoe Bend. Since that awful spring day, Houston had traveled across Alabama many times, visiting Mrs. Lea, courting Margaret, or making his way to Nashville or Washington City. Never, however, had he returned to that turn in the Tallapoosa River.

War turned men into savages. He had seen that

when he was but twenty-one. Years later, he had watched his own men butcher Mexican soldiers trying to surrender at San Jacinto.

And now, across the bays called Trinity and Galveston, his oldest son prepared for war. No one could truly prepare for such madness.

Yet he also wondered what would have become of Sam Houston had he not enlisted in the army and followed Old Hickory into battle. Would he be back in Maryville, charging $8 to educate a bunch of children whose parents lamented the fact that their kids were being taught by a wild man who wore a hunting shirt made of flowered calico and wore a long queue in Cherokee fashion that hung down his back? Would he still need the leaden knuckles to make some of those boys pay attention in class?

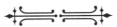

The Creeks, eventually, had signed the treaty, and Andrew Jackson saw his star rise and rise and never set. Horseshoe Bend had made him famous. New Orleans had made him legend and would send him to the presidency, where President Jackson never forgot his friends, or forgave his enemies.

Houston had survived the agonizing trips on litters. He had survived doctors in Knoxville, New Orleans, and New

York City. He had been promoted and promoted and by the fall of 1817 he had found a job that suited him: sub-agent for the Hiwassee Cherokees. He had kept the Cherokees out of a war with the United States, an act he sometimes regretted but one he understood that he had to do. That had brought him to Washington City, where he had met with President James Monroe and made a bitter enemy in John C. Calhoun, the South Carolina fire-breather then serving as Secretary of War. Which had given Houston his first taste of politics. He savored that flavor.

From there, he had moved into law, reading in Judge James Trimble's office in Nashville. He had hung a shingle in Lebanon, just east of Nashville. Within ten months, he found himself serving as adjutant general of Tennessee. Everything came like a whirlwind: attorney general of the Nashville district in 1819 . . . major general of the state militia in 1821 . . . elected to the U.S. House of Representatives in 1823 and again in 1826 . . . governor of Tennessee in 1827, one year before Old Hickory became President of the United States of America.

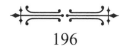

"You promise me, Master Sam," Jeff said, "that you ain't gonna join up to fi't the Yankees like Young Master Sam up and done?"

Houston smiled. "They won't have me, Jeff," he said.

"So why you have me get you all duded up in that ol' uniform of yours, sir?"

"I want to show those young whippersnappers what a real soldier looks like," Houston said as he tugged at the jacket, almost too small to fit him anymore.

Jeff cackled.

A pelican glided over the boat and skidded to a stop in the calm bay.

Houston wore the uniform he had donned at San Jacinto: pants the color of snuff—and likely stained with snuff, not to mention whiskey—tucked inside worn, black boots; the jacket frayed at the collar and cuffs and missing a couple of buttons; the old planter's hat, practically battered into oblivion, with the left side pinned up. His belt lay on the bench, the scabbard and sword's hilt reflecting the sunlight.

"I reckon they'll ask you to give a speech," Jeff said. "Don't you reckon, Master Sam?"

"They usually do." The city of Galveston drew ever so closer.

Frank Lubbock, Texas's newly elected governor, rambled on about this and that to the good citizens on the street front. Houston listened for a few minutes before stepping inside the post office to collect his mail: newspapers mostly, two magazines, a letter to Margaret from her mother, and one to him mailed from Tennessee. He did not know if he wanted to learn of any news from Tennessee, so he stuffed that letter inside his pocket next to the crumpled envelope of a letter Ashbel Smith had sent him. The rest he gave to Jeff as they walked outside.

"Let's go," he said, but Frank Lubbock called out his name.

"I've told you what I think, folks," Lubbock told the crowd. "And my plans for Texas, and for the South. Now let's hear from a true patriot, a bona-fide hero. General Sam Houston. Get up here!"

At first, he frowned, but then he heard the cheers and applause—sounds he had not heard in months.

"Go on, Master Sam," Jeff whispered, and Houston stepped onto the street. The crowd parted, and Houston moved forward, feeling their stares, hearing a few whispers. Frank Lubbock's weak hand helped pull him into the back of the wagon.

Although Lubbock had served under Houston as comptroller during the republic years, Houston would not call him a friend. A die-hard Democrat, Lubbock had defeated Houston's run for governor back in 1857, only to see Houston win two years later. Lubbock seemed to be better at running that store he owned in Houston City than in politicking. After all, he had barely defeated Edward Clark for governor, and a dead pack rat would have defeated Clark in a landslide.

Lubbock grinned, and pointed at Houston.

"By thunder, this is indeed General Houston, folks! And he's dressed for battle!"

His face flushed. Lubbock had played him for a fool, but now the new governor yelled: "Hurrah! Hurrah! Hurrah for Sam Houston! Remember the Alamo. Remember Goliad. Remember Sam Houston!"

The crowd took up the cheer, and Houston's anger was replaced with tears in his eyes, which he quickly blinked away. He held out his hands in a feeble attempt to silence the throng. Eventually, the din died just enough so that he could be heard.

"We have had our differences," he said, "but this is not the first time people have disagreed with Sam Houston. Ask Governor Frank, here. Governor Frank has called Sam Houston a fool, and Governor Frank was right." He enjoyed the laughter, and tried to think of the last time anyone had laughed during one of his stump speeches. "Old Sam Jacinto, on the other hand, has called Governor Frank worse, and I, God, and all of Texas . . . even Governor Frank himself . . . know well that Sam Houston was absolutely right."

They roared.

"Yet now we are at war." Smiles vanished from the faces in the crowd. "It is time to set differences aside. We are in this together, as friends, as neighbors, as Texans. Thank you."

They cheered, and he shook hands with Governor Lubbock, made his way off the buckboard, and back through the crowd. Once he reached Jeff, he hailed a carriage to take them to Houston City and on to the flatlands outside of the city that had been rechristened as Camp Bee.

The soldiers stood at attention as Houston shook hands with Ashbel Smith and Colonel John Moore. No longer just Smith's Bayland Guards, these boys had become the 2nd Texas Infantry.

"Would General Houston care to drill the regiment?" Moore asked as he unsheathed his saber.

I guess my sword is too old, too dull, Houston thought, but he felt the excitement swelling inside him, and gladly he took the offered saber, stepped off the stand, and walked to the men. His eyes scanned the faces, stopping ever so briefly on Sam Junior.

He straightened. "Shoulder arms," he commanded. "About face."

They snapped as one. He thought: *By thunder,*

the men I led at San Jacinto never could have done that.

"Do you see anything of Judge Campbell or Williamson S. Oldham here?"

"No!" they snapped.

Damned right. Campbell and Oldham were a couple of blow-hards who would turn tail at the sight of a musket aimed in their direction—even if Oldham had helped get Sam Junior a commission as a lieutenant. An offer that made Houston's heart sink, but he refused to show any emotion now. Just fatherly pride.

"Well, they are not found at the front, or even at the rear. Right about, front face! Eyes right!"

Again, they moved in unison.

"Do you see anything of Judge Campbell's son here?"

"No!" they shouted as one.

Then one sang out: "He has gone to Paris to school!"

Houston grinned. Campbell and Oldham were nothing but talk. They bragged. They preached. They let others fight, and die.

"Eyes left! Do you see anything of young Sam Houston here?"

"Yes!"

He felt something in his throat, and wondered if he would be able to finish. He coughed. "Eyes front!" He drew in a breath. "Do you see anything of old Sam Houston here?"

They cheered. He beamed. And he could let this go now, let them feel the glory, the pride, but he had more to say.

"Gentlemen of the Second Texas Infantry, I am Sam Houston." He would not speak of himself in the third person. Not this time. These brave boys deserved better. They also needed to know the truth. "I made Texas, and you know it. You have prospered most when you have listened to my counsels, but now you have listened to others. You march into battle, and you desire glory. But, hear me and hear me well, there is no glory to be found in war, and I fear that you will sink in fire and rivers of blood."

He saluted, and returned to Ashbel Smith and Colonel Moore, handing the saber to the latter.

"Where are you staying tonight, General?" Colonel Moore said.

"The Fannin House," Houston replied.

"Very well." Moore looked around. "I fear your hack has abandoned you. Captain Smith."

"Yes, Colonel," Ashbel Smith said.

"Find a suitable soldier and have him escort General Houston and his slave to the Fannin House."

"Very good, sir." The doctor stepped toward the soldiers who remained at attention. "Private . . . Houston."

Sam Houston grinned.

・ ・ ・

When they reached the hotel on the corner of Fannin Street and Congress Avenue, Houston and his son sat in the Army ambulance in silence as Jeff gathered the grip.

"Doctor Smith wrote me about your decision to turn down the lieutenancy," Houston told his son.

"Yes, sir. Captain Smith told me he was doing that."

He nodded. "When do you move out?"

"In two days."

Had his son accepted the commission, he would have remained in Texas. And now?

"Are you permitted to tell an old general where you are bound?"

His son shrugged. "We know we take the train to Beaumont, then a steamboat north. Alexandria is what most of us guess."

Louisiana then, Houston thought. *But not forever.* Two forts in Tennessee, Donelson and Henry, had fallen last month. The Union Army kept moving south. The 2nd Texas, in all likelihood, would join a major army to meet the challenge.

"Your mother asked me to tell you that she received your letter," Houston said. "And the drawing you included."

"Tell Mother that I shall continue to write."

His heart pained him. "And draw," he said. "I hope."

"I shall gladly send my sketches to her," Sam Junior said. "And you."

His head bobbed once more. It seemed that was all he could do. Just nod his big, fat head.

"You do have a gift." Houston wondered why he had always found drawing such a waste.

"Thank you, Father."

Jeff had returned from leaving the luggage with the hotel desk clerk. He opened his mouth as if to speak, but stopped, and stepped away, waiting patiently.

"Ashbel is to meet me here for supper," Houston said. "It would honor me, and your captain, were you to join us."

"Thank you, sir, but . . ." His son smiled, and Houston knew his son was full grown, his own man, and had been for a long time. "But . . . well . . . we have been invited to Perkins Hall for a dance and feast. They haven't finished the playhouse yet, but . . . well, Perkins Hall as it is will do for the boys of the Second. I . . ."—he held out his hand—"I should be going, Father. It was wonderful to see you." After they shook, his son's fingers traced along the lapel of his old coat. "The boys will be talking of your speech, and your uniform, all the way to wherever we are going."

Somehow, Houston managed to laugh. "I suppose they will." As his son climbed out of the wagon, he held out his hands. Now Jeff came forward, and the two of them helped Houston onto the boardwalk. Houston handed his cane to the slave, and reached into an inside pocket.

"Your mother sent a present for you," he said, and held out the pocket Bible to his son. "I believe she has inscribed a sentiment."

Sam Junior opened the Bible, smiled, and closed it.

"Send her all my blessings, and my love, and tell her I shall carry it with me till I return home."

"You do that, Private Houston." He snapped a salute, and watched his son perfect the return. Then, Sam Houston Junior climbed back into the driver's box, released the brake, and urged the mules into a walk.

Houston just stood there, with Jeff at his side, watching the ambulance disappear in the darkness.

"You do that, Sam" he said in a choking voice. "Return home."

Sautéed shrimp, stewed onions, buttermilk biscuits, and Texas beef. Dr. Smith sipped red wine. Houston drank black coffee.

"Do you know where you're bound?" Houston asked after the waitress removed their empty plates.

"Corinth," Smith whispered.

In northern Mississippi. Houston frowned.

"We'll be under General Johnston's command, Sam," the old doctor assured him. "You know Albert. There is no better leader of men, other than the strapping young man sitting across from me."

Houston ignored the compliment. "Albert's a fine gentleman but no general, nothing but a mechanical soldier."

"Well." Smith frowned. "Not everyone can be Old Sam Jacinto."

He had hurt the doctor's feelings, had insulted an officer of the Confederate army. Houston did not apologize, but changed the subject. He pulled both envelopes from his pocket, finding the one that had contained the short note from Ashbel Smith, the one saying that Sam Junior had rejected a promotion, and that the 2nd Texas would be leaving Texas. He fumbled with the envelope before passing it on.

"Do not take this as a bribe," Houston said. "Money. For Sam, if you determine he needs it. And . . . you. Remember those early years in the Republic? Mostly, this is state script, but some old Union notes as well. And a couple of gold coins."

"Sam," Smith said, "you need not . . ."

"No." Houston held up his big hand, and Smith, conceding defeat, slipped the envelope into his inside coat pocket.

"You should hold on to your cash, Sam," Smith

said. "Inflation and all. By thunder, do you know what coffee costs these days?"

Pushing close to $4 a pound, and rising practically every day. Houston had to keep making his slaves chop cordwood for money. He smiled at Smith and sipped his coffee. "Then I had best drink while I can afford it."

Smith laughed with him, but it was not funny. Houston stared at his old friend, remembering that Smith and others had laughed at Houston's suggestion that the Union blockade would devastate the Texas economy. Now he had been proved correct.

"Have you seen the *South Carolina*?" Smith asked.

The U.S. Naval ship had arrived back in July. From what Houston had learned, the screw-propelled steamer had already captured a few blockade runners. Other ships had since arrived. The blockade became a python. The stranglehold was just beginning.

"No," Houston answered.

"Our governor suggests that we abandon Galveston," Smith said. "Put the torch to her and all that cotton."

"That would be a travesty," Houston said. "She is a beautiful city."

"Quite true." Smith stared at his napkin. "And cotton is selling at nine dollars. But you know better than anyone that Galveston cannot be defended. In time, the Yankees will occupy her. Sam, if I were you, and not a captain in the Confederate army, I would consider moving away from Galveston. Head inland. Huntsville perhaps."

Houston's head bobbed with a weary sadness. Similar thoughts often occupied his mind.

"But enough talk of war and Yankees. What's in that other envelope?" Smith pointed at the letter from Tennessee. "Is that . . . ?"

Houston picked up the envelope. "This is . . . I do not know. From Nashville." Sighing, he decided to open it. He found the knife, slit the paper, and withdrew a piece of yellow paper. It came from a Baptist minister named Stan Sullivan that Houston had known years ago. A short note.

The letter fell next to his coffee cup.

"Sam?" Smith leaned forward.

"Eliza," Houston gasped, "is dead."

CHAPTER NINETEEN

Eliza

These phantasms have always visited him as he remembers them—or how he wants to picture them: Crockett in all his middle-aged vibrancy; his mother, old, yes, but full of life and wisdom; Jackson as he might have been while entertaining at the Hermitage or White House. But Eliza Allen is different. Much different.

Fifty-two years old, looks twenty years older. No longer slim and fit, but haggard, fat, decrepit. The blonde hair is gray, disheveled, and her eyes, once vibrant and daring, are hollow, bloodshot, dead. He recalls her jewels, and gowns of the best fashion, but she dons a dress of coarse black wool and a Spartan wedding band. She smiles at him, revealing yellowed teeth, one rotten, two empty spaces.

"Surprised to see me after all this time?" Her voice is mocking, thick with rage.

Except for Crockett, his first visitor, he has rarely trembled upon seeing such specters, but Eliza Allen Houston Douglas, his first wife, terrifies him.

"Can't you even look me in the eye, darlin'?" Taunting him, Eliza spits into the bay. She sits on the middle seat, between Houston in the front and Jeff, who continues to guide the skiff toward Cedar Point, oblivious to this permutation of what once had been a beautiful girl from one of Tennessee's most prominent families. "Sam, you ain't exactly what my mama would've called a catch . . . not no more, you ain't . . . darlin'." Bitterness fills her laugh.

Which is one thing that has not changed in thirty-three years.

"How is your husband?" he manages to ask. "The doctor?"

"Sicker'n a dog. He'll be followin' me directly. Straight to perdition. But the kids, the ones still livin', they's old enough to take care of 'emselves now. Mostly, anyhow."

Once, Eliza would have spoken in proper English. He smells rum on her voice. During their courtship, she never imbibed. Perhaps he is to blame.

"I never loved you," she tells him.

Bitterness enters his own voice. "As you mentioned many a time . . . after our wedding."

She waves him off. "Bad luck. I always had bad luck. And Ma and Pa, well, they loved you enough. At first, I mean. Till I told them all about you."

"Yes," he says. "I remember."

"Do you, Sam?" she rages. "Do you really?"

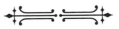

He can never forget. Seeing her that first time at Allenwood Plantation on the Cumberland River. A young girl of sixteen riding a white Arabian mare, riding with authority and experience, and not a touch of trepidation . . . even when she made the horse leap over a three-rail fence. Laughing, when she reined up in front of Sam Houston.

"Good evening, Uncle John." Addressing the Congressman standing next to Houston. But looking directly at Houston, who finds her blue eyes hypnotic.

"Eliza, allow me the honor of introducing you to Sam Houston."

"The Sam Houston who Mister Jackson goes on and on and on about, Uncle John?"

"Indeed. Although I should say Governor Houston. As you mean President-Elect Jackson."

He cannot move as she slides off the stallion, curtseys, and offers a hand.

" 'Tis my pleasure, Governor. I do declare. I have heard so much of you from my mother and father, from Uncle John, and practically all of my friends in Gallatin."

That mocking laugh snaps his vision.

"I was pretty, wasn't I, Sam?"

His head bobs. The boat rocks gently. Jeff expertly maneuvers the skiff through the water.

"Oh, to be young . . . and in love." She shifts in the seat. " 'Course, I wasn't in love with you. Poor Will Tyree. If God ever existed, He frowned on me, Sam. He surely did."

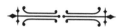

For years, Houston has tried to purge William Tyree, the young attorney claimed by consumption, from his memories. Houston also remembers his own feelings, of lust, and of the fact that he was governor of Tennessee, a friend of President Andrew Jackson, and a man who constantly heard that a governor—and, mayhap, one day President of our United States—must be married. To the right woman, of course. To the right family.

Young Elizabeth Allen would be such a woman. Or so Houston had thought. From a wealthy family with political influence. So, he had proposed. And Eliza's parents had forced their daughter to marry.

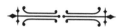

"We had us a whirlwind courtship, didn't we?" she asks.

"A tornado," he corrects. "A hurricane."

"Yeah. I'd rile you. You'd anger off. Then we'd kiss and make up, and I'd keep tellin' myself . . . make Pa happy . . . make Ma happy. You wasn't a bad-lookin' fellow back then. At least . . ."

He waits, feeling the anger, the betrayal, that he had tried to forget after all these years.

✦══✦══✦

Oh, the wedding is wonderful. At Allenwood on a Thursday evening, Eliza wears an elaborate white gown, Houston in tails, the fires blazing in the fireplaces, and Reverend William Hume so reverent. The supper lasts forever, but then Houston takes his young bride upstairs.

✦══✦══✦

"Our first night in an upstairs bedchamber in the house of your parents," Houston recalls. "Perhaps that is what doomed our nuptials."

"What doomed us, Sam," she snaps, "was you. You and your . . ."—now she shakes with rage—". . . heathen customs and . . . your . . ."

"Yes," he fires back. "If it pleases you, my wounds still leak, and I earned more wounds after our marriage." He points to the ankle shattered at San Jacinto.

She jabs him with: "You were never no Will Tyree."

213

"I never tried to be."

"Walkin' around, naked, no shame at all. Chantin' some heathen prayer. Talkin' 'bout *Kanati* and *Selu*."

"First man," he tells her. "First woman."

"You and those damned Cherokees." She snorts out a laugh, and wipes her nose with the back of her black sleeve.

"I was already disgusted by your nakedness, and the . . ." Now she howls with laughter. "You show me a damned piece of ham you brought up. Hell, I thought you was hungry."

Meat, he remembers. Cherokees brought no rings to a wedding. The groom would show meat, revealing that he would provide for the family. The bride would bring corn, perhaps bread, to show that she would care for and keep the family fed. And then they would drink from a wedding vase.

"I wasn't a damned Cherokee, Sam. I'm white."

He does not speak.

"You never was."

He looks past her now, at the calm waters, at the gulls flying over a boat where men cast nets.

"Did she make you happy?"

He turns back to her, his eyes questioning this grotesque permutation of what had been a beautiful young woman.

"The Cherokee whore you took up with after you left me! Did she make you happy?"

"She was a good woman."

"Yeah. So I hear. Good at lettin' you drink yourself half to death. Good at mindin' a store so you could take her money to buy yourself more rot-gut. Good at not raisin' a stink when you left her, too."

He does not speak. He has no defense.

"You." She spits at him. "You was always so . . . virtuous."

"What," he fires back, "did you ever know of virtue?"

Her laugh sounds like that of a witch in "Macbeth." "You married me for one reason. So you could get re-elected as governor of Tennessee. You figured sweet Eliza Allen Houston would be all you needed to whip Billy Carroll's arse in the election."

"Perhaps," he says softly. Perhaps Houston had just liked the idea of marriage, and he could not deny that few women stirred his blood like Eliza. Until he understood how much he repulsed her.

"What I really enjoyed was watchin' you squirm. Hell's fire, Sam, you didn't even go see Ol' Hickory inaugurated in Washington City. Because you just couldn't trust your devoted young wife to be left alone."

"Not with Will Tyree and who knows else hanging around Nashville," he snaps.

"No, damn you!" She starts to rise, and Houston fears the boat will capsize, but he feels no movement, and Eliza points a crooked finger at him. "You don't dare speak of Will like that. Don't you dare."

She settles back into her seat, and he sees the tears leaking from her eyes, to be consumed by the wrinkles in her old face. He feels it then, what he had felt when he sent her back to her parents.

Shame.

Only, back in the spring of 1829, when he understood that his marriage, ever so brief, was over—if it had even been a marriage—he had felt shamed by her. Now he understood that the shame was his own making. He was ashamed of himself.

"I remember that night at Martha Martin's," she says. "At Locust Grove. You remember Martha?"

He nods. "And her daughters."

"Yeah. That's right. Colder than a witch's teat it was, snowin', and you go down out into the yard and have yourself a snowball fight with the girls. They're laughin' and carryin' on, peltin' you with snowballs, and then one even knocks you on your arse. And I'm watchin' upstairs with Martha, and she's laughin' and all, and she tells me . . . 'Your husband needs some help.' Meanin' that I ought to go out and join the frolic. But I'm in no mood. And I tell her . . . 'I wish they would kill him,' . . . and when Martha lets out a gasp, I tell her what

I really feel. I turn to her and I tell her again . . . 'Yes, I wish from the bottom of my heart that they would kill him.' "

He has never heard that confession. His head falls.

"Tell me, Sam. Did the Creeks fight as awful as we did?"

He does not answer.

"Four months. We don't even live together four full months." Her head tilts back as she laughs. "It took me just shy of four months to have you see the light, throw my clothes in a grip, and shove me out of the door into the hallway at the Nashville Inn. With a letter to take back to my good, God-fearin' daddy." She mocks him. "I was 'cold' to you, you tell Father. Oh, 'I have and I do love' her so much, but, you had believed me 'virtuous'. That's what you wrote. He read the damned letter to me. In front of my mother! Aloud. God, you shamed me enough." She bawls now, choking sobs, and he tries to look away, to stare at the water, at his boots, at anything but this woman whose life he ruined, who, for a while, destroyed his own. "Oh, my . . . you was so damned noble. And you had the gumption to say you forgave me. Hell, do you think I ever forgave you?"

For an eternity, he hears not the snapping of the sail and the rippling of the water, but only Eliza's sobs.

• • •

He remembers writing that bitter note to Mr. Allen, just as he recalls tendering his resignation as governor of Tennessee. Of boarding the *Red River* and steaming down the Cumberland River. To Arkansas. And then, in an alcoholic haze, making his way to the Indian Territory, to reunite with his Cherokee father. To become The Big Drunk. And to meet Tiana Rogers, who would, along with *Oo-loo-te-ka*, let him find his dignity again. Until he left them, too, to follow . . . what? Ambition?

"I am deeply regretful for the pain I caused you and your family," he tells Eliza.

"I don't want no sympathy from you, Sam Houston," she snaps. "You know what I told Preacher Stan?" She does not wait for a response. "I told him . . . 'When I'm gone, you can preach whatever you want. Be it Baptist or pagan. You can sing hymns and try to make my widowed man and our young 'uns feel better. I don't give a tinker's damn. But the tintypes of me are buried with me. The portrait my daddy had done back in Gallatin, it's to be burned. No one's ever to remember what Sam Houston's first wife looked like. God knows, no one would want to know what she looks like now. And there ain't ever to be no damned marker on my grave. Ever.' That's what I told him. And you know why? Because

I don't want no busybodies hoverin' over my grave, sayin' . . . 'What on earth caused their separation and divorce?' That ain't how I'm spendin' eternity, darlin'."

The tears have vanished. The eyes are dead once more. She laughs again.

"You wasn't always the hero, was you, darlin'?"

"I was never a hero," he tells her.

"Yeah. You know somethin' else, Sam?"

He cannot answer, cannot move.

"I waited for you."

His eyes widen in surprise.

"I thought you'd come back to me. I mean . . . hell's fires, I was something to behold back then. When I was young. Maybe I wanted you to come back. I reckon my daddy wanted you back. After all, you was one of Jackson's Tennessee boys. So I waited. Five years. Six. I don't know offhand. Finally, it struck me that you was gone, never to return. Well." She shrugs. "Elmore shows up, he's a doctor, nothin' fancy 'bout him or nothin', maybe not even that good of a pill-roller. So I marry him."

"I hope he made you happy," he tells her.

She laughs again. "Sam Houston, the last time I was happy was that day Uncle John brung you to Allenwood. And I laid eyes on you for the first time. We ain't all blessed by the Lord . . . like there ever was a God . . . to be happy. That was

my curse. I reckon . . ."—the tears begin again—
"I reckon . . . maybe . . . I guess maybe that . . .
well, at least you found happiness. 'Cause you
never would've found it had you stuck by me."

CHAPTER TWENTY

April 10, 1862

The hard part, he finally accepted, was filling each day. Retirement disgusted him. With the war but a year old, the call for him to speak in public rarely came. Everyone had predicted a quick victory for the Confederacy, but now they had resigned themselves to a war with no foreseeable end. Inflation was on the rise in Texas. Sugar became more and more scarce, as did molasses. Coffee? Even Aunt Liza roasted acorns as a substitute.

He had tried to fill his time with other things. Fancy fairs at one of the churches. Tent revivals. Evenings at an opera house to see "Catching an Heiress" and "Charles the Second; or, The Merry Monarch," neither of which he found amusing although Margaret and most of the audience had laughed. *The Tri-Weekly Telegraph* reported that, fearing a Yankee invasion, more and more Texans were fleeing the coast.

The Houstons traveled, too, to Independence to visit Margaret's mother, and see their daughters who still attended school. Yet always, Houston and his wife returned to Cedar Point, especially during the summer. Margaret kept mentioning how she wished they could go back to their old home in Huntsville, away from the Gulf and the Yankee blockade.

When she spoke to Houston, anyway. With Sam Junior off in Mississippi, closer to the real battlefields, Margaret mostly spent her days fretting, worrying, reading the Bible, praying.

So Houston sat in his library, or on the porch, and did . . . nothing.

"Write your story," a friend of his, Russell Witherspoon, said on one visit. "The Autobiography of Sam Houston. What a hoot that would be."

"A pack of lies," Houston told Witherspoon.

"Even better," Witherspoon said.

He considered it, but his shoulder ached so much these days he rarely even wrote letters to the newspaper editors. In fact, during their current visit to Independence, he had asked his daughter Maggie to write a letter for him. Now her penmanship far surpassed his, and he did not think he could grip a pen long enough to finish a note, so he had dictated it to Maggie.

That afternoon, he asked Jeff to take him to the post office. To mail the letter. To give him something to do other than listen to his mother-in-law talk about her impending death, or ask if he wanted to see her coffin. Or sit on the porch, bored, and hear Margaret and her mother talking in the parlor, letting Mrs. Lea ask if Margaret has noticed how much her husband's health is failing, or that he isn't as sharp as he had been even just last week, or . . .

It was an uneventful trip to town. He posted the letter, and nodded when the clerk told him: "It might take a week to get it to Nacogdoches, General. It might take a month. It might take till hell freezes over."

He tried to think of something else he could do, just to while away another ten minutes or thirty. Haircut? No, he had done that two days ago. Dinner? He rarely felt hungry these days, and the last time he had eaten in the café, he had been outraged by what the owner charged for grits and sausage.

"Don't you have no friends you can visit here, Master Sam?" Jeff asked.

He snorted.

"Marco Pierce?" His head shook. "He's dead . . . Roland Hewitt?" He let out a sigh. "He's dead, too. So's Pete Oliver . . . Larry DeFee . . . Sam Walker . . ." He did not finish. "Let's just go back and see what the old biddy's saying about me now, Jeff."

"You be nice, Master Sam." The slave turned the buggy around in the center of the deserted street. "She the only mother-in-law you's apt to have."

"Thank the Almighty for that blessing."

"Master Sam!" Jeff tried to hold a stern look, only to break out laughing.

So there he sat, in a damned rocking chair on the front porch, as Jeff unhitched the mules. Pearl came out, bringing him his dinner, which, for once, made him happy. Few things tasted better than day-old cornbread crumbled into a glass and covered with cold buttermilk. His appetite returned, for at least this afternoon. He relished every bite, then finished the milk, spooned out the soggy remnants to polish off his meal, and set the glass and spoon on the table.

Pearl had also brought him *The Iliad*, which he opened.

"You need something else, Master Sam?" Jeff had returned.

"No." Houston changed his mind. "Yes. Take the glass and spoon to the wash basin."

"Yes, sir."

The spoon rattled in the glass as Jeff headed back down the steps, bound for the back door, when he stopped. Houston also heard hoofs on the cobblestone street.

"Why, ain't that Tom Blue?" Jeff called out.

With a grunt, Houston came out of the chair, retrieved his cane leaning against the wall, and moved with remarkable speed to the top of the steps. He stopped, glaring down the path, rage boiling inside. He quickly turned that anger onto Jeff.

"That's not Tom Blue, you damned fool," he snapped.

"Yes, sir. I see that now, sir. Sorry, Master Sam." The young Negro moved toward the black man who slid from the saddle and handed the reins to Jeff. "It be good to see you, T.J."

T.J. Roland, the black preacher, carpenter, and handyman—as fine a man with a paintbrush as one would find in Independence—walked up the path. Roland was lean, blacker than a raven, but with graying, close-cropped hair. Apparently, this day had found him painting, for his overalls were stained white.

He was not Tom Blue. *Be glad you are not,* Houston fumed to himself.

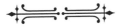

Tom Blue had been—still was—one of Houston's slaves. A strapping mulatto from the West Indies, Tom Blue had served as Houston's assistant, then as coachman . . . and then, with no call, back while the Houstons lived in Huntsville, he had run off. But not alone. No, Tom Blue had talked Uncle Strother, one of Colonel Hume's boys who worked at the blacksmith shop in town, into escaping with him. They had crossed the border into Mexico. Free.

Old Hume wanted to hire someone to fetch those boys back, to give Uncle Strother a sound whipping, and had asked Houston to help pay the slave hunter. Houston had refused. Oh, he felt betrayed by Tom Blue, but he had never whipped any of his slaves the way Old Hume and many others did. He had never separated any families. He had let them attend church services, had taught them trades, even shown many how to read and write. And this was how Tom Blue had paid him back.

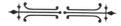

He shut out the memory, and lowered the cane as T.J. Roland stopped at the bottom of the doorsteps.

"Mister Houston, sir." Roland removed his porkpie hat, crushing the brims with his paint-stained hands. "How you doin', sir?"

"Fair to middling, T.J. What can I do for you?"

"Well . . ." The man stared at his brogans.

Houston stepped back. "Come out of the sun, T.J." He pointed to another rocking chair. "Have you had your dinner? Pearl just brought me some cornbread and buttermilk. And I do believe we have a slice or two of pecan pie left."

The freedman climbed the steps, shaking his head.

"You thank Miss Pearl and Aunt Liza, Mister Houston, but, no sir, my stomach's full."

The hat, Houston notice, rotated, and the big hands of the painter kept crushing the brims. Houston frowned. He had started for his own rocking chair, but now he stopped. He moved toward one of the wooden columns, and leaned against it for support.

"Mister Houston . . ." T.J. Roland stopped.

Houston looked at the window to the parlor. No movement came from behind the curtains, and no voices could be heard. His wife and mother-in-law had gone to another part of the house. Obviously, for a busybody like Nancy Lea would have been out the front door and standing on the porch to see who had decided to pay Sam Houston a visit.

"Sir." The freedman's Adam's apple bobbed. "You heard from Master Houston, sir? Sam Junior, I mean."

"No." Houston inhaled deeply, held the breath, finally let it out. "I mean, Missus Houston received a letter a week or so back."

"Yes, sir. Well, I was down at Washington-on-the-Brazos. Paintin' Missus Hatchell's fence for her. That's how I'm all painted over, sort of, sir." He frowned, and at last let the hat fall to his side. "Steamboat docked, Mister Houston. They don't come down the river so much no more. And the white folks, and even some colored boys workin' as deck hands, they was talkin' up a storm. Been a big fight, they's sayin', and I means a big, awful battle. Way up north somewheres."

"Virginia?" Houston asked, pleading for Roland's affirmation.

"No, sir. Place in Tennessee. Never heard of it my ownself. They calls it Shiloh Meetin' House."

CHAPTER TWENTY–ONE

April 10–May 5, 1862

Inconsolable, sobbing, irritable, Margaret took to bed. Houston tried to assure her that her son, their son, was all right. "God will not allow him to be harmed!" he roared.

She fired back: "You are not God, Sam Houston. I know you think you are, but you are not!"

She lost interest in the chickens and turkeys she had been raising, turning the care over to the children and slaves. Winds blew hot and steamy off the bay, with no clouds, no rain, nothing to relieve the oppressive heat. The crops suffered. Houston doubted if they would have any corn.

Temple and Andrew picked primroses and China blossoms, but those did not make Margaret smile.

Houston felt little better. His appetite again disappeared. Even cornbread and buttermilk no longer appealed to him. He survived on what passed for coffee these days. Coffee . . . and waiting.

The letter arrived on the 16th, addressed to Margaret, but he ripped it open on the porch. Sam Junior had not written this, Houston knew, for he did not recognize the handwriting. He read, frowning at the first words:

Corinth, Mississippi, April 2 1862
Dear Cousin Margaret:
I am amidst 100,000 men. Emmet and Sam are talking outside the tent—(God bless & protect the boys). I know full well your anxiety and solicitude about your boy . . .

The letter came from one of Margaret's cousins, C.W. Lea, who had likewise joined the 2nd Texas Infantry. Houston sank into his rocking chair. His chest screamed in agony, and he fought for breath. Houston had found enough maps to determine that a church known as Shiloh—near Pittsburg Landing on the Tennessee River—lay marching distance from Corinth, Mississippi. His son would have taken part in the big battle T.J. Roland had told Houston about. The rest of the letter seemed trivial, written a few days before the battle.

He ordered Joshua and Lewis to hitch up the team, then made Jeff drive him into Houston City, where he collected every newspaper for sale at Dottie McGee's Book Store. The merchant's husband served as postmaster, but Ike McGee had no letters for Houston.

First newspaper reports of the battle seemed,

typically, sketchy. He wondered if his mother had felt as he did now, or as Margaret must have suffered, after hearing of the slaughter at Horseshoe Bend. Yet there had been no newspapers in Maryville, Tennessee, in those times—Houston doubted if you could find a newspaper there today. Word would have come by courier. Or, rather, wagging tongues. Which is what filled most of the newspaper reports.

The first articles assured that Albert Sidney Johnston had driven Grant's army into the Tennessee River. Houston did not believe it.

He went home, and returned the next day, returned every day for more newspapers, and to see if any letters came for him, or Margaret. Sam Junior would have been more inclined to write his mother.

By then, the newspaper articles had changed. Somehow, General Grant had held strong on the banks of the river, reinforcements had arrived, and the Union Army had driven the Confederates off the battlefield. General Albert Sidney Johnston was dead, killed in the first day of slaughter. Houston had been right. Johnston was a gentleman, sending his surgeon away to help wounded Union soldiers. The gentleman had bled to death in a ravine. Afterward, a tourniquet had been found in one of Johnston's coat pockets.

At first, Houston City seemed in shock. Then horrified. Sometimes, Houston could hear men yelling inside the grog shops, blaming the disaster at Shiloh on the generals, others calling the reports nothing more than bald-faced Yankee falsehoods. Church bells pealed. Women wore black armbands to mourn the fallen heroes, whether they had sons or fathers in the war or not. Outside Oliver's Saloon, the whitewashed board keeping a tally of those killed in Houston, Richmond, and Hempstead was ripped off and smashed to pieces.

Margaret prayed and cried at Ben Lomond. She went to church on Sundays and Wednesdays to pray and cry with others. On Mondays, Tuesdays, Thursdays, Fridays, and Saturdays, she lay in bed, reading the Bible, rereading Sam Junior's letters, sobbing over his sketches and drawings.

Houston continued to go to town every day. No letters came from Sam. Few letters came at all, and the newspapers—what few arrived now— never answered the most important question Sam Houston had.

He stood in line at Dottie McGee's store, waiting for some lady to decide between two novels by Dickens.

Finally, Houston snapped. "Read *Bleak House*, madam."

She turned, lowering her spectacles. "And why should I, sir?"

"Because it's shorter than *David Copperfield*, madam, and if it takes you as long to read a book as it does to choose one, you'll never finish the latter before you're called to Glory." He ripped another book from a table. "Or here. This one . . ." The title stopped him, and he tossed *A Christmas Carol, in Prose, Being a Ghost Story of Christmas* back onto the table.

"No," he whispered, "not . . . that one."

He did not realize the woman had slammed both books onto the counter, and stormed into the muggy afternoon.

"General?"

Blinking, he remembered where he was, and regretted his anger, especially when he saw the expression on Dottie McGee's face.

"I shall buy both copies, Missus McGee," he said. "And any new papers that have arrived."

"I am not upset, General," the woman said. "The Widow Petty would have left without purchasing either edition. I doubt if she has ever read a book in her life, including the Bible." She drew a deep breath, let it out, and reached underneath the counter. "Here are the latest papers, sir. The Dallas paper . . ."—Mrs. McGee paused—"it has . . . some of the first . . . casualty reports."

Houston picked up the *Herald*. The thin paper shook in his hand.

"Casualty . . . reports . . . ," he whispered.

"Ike calls them 'the butcher's bill.' " The owner also brought up a letter. "Ike brought this over during dinner. To give to you, sir."

233

Scanning the item in the *Herald*, he froze as he read: *We have reports that Sam Houston Junior, son of the hero of San Jacinto, is among the thousand gallant Texians slain in defense of our homeland.*

"Oh, God in heaven, no," he muttered.

"General . . ." Dottie McGee held out the letter.

He almost collapsed when he recognized the handwriting of Captain Ashbel Smith.

A mile out of the city, Houston ordered Jeff to steer the buggy to the side of the road. He had yet to open Smith's letter, and now he passed it over to the young slave.

"Jeff . . ."—he steeled himself—"read this."

"Your spectacles not workin', Master Sam?"

"Something's not working. Read it, Jeff."

"It starts 'April Sixteenth, Eighteen Sixty-Two.' He says . . . 'My dear Old Chief, Writing is extremely painful—a wound involving the right armpit and weakness from many days fever . . .' "

Even Ashbel Smith had been a casualty at Shiloh. Newspapers from New Orleans and Dallas had said the number of dead would reach the thousands, and the wounded in the tens of thousands. More, Houston knew, than the casualties during the entire Creek War and the campaign for Texas's independence combined.

234

Houston had to help Jeff with some of the words: *amanuenses, plantation, apprehensions*.

" 'I shook hands with Sam on the morning of the Seventh,' " Jeff read. Houston feared he would throw up. " 'Sam and some seven or eight others were in no way accounted for. . . . On the Ninth, I was sent to the hospital in Memphis. . . . Since leaving, I have not heard a word from Camp.' "

He frowned. Silently, he prayed.

" 'I by no means despair of Sam's safety—indeed I think he may now be in camp. . . .' "

Then Captain Smith shattered Houston's prayers.

The battle had been fought "gallantly." Sam Junior "fought like a hero and with the coolness of a veteran." He had marched in "the first rank." Tears blurred Houston's vision. " 'I occasionally cautioned him with a friendly threat to tell his mother of his so expressing himself. Sam always replied with a pleasant smile and a cheery word.' "

Jeff read: " 'I trust my dear General that Sam will soon send to yourself news that he is safe and well.' "

Houston barely heard the rest.

"And he signs it . . . 'Truly Your Dear Friend, Ashbel Smith.' That's all it says, Master Sam."

His eyes opened. "I know he's all right, Master Sam," Jeff told him. "It's like you tol' Missus Houston, sir, that time. God won't let young Sam get killed. Remember, Master Sam?"

"And . . ." Houston fingered the pages of Smith's letter and stuffed them back inside the envelope, "as Margaret reminded me . . . I am not God."

Another letter arrived a week later, but it held no news about Sam Junior. It had been addressed to Margaret, a short, grim note that word had reached Alabama that Margaret's cousin, William P. Rogers, had been killed at Shiloh.

"Another addition," Houston whispered to himself, "to the butcher's bill."

CHAPTER TWENTY-TWO

May 6–June 12, 1862

His mother-in-law arrived that morning, had her servants take her grips to the guest room, and walked past Houston—never making eye contact with the giant—and on into Margaret's room. He had started to say something like: *You didn't bring your casket. What'll you do if you up and die, Nancy?* He curbed his tongue, though, and prayed silently to the Lord to forgive him for vindictive thoughts. He blamed this on the bitterness, the crushing anxiety of not knowing.

Behind the closed door of Margaret's room, his wife sobbed. "Oh, Mother, what shall I do? How shall I bear it?"

Houston went to his library. He had stopped going to Houston City for newspapers. The papers all reported the same. The butcher's bill grew, and Sam Junior's name appeared in many of them, sometimes as killed, sometimes as wounded, often as missing, twice as captured. No more news had arrived from Captain Ashbel Smith, but for all Houston knew, the good doctor had died in Memphis. Or his arm could have been amputated. Or he could have been captured and sent on some prison ship up north.

Now he knew what the phantom of Andrew Jackson had meant in that dream—or whatever the hell it was—when Old Hickory had warned Houston that his heart would be shattered.

That was the hell of this. Waiting. Not knowing. Governor Lubbock had written him. The Austin papers must have reported that Sam Junior was missing, and Houston found a pen and wrote a brief, strained reply. He sealed the letter with wax, and pushed himself away from the desk. *The Iliad* lay within reach, but Homer could not carry him away from his weakness, his troubles. He stared at the corner table and saw the bourbon and rye, and his hands clenched into balled fists.

"No," he told himself. Beads of sweat popped out on his forehead.

Suddenly, old Lewis stood in the open doorway.

"Master Sam!" the slave called out.

Houston steadied himself. "What is it, Lewis?"

"They's a lady here to see you, sir. Had her manservant drive her in from Galveston, sir. Name Jones."

"Jones?"

"Yes, sir. A widow Mary Jones."

Once, her late husband had been one of Houston's strongest supporters, and best of friends. And Mary had shared many cups of tea with Margaret. Anson Jones had fought at San Jacinto, had served as Houston's minister to the United States during that raucous first term as president of the Republic of Texas. Later, he became Houston's secretary of state. Finally, he had been the last president of the republic, and had fought with vigor and foolishness against annexation.

"He does not want statehood for Texas," Houston had said. "He wants a throne for himself. He sees himself as King Arthur. He sees himself as God."

But when Texas became a state, and Jones had not been chosen senator, he grew to hate Senator Sam Houston. In 1857, he had tried for the U.S. Senate again, and received no votes. He blamed Houston. Mary stopped speaking and writing to Margaret. In January of 1858, Anson Jones had killed himself in Houston City.

What would his widow want of me? Houston thought. He found a handkerchief and wiped sweat from his brow, rose, and moved toward the coat rack. It was too damned hot to be wearing a frock coat, but if Mary Jones came from Galveston to see him, he must look dignified. Lewis helped him into the coat, and Houston settled back into his chair.

"Show her in, Lewis," Houston said, and waited.

Mary had always been a beautiful woman, probably twenty years younger than her now dead husband. She had not changed, but after four or five years since Anson's suicide, she still wore black. She had been forced to sell the plantation in Washington-on-the-Brazos—the money going to her husband's creditors—and if not for Ashbel Smith, the widow and her children would likely have been living in some hard-scrabble hut in the woods. Dr. Smith had managed to buy land for her in Galveston.

Despite the pain in his leg, Houston pushed himself to his feet without a grimace and bowed. *Should I go over to greet her?* He could not decide. *What is proper?* Her eyes were rimmed red, which could have been from the dust from the drive as fierce bay winds had not abated. Or she might have been crying. He gestured toward a chair.

"Have a seat, Missus Jones." *Missus Jones.* Once he could have called her Mary.

"Thank you, no, General."

Once I would have been Sam.

"Your boy told me," the widow said, "that your wife is indisposed."

Houston nodded. "She has worried herself sick fretting over Sam, our oldest."

"Yes. My son was at Shiloh, too."

He stiffened, and felt the dread as she opened a purse and withdrew a letter. "Have you word from . . . ?" He could not remember her boy's name. She had more than one son, and a daughter, if he recalled correctly. But which boy had been closest to Sam's age? Which had he seen at Camp Bee with the 2nd Texas?

"Charles," she said. "Yes." The red in her eyes came from tears, not dirt, not dust, for the tears leaked down her cheeks, and she weaved. Houston came to her, limping, but she steadied herself before the envelope fell to the floor. The yellow piece of paper shook in her hands.

"Lewis!" Houston barked, and the slave reappeared in the doorway. "Pick up . . ."—he fought for control—"the envelope." He could not bend down himself. "Please."

The slave obeyed, but now Mary Jones began speaking.

"This came from Jim Hageman, a friend." The tears turned into a torrent, and the widow spun, brushed past Lewis, and disappeared out the door. In his massive right hand, Houston caught the letter the widow had dropped.

Houston burst through the door of Margaret's room. His mother-in-law screamed, and Margaret, pale, face flushed, eyes red, sat bolt upright.

"He's alive!" Houston roared. "Thank the Almighty, Sam is alive!"

He would have trampled Nancy Lea had she not spun out of his way, and he sank onto the bed. His bed. His room. They had shared it until the melancholy took hold of Margaret. Of late, he had slept in Sam Junior's room—whenever he could actually sleep. Margaret's eyes widened. He held the letter, slightly crushed.

"Mary Jones brought it. Just now. She received it." He spoke in rushes. "Cromwell. No. No. Sam. No." He laughed. Now he remembered all of the Anson children's names, even Sallie, the youngest. "Charles. Charles was in the Second with Sam. Her son, Charles. You remember him. A cat-tail weighed more than he did, and he was just as tall. Mary got this letter." He thrust it before her. "See. See. It's from one of the Hageman brood. Charles received a wound in the arm. Just a flesh wound, though. Sam was captured."

"Captured?" Margaret blinked away the disbelief.

"Yes. Yes. He's a prisoner of war. But he's alive, my darling. Our boy is alive!"

He wrapped his massive arms around his fragile wife, and pulled her close. She bawled then, tears of joy. Behind him, Nancy Lea muttered something.

"I must write Mary," Margaret was saying. "I must . . . I . . . Sam . . . oh . . . Lord have mercy. Lord have mercy. Blessed be our God in heaven. Oh . . . Sam."

For the longest while, he hugged his wife.

Margaret returned to him. Nancy Lea left for Independence and her steel casket. Houston could eat again, and he delighted in watching Margaret, Andrew, Willie Rogers, and Temple caring for the goslings, poults, and chicks. Margaret quilted. She knitted. They talked again. They even laughed.

Oh, they still felt the stress, that fear of the unknown, but the last word they had received told them that Sam Junior was alive. A prisoner of war. But alive. At some point, they told themselves, he would write them. So, they waited, no longer fearing the worst.

He thumbed through Homer and Virgil. He fished. He read newspapers, and what little mail came. And when he needed money, he ordered the slaves to chop cordwood.

Weeks later, Ike McGee brought the package.

"I don't know what it is, General," the post-master said. "Feels like a book. And there wasn't enough postage on it, so I got to ask you for . . . well, sir, you know what a Confederate dollar's worth these days, General."

Houston held the package, and handed it off to Joshua. He called for Jeff to find his billfold and paid McGee. After taking the package from Joshua, he saw that it had been mailed from Corinth, Mississippi.

A few days back, word had reached Cedar Point that the Confederates had withdrawn from Corinth, abandoning the city to the Yankee Army.

Senator Samuel Houston, Esquire
Dear Sir:

I am certain you do not remember me, but I shall never forget you. Years ago, I met you as among the petitioners fighting against the repeal of the Missouri Compromise, and your defense of us was honorable and heroic.

I wear the blue, sir, and was at Pittsburg Landing. While crossing the battlefield after the carnage, I came across a young Rebel soldier who had been grievously wounded by a rifled Minié ball in his thigh. At first, I thought the young, lean lad to be among the dead, but when he moved suddenly and let out a groan, I dropped by his side to give comfort and, I feared, the last rites. Finding his knapsack, I opened it and withdrew the enclosed Bible. When I opened it, I saw the inscription almost at the same time the boy opened his eyes and locked onto me.

"Are you," I asked, "related to General Houston of Texas, who served in the United States Senate?"

The lad wet his lips and said . . . "My father."

Various emotions tore at me, and I had seen enough carnage over the past two days. I had seen a pond in which the water had turned red from the blood of soldiers, in blue and gray, who had bathed their wounds. I had seen the ground covered with dead. Your son said to me . . . "The surgeon says I am dying."

"You," I told him, "will not die." I called another surgeon over, told him that this boy, an enemy perhaps but the son of a great man, needed the best care we could provide. The surgeon said that the femoral artery had been severed and there was nothing he could do. I begged him to look again.

God in His mercy opened the surgeon's eyes. The artery had been missed. Thanks be to our Lord.

General Houston, I return the Bible to you now, in hopes that it will reach you in good health. I hope that this will help ease your suffering. Your son is alive. His dreadful wound shows no signs of infection, and the bleeding has been stopped. I can be of no more assistance to him, or you, Senator, other than to tell you that he is to be sent to Camp Douglas near Chicago, Illinois.

For him, sir, I pray that the war is over. And I pray that this carnage will end for all of us soon, His Will Be Done.

· · ·

He found Margaret on the settee, knitting. Holding the Bible in his hands, he sat beside her. She recognized the book instantly and gasped.

"Sam's in a prison camp near Chicago," Houston told her, then began to sob, burying his head against her shoulder. He felt her arms around him, and he straightened. He told her of their son's wound, of the surgeon, of the chaplain Houston had met years ago. He handed her the small Bible, the one Houston had handed his son in Houston just before he had left on the train. Margaret opened the Bible, and through blurred vision, they read Margaret's handwriting.

Sam Houston, Jr.,
From his mother,
March 6, 1862

She pointed to a hole toward the bindings.
"A bullet," Houston said.
"Not the one that wounded him."
He shook his head. "Your gift, my darling, likely saved our oldest son's life."
Her fingers trembled as she turned the pages, stopping at the 70th Psalm.

Make haste, O God, to deliver me; make
haste to help me, O Lord.
Let them be ashamed and confounded that

seek after my soul: let them be turned backward, and put to confusion, that desire my hurt.

Let them be turned back for a reward of their shame that say, Aha, aha.

Let all those that seek thee rejoice and be glad in thee: and let such as love thy salvation say continually, Let God be magnified.

But I am poor and needy: make haste unto me, O God: thou art my help and my deliverer; O Lord, make no tarrying.

CHAPTER TWENTY-THREE

September 30, 1862

He busied himself, protesting martial law—
"We are back to the days of the Inquisition," he
told Margaret—but spending more time sending
money and letters to friends he had in Chicago.
Brokering, he secretly knew, a prisoner exchange.
He would do anything to get his son home. Yet
Cedar Point began to lose its appeal. Once,
Ben Lomond had been a respite, but no more.
Oysters lost their flavor. The heat kept its grip,
even though the calendar read fall. His neighbors
turned into conniving cowards.

On this Tuesday afternoon, two provost
marshals knocked on the door. Sighing, he told
Lewis to send them in, and he hurriedly finished a
letter to a solicitor in Chicago named John Rose,
Sr. He stuffed a few federal banknotes into the
envelope and sealed it before the two marshals
came to see him. Outside his chambers, he heard
the voices. He waited. Then understanding what
those visitors were doing, he felt the blood racing
to his head and he pushed himself to his feet. He
had to use a damned crutch these days, but he did
not care. Limping to the door, he stepped into the
hallway and roared.

"Lewis! I told you to send them in to the library. I did not say they were to question my children!"

He knew one of the marshals, Jimmy Donahoe, and knew of the other, a one-armed, dark-haired scoundrel named Moody. The latter had squatted to talk to Andrew Jackson, all of eight years old.

"Yes, sir," the old slave stuttered, "but they says . . ."

"I give not a tinker's damn what they say. This is my house."

Marshal Moody slowly rose. "General," he began, but Houston cut him off.

"Do you take especial interest in what my children prattle about in my own home, sir?"

Lewis took the opportunity to grab Andrew's hand and rush the boy away from an approaching battle.

"This way." Houston returned to the library.

"Did Governor Lubbock send you?" he asked once they were settled. He had skewered the governor with ink and paper over the martial law.

"General," Jimmy Donahoe said. "The governor is used to your letters, sir. But others . . ."

Houston shook his head. This meant his own neighbors were conspiring against him, accusing him of disloyalty to the Confederacy, or, even worse, to the state of Texas.

"I claim no more than the humblest man in the community," he told the lawmen, "and I am always ready to answer to the laws of my country.

Or do you plan to arrest me as you have done in Gainesville and Sherman?"

That news had reached him the other day. North Texas had been divided during the Secession movement, and the latest conscription act had caused a protest among those who abhorred the idea of Secession, who remained loyal, or as loyal as one could be in these trying times, to the Union. Men who had refused to report to duty had been arrested. If that were not horrifying enough, a few days earlier other citizens had been arrested.

"General," Donahoe, ever the peacemaker, began, "what happened up north . . ."

"Is abhorrent," Houston said. "Does anyone believe those poor farmers and merchants actually planned on pulling off some John Brown raid of the arsenals in those towns?"

"That ain't our reason for comin' here," Moody said. "And that ain't our jurisdiction nohow, Gainesville, I mean, Sherman. But you ain't never been one for the Confederacy."

"But," Houston roared, "I have always been for Texas. Say otherwise, Marshal Moody, and we shall meet on the field of honor, sir."

"General," Donahue began. "Governor Lubbock simply wants . . ."

That's when Houston understood. Laughing, he shook his head. "Frank is scared. Scared of an old man like me. By Jehovah, boys, send word to

250

Austin that I have no plans to run for governor. I oppose the conscript law. I oppose martial law. I said it in 'Sixty, I said it in 'Sixty-One, I repeat it today, and I will continue to say that war will be disastrous for the South. Is that treason? I think not, gentlemen. I think it is factual. I speak my mind. That's all I have to do these days." He held out his big hands. "Slap on your manacles, gentlemen. Haul Sam Houston to jail or hang him."

When they left, Houston settled back into his chair. He picked up the letter to the Yankee lawyer named Rose, spinning it end over end before dropping it on the desk top and reaching into his pockets. The knife came out, and he unfolded the blade, gliding his thumb across the keen edge. Next a scrap of wood came out—hickory—and he pushed himself away from the desk.

The blade glided with the grain. He studied the work, and continued to whittle.

Eventually, he found Margaret standing before him. Dusk had settled over Cedar Point.

"They did not arrest you, I see," his wife said softly.

"Mayhap you would have been better off had they done so." What was left of the hickory he placed on the top of his desk and closed the blade before dropping the knife into his pocket.

"I miss Huntsville," Margaret said.

He smiled at the memory. Over the past months, he had kept busy touring east Texas, lighting out with Jeff in the buggy, making stops at towns, including Huntsville. "It was a bang-up house we had at Raven Hill."

"Yes. I wish . . ."

"The owner will not sell." He realized his mistake.

"What have you been doing on your buggy rides, Sam Houston?"

He shrugged. "I have made inquiries, my darling." Those journeys had left him exhausted, and recently Margaret had asked him to stay home. He had rarely found strength to refuse her.

"Perhaps I should rethink keeping you about the house." She smiled, but it did not last. It rarely did.

The concussion of a shell from the *U.S.S. South Carolina* rattled the house. Sounds of war. So close. And, of late, more and more frequent.

"Probably just another blockade runner," he told her. "Those forty-four-pounders are quite loud."

"I hate this damned war," she said.

His eyebrows raised. Never had he heard Margaret utter an oath. Now, with a sigh, he closed his eyes. "From one nation, we have become two." His head shook. "That attests how vain were the dreams of those who believed that the Union could last forever."

"It might yet," she said.

"No." His eyes opened. "No . . . ," he said again. "I wonder if Adams and Jefferson and Franklin thought it would last as long as we have." He paused. *"Had,"* he corrected. "Crockett once told me that he pitied me for living to see everything I fought for crumble into ruin."

Her face turned pained. "When did Crockett tell you that, Sam?"

He blinked. Trying to smile, he waved her off. "It does not matter. You are here to tell me that you have sent Lewis or Jeff umpteen times to call me to supper. Well . . ."

Margaret's head shook. "No, Sam. Not yet." She crossed the room, and he saw the newspaper in her hand. "Ike McGee brought this from Houston City, Sam." She laid the paper on his desk, and pointed at a headline from a New Orleans newspaper. Since spring, New Orleans had been under Union control.

Houston stared at the paper. He read the item quickly, digesting its meaning.

"This means nothing." He glanced at his wife. "It is an act that cannot be enforced."

"You know and I know that this does not mean nothing, Sam. It means everything." She turned away, her skirts rustling as she left his library. "I will send Jeff when it is time for supper. Do not be late. We are having shrimp and grits."

He sat for some time before he reread the

article. Then read it again. On his next pass, he understood that Margaret had been right.

Jeff came to the open doorway and knocked on the frame.

Houston looked at the slave, who said softly: "Aunt Liza and Missus Houston, they say it's time for you to come eat, Master Sam. You ready?"

"I'm ready."

"Let me get your crutch, Master Sam."

"Jeff," Houston said, stopping the slave from moving. "Come here. I want to show you something."

The slave moved uncertainly, and Houston rose from his seat.

"I'll clean up them shavin's, directly, Master Sam," Jeff said, and Houston saw the remnants of his afternoon of whittling on the floor at his feet. "I can do it right now. . . ."

"No." Houston smiled warmly. "The shavings can wait." He tapped the headline on the *Daily Crescent.*

The young man frowned, his head shaking. "Master Sam, I sure ain't never seen that word before." He struggled trying to pronounce it.

"Emancipation," Houston told him.

Jeff blinked. He tried saying it. Houston helped him.

"What do it mean, sir?"

Houston shook his head. "For the moment,

nothing. But in time, it will be a word you and your sons and your son's sons and their sons will say, will remember, forever."

"E-man-ci- . . . ?"

"Emancipation."

"E-man-ci-pa-tion."

Houston felt light-headed. "Yes," he said. "That's it."

"And Father Abe . . . I mean . . . Mister Lincoln, he done this?"

"Yes."

"You want me to read more of that story, Master Sam, or just that big word?"

"The big word for now. Let us eat. No one makes shrimp and grits better than Aunt Liza."

"It's on account of the bacon and butter."

"That's right."

Using the crutch, Houston walked out of the library, through the doorway into the dogtrot, and into the adjoining cabin.

President Abraham Lincoln had announced this Emancipation Proclamation a week after a savage battle near Sharpsburg, Maryland, either a Union victory or a draw, but from some reports a more costly bloodbath than Shiloh.

As of January 1, 1863, slaves in all territories still in rebellion would be free.

It took a while for that to register. Of course, anyone could make such a boast. How could you enforce any law in a state in which your government had no authority? Free the slaves in South Carolina? In Mississippi? In Texas? Balderdash. But the more Houston had studied it, the more he realized just what a brilliant political maneuver Mr. Lincoln had managed.

This war had just become a different type of war. Not for the Confederacy, but to free men in bondage. No matter who Jefferson Davis sent to England or France, now that Lincoln had changed the purpose of the war, no skilled orator, politician, or broker could persuade any country of power and prestige to recognize the Confederate States of America. With one brilliant stroke of his pen, Abraham Lincoln had perhaps just won the war, or, at the least, prolonged it.

In the long run, Houston realized, Lincoln would have to adjust his proclamation. In the end, Houston understood—and so, he thought, did that raw-boned lawyer from Illinois—all slaves would be free.

The Confederacy was suddenly alone in the world. The Confederacy was lost.

Chapter Twenty-Four

Tom

The figure sits on the edge of Houston's desk, so cocksure and haughty, grinning with a set of teeth that seem even whiter against his dark black skin. His eyes sparkle. He is dressed in the proper outfit of a gentleman's coachman.

Houston cannot believe the audacity. He starts to mouth one word, but stops himself before he can call Tom Blue uppity.

The one slave who had run away from Sam Houston must be able to read his mind, for Tom Blue laughs.

Houston shakes from a deathly chill. Another ghost has come to visit him, but Tom Blue frightens him more than Crockett, his mother, or Old Hickory. Perhaps Tom Blue scares him even more than Eliza.

"Tom," he manages to say. "Are you dead, too?"

The slave slaps his thigh and slides off the desk. Tall, he speaks like a man with education. Well, Sam Houston had sent him to school—over protests from Texas officials and neighbors—but Tom Blue had already been a man of letters, it appeared, long before Houston had purchased him at auction.

"Must I be dead to come see you, Boss Sam?" The last words come out in a thickened accent. Houston bristles. *This runaway dares mock me?*

"Oh, Boss Sam, I's so sorry. I sure didn't mean to insult your pride, Gen'ral. Please don't whup me. I promise, Master. I be a good boy . . . an obedient darky . . . from now on, Boss Sam."

Blood rushes to Houston's head. He pushes himself up. "By thunder, Tom Blue. . . ."

The runaway slave laughs.

Houston tries to calm himself. He tells himself that he is dreaming again.

He bought Tom Blue in Washington-on-the-Brazos. The auctioneer said the strapping young buck was a "quality folk" of good breeding—as good as a colored boy could get—and had been born in the West Indies. *That had been . . . ?*—he tries to think—when talk of independence could only be whispered, when he had been new to the state, without any slaves. *1833? Something like that.*

"Why have you come to haunt me? Did you die in Mexico? Well, had you not run off, I would have cared for you. I always cared for you, and all my . . ."

"Property?"

Houston clenches his fist. "I treated you right, Tom Blue."

"Did you?" There is no mockery in his accent now, just anger. Those black eyes match the intensity of the slave's voice.

"You never chopped wood," Houston barks. "You never worked the fields."

"Because I was your coachman . . . once you bought that fancy yellow wagon to impress your wife. How is that barouche, General? That new boy of yours, young Jeff, does he have a touch with the leather the way I do? Does he know how to get mules or horses moving at a good lope?"

"I do not deserve this, Tom Blue."

"Don't you?" The Negro crosses the room, finds a glass, and fills it with brandy from a decanter. He drinks it down in one gulp, tops the glass again, and returns to Houston's desk. "You think you're a good man, a hero. The father of Texas. Ol' Sam Jacinto."

"I have lived my life with honor."

"White man's honor. Slaveholder's honor. That's what you mean." Tom Blue sips the brandy. "Oh, how you were something else speaking for the rights of your Cherokee Indian pals. But they were more family to you. Me and Aunt Liza . . . and old Esau. You remember Esau? How many years did he work for you . . . before he died?"

Houston frowns.

"How many slaves do you own now? Ten?" The mockery returns as Tom Blue sips more brandy.

"Nah. Gots to be more'n that. A dozen, maybe. I mean, slaves that you owns and Margaret . . . you don't mind my callin' her by her first name, does you, Master? Oh, I reckon that ain't fittin'. Reckons that I be actin' a mite uppity for a runaway slave hidin' out from all the greedy white bastards who wants to collect a bounty? So, combined, your darkies and Missus Houston's boys . . . gots to be an even dozen. Let's say, eight hundred dollars each. I know. That ain't right because a strappin' young buck like Jeff and Joshua, they be worth two three times that much. At auction, I mean. So that puts your wealth at . . . ? So . . . hm-m-m. Cypherin' never was my best skill in that school you sent me to. Nine thousand dollars? Somewhere along that. That be a lot of money, Boss Sam. Lots of money."

Houston rears back, pointing a massive finger at the runaway. "You got an education, Tom Blue. I saw to that. You were allowed to go to church, too. I allowed that."

"You *allowed* that." Tom Blue's head shakes. "You don't see for anything, Sam Jacinto. Because you're just a rich white man. Me? I'm just an animal to you, like one of your mules or pigs or one of those baby geese and turkeys and chickens that Missus Margaret loves. But an animal, now, like that fine horse of yours. An animal has a soul. But a Negro? No." His head shakes faster and faster. "No, sir. A Negro is an animal, but a Negro ain't got no soul."

Houston opens his mouth, but no words of protest form. He slumps back in the chair.

"You did let us go to church," Tom Blue tells him, "but after we had stayed outside to hold your horses while you attended the white services. And you did teach Jeff how to eat with knife and spoon and fork. Yes, sir, Boss Sam, that was mighty white of you."

Houston finds another argument. "Do you think Jeff would have been better off had I let him be bought by that son-of-a-bitch Moreland? Moreland would have whipped the boy for spite. Or maybe I should have sold Jeff back to that bastard McKell, who needed to sell Jeff to pay off his whiskey debts."

"What'd you pay for Jeff, Sam? Five hundred dollars or something like that. Bargain you got."

"Jeff was better off . . . is better off . . . with me than he would have been with Moreland or McKell."

"Right. You took him straight to the mercantile, bought him new duds, some ginger cakes. You were a fine boss, General Houston. A fine master. You're eatin' oysters on the half-shell. Aunt Liza and the rest of us would be eatin' 'possum and sweet taters."

"I do not deserve this treatment, Tom Blue."

Now Tom Blue laughs. "Well, Aunt Liza made

real fine 'possum stew and sweet taters. I'll give you that."

"McKell and Moreland were slave beaters. They would have . . ."

"McKell and Moreland never owned me, Sam Jacinto. Never would have, either, unless you ran out of money and had to sell me to pay off your own whiskey debts. Then again, maybe you'll have to sell Jeff or Joshua or even Aunt Liza. War's not going too good for your Texas, General. And firewood don't last forever, Boss Sam."

"I never beat you, Tom Blue."

The runaway tests the brandy on his tongue, swallows some more, and sets the glass on the desk. "Because you knew I would have torn your damned head off if you laid a stripe across my back."

Houston almost rises in fury. "If you'd done that, by God, I . . ."

"What? Would've castrated me? Crippled me? Give me a good Come-to-Jesus beatin'?"

"I never beat you," Houston says again. "I never beat any of my slaves. And you know that's the gospel truth, Tom Blue."

The slave grins again, and retrieves his glass. He swishes the amber liquid around the crystal, admiring it, and drains the brandy. "Didn't you?" he says.

Houston stares across the library, seeking help. But he's alone with a runaway slave. He wets his lips. Sweat stains his armpits, and his damned hands turn clammy as they had done at Horseshoe Bend, at San Jacinto, and countless times before and after.

"I never beat . . ." He stops.

He remembers.

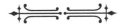

Huntsville at Raven Wood plantation. Four years ago. Maybe five. Jeff has put a halter on Houston's fine stallion, Old Pete, and leads the horse to the spring a few hundred yards from the house, the spring everyone called the "baptizing pool". Houston's daughter Nannie, not yet in her teens, runs down to the horse. She has been playing musketeers with Sam Junior and Maggie, so she holds a switch that has become a make-believe sword. Jeff knows better, but he jokingly tells Nannie to swat that fly on Old Pete's nose. With a childish laugh, she smacks the horse. Old Pete is a hot-blooded stallion, tolerates little nonsense, and he rears. Nannie winds up in the spring, Jeff releases the reins, and dives in after Nannie, lifting her up, and pulling her out, barely getting himself onto dry land. Old Pete gallops down the road.

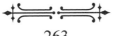

"Yeah," Tom Blue says. "You remember. So do I. I heard the ruction, came out of the wood-shed, hurried to the baptizing pool. Poor Miss Nannie's bawling her fool head off, and Jeff . . ." He laughs. "Hell, he's practically white."

Houston feels shamed.

"So, I run off to fetch Old Pete, leaving you and your missus to conduct your own inquisition . . . isn't that what you called those Rebel law dogs who come visiting you today of doing? Well, y'all ask Miss Nannie and poor, scared-to-death Jeff anything you can think of. By the time, I'm back, you've handed Jeff your knife. You tell him to go cut a good switch, and it better not be a small one. Then you led him to the stable. That's how it happened. Or am I wrong, Boss Sam?"

For a moment, Houston cannot answer. He sees himself, though, slashing with the switch, and he remembers the welts on Jeff's back. He cannot forget the tears in the young slave's eyes.

"I would . . ."—he tries to explain—"had it been my own son." He nods, as though to confirm what he is saying. "I would have whipped my own son for . . ."

"For what? A foolish prank? That's what it was. Nothing more."

"Jeff . . ."

"Jeff pulled your daughter out of that spring, Sam Jacinto. He likely saved her from drowning.

And Jeff . . . he can't swim, not any better than Miss Nannie."

"Yes." He is a former lawyer, a former senator. He finds his argument. "But Jeff was responsible. He told Nannie to strike Old Pete's nose."

"Yes, sir. So you beat him."

"As I would have whipped Sam Junior had it . . ."

The runaway laughs. "Sam Houston," he says, "tell me something. When did you ever beat any of your children?" A long pause fills the room, and then Tom Blue is walking away, toward the door. "Everybody calls you a hero, Sam Jacinto. The newspapers. The rich white folks, and the poor white folks. The preachers. Your kids. Your wife. You even call yourself one, too. But you ain't no hero, Boss Sam. You ain't nothin' but a rich white man."

CHAPTER TWENTY-FIVE

October 1–15, 1862

The next morning, he brought Jeff back to the office, and again pointed to the New Orleans *Daily Crescent*.

"E-man-ci-pation!" Jeff grinned widely at his accomplishment.

"That's right. This is a proclamation from President Lincoln. It says that on the first day of next year, you will be free. All Negroes will be free."

The young man could not comprehend.

"Well," Houston said. "Maybe not immediately. But in the end, when peace comes, you and Joshua and Aunt Liza, Aunt Mary, Pearl, Lewis . . . all of them . . . you shall all be free."

"Free?"

Houston nodded vigorously. "Yes. Do you understand?"

Jeff shook his head. "No, sir. And I don't rightly think Aunt Mary or Aunt Liza wants to be free, sir."

Houston frowned. "Well, you just remember. Abraham Lincoln will set you free. Eventually."

"Like God will."

"No. Not like God. Just . . ." Sighing, he

gave up. He picked up the letter to lawyer John Rose, Sr., in Chicago. "We should take this letter to town to post. And . . ." He thought of something else, something he and Margaret had discussed. "Give me an hour to pen another correspondence, Jeff. Then take me to Houston City."

"Yes, sir." The slave walked away, and Houston sat in his chair, opened a drawer, and found stationery and an envelope.

"Master Sam?"

It sounded like Tom Blue's voice, and Houston shivered before looking up only to see Jeff standing there. Gathering his composure, Houston said: "And one more thing, Jeff. I would prefer if you no longer called me master." With a smile, he pointed toward the ceiling. "We have but one master, and he watches over us from heaven."

Jeff swallowed. "But, Master . . ."

"No. Not 'Master Sam.' Our master is the Lord."

"What you want me to call you then?"

"Mister Houston will suffice."

"Yes, sir, Mister Sam . . . I mean . . ."

"Mister Sam is fine. I like the sound of it."

The slave tried to twist all this until it made sense. Apparently, he failed.

Houston asked: "Is there something else, Jeff? Something I can explain?"

"No, Mas- . . . I mean, no, Mister Sam. But . . . well. Yes, sir. So, we gonna be free on the first day of January, but we ain't really gonna be free?"

Houston sighed. "Something like that, Jeff. It is difficult to comprehend or explain."

"And Mister Lincoln, he's freein' us? But he ain't quite able to do it?"

"Yes. That's about how things size up."

"But . . . well . . . sir . . . ain't you . . . I mean, don't you have that power? Couldn't you free us, Mas- . . . Mister Houston? You, sir? And not Mister Lincoln?"

Sliding the pen back into its holder, Houston swallowed. He seemed to hear Tom Blue laughing at him again, but he saw no one in the room, only his own reflection in the mirror and young Jeff standing at the door.

"It is . . . hard . . . but . . ." He could not look Jeff in the eye. "You will be free, Jeff. In time. Remember." Then he recalled a fact to help him. "When our new leaders adopted the Confederate constitution for our state, they made it illegal to free slaves." He felt despicable, letting an illegal constitution in a traitorous state get him out of this trap he had set for himself. "Have faith, though, my loyal servant. You will live to see you and all your race freed. See to your chores, Jeff, and fetch me in an hour."

He found the pen, dipped it in the inkwell, and

placed it on the stationery. He could not write. His heart pained him.

He could not free his slaves—but not because of any state law. He just couldn't do it. Not with the little time he had left on this Earth. Margaret and the children would need something left behind, and Houston had little money. He would not leave them destitute as poor Mary Jones had been after Anson's cowardly suicide. He had to think of his family first. He had to . . .

Returning his pen to its holder, Houston pushed back in the chair.

"You were right, Tom Blue," he said in a ragged whisper. "I am no hero. I am but a weak, cowardly man."

Trips to Houston City he could take, but no more journeys to Brenham, Bastrop, Washington, Huntsville, Nacogdoches. Margaret even stopped traveling to see her mother in Independence. On this day, Jeff drove him to his namesake city to see the barber, Perry Stokes. As far back as Lebanon, Tennessee, Houston had learned that barbers were not only good for shaves and haircuts.

What shocked him was finding the Confederate and state flags flying at half-staff. One woman walked out of the store across the street and dropped her basket of eggs. The gray-clad soldier coming forward to ask for Houston's pass stumbled, dropped his musket, and gawked.

Stepping out of his tonsorial parlor, Perry Stokes turned pale, blinked, and leaned against the wooden wall.

"By . . . ," he started, laughed, then roared. "I told you dumb oafs it was a lie! He ain't dead!"

"Who's not dead?" Houston demanded.

"Why, you, you old reprobate!" the barber shouted.

"I live just down the road," Houston told the barber as he settled into the chair. "Who sent the telegraph?"

"I don't know, General. Someone said you had taken sick and up and died. Folks were wearing black armbands in Galveston, Houston City, maybe all the way to Nacogdoches, Austin, and Dallas."

The windowpanes rattled. Another ship had fired another shell.

"Been to Galveston lately, General?" Stokes asked as he combed what was left of Houston's mane.

"Not in months," he answered.

"No reason to go. Hardly anyone left, except for green Confederate troops. They've hauled all the guns off, except for one big one at Fort Point. Army up and left. The island, I mean."

"It could not be defended anyway," Houston said. Another cannon boomed. He frowned. Back in the summer, the *South Carolina* had bombed

Galveston and the North Battery. Men, women, and even children had rushed out onto the beach to watch the show—until a shell blew a man to bits and wounded three others. He did not want to think about war now.

"Don't you find it odd, Perry?" he asked.

"What do you mean, General?"

"That the citizens here find my demise to be of enough significance that flags are lowered, but no one bothers to bring ham and cake to my wife and family, no newspaper editor sends a reporter to learn the particulars of my death, or to jot down a quote from my widow, or even learn of my funeral arrangements."

The brush whisked across the back of Houston's neck.

"Folks got a lot on their mind, I reckon," the barber said.

Back at Ben Lomond, Houston retired to his library with the letters he had gotten at the Houston City post office, leaving Jeff alone with Margaret as she instructed the slave on something to do with the flower garden. Aunt Liza had vegetable soup cooking in the kitchen, but the aroma did nothing for Houston.

He opened the first letter, read a few lines, discarded it. He placed a bill atop *The Iliad*. He started on the next letter with excitement and perhaps a little anxiety when Margaret screamed.

After the buggy ride to Houston City and back, he had to use the crutch—not even a cane would help on days like this—and limped outside, moving as fast as his aching bones and overworked lungs could carry him. Andrew Jackson and Temple hurried from the back yard, but Houston growled at both: "Stay here!" He told the slaves Lewis and Joshua the same, and stepped onto the porch.

Jeff stood in the garden holding some trimmings and a pair of shears. Margaret had buried her head into the shoulder of some tramp, a scarecrow in rags, pale, bearded, filthy. The stranger held a crutch, too.

Instantly, Houston's heart exploded and tears blinded him. He gripped the column for support, and muttered a name, inaudible at first. When his crutch clattered onto the porch floor, Jeff saw him. The young slave raced across the garden, trampling plants, but Houston recovered and raised his hand. Jeff stopped.

"Sam!" Houston said, and his son looked up over his sobbing mother's shoulder.

Sam Houston Junior grinned, and Houston no longer needed the crutch. He stumbled down the steps, and hurried to the garden. Margaret pulled away, and father and son embraced.

"All morning," Houston whispered, "all day . . . something told me…that you would return to us . . . that you would come home."

The boy ate. The boy slept. Houston let him.

As dawn broke on the 4th of October, eight Federal warships arrived at Galveston Bay. The Confederate artillery opened fire. The Yankees quickly silenced the Rebel guns, and the Confederate navy, at least in these parts, consisted of a handful of old river steamboats with bales of cotton instead of armor. "Cotton-clads," folks called them. Cotton-armored, decrepit ships against a federal flotilla of ironclads, forty-four-pounders, mortar schooners, and transport ships. Houston wondered what had taken the Yankees so long.

"The Runaway Scrape again," Houston whispered, watching men, women, children, carts, horses, mules plod down the road in front of his house.

"I should get to Houston City, too," Sam Junior told him. "I remain a soldier."

"In good time," Houston said.

"But, Father, if there is to be a battle . . ."

"What battle, Son? Our army has withdrawn to Houston City. And you are not fit for guard duty, let alone battle." He saw the rebellion in his son's eyes, so he found a different approach. "In time, you will return to the field. But for the moment, your job is to eat and sleep and watch. We need you to help us move."

Two of the slaves hauled chests to one of the wagons.

"I find it hard to believe," Sam Junior said, "that you are leaving Ben Lomond."

Houston chuckled. "Before you came home, I told Lewis and Joshua to go chop some cordwood. Lewis told me . . . 'Mister Sam, there ain't no more wood to chop.' I barked some unkind remarks at his ignorance, and stepped outside. And saw that he was right. Even Sam Houston has to make a living, Son. We are going home. Home. Home at last."

For three days, they caravanned north. Through Presswood on Caney Creek, following the paths through the thick forests, Dry Creek, the Little Caney, to the Dallas Pike. The second Runaway Scrape, which never really came close to that horrible journey, had long faded before they crossed Shepherd Creek and came into Huntsville.

"Turn here." He wrapped his cane against the wall of the yellow barouche, finding it difficult to contain his grin, and squeezed Margaret's hand. A youthful exuberance overwhelmed him. He felt damned near giddy, one reason he had let Sam Junior ride in the black buggy. He wanted to be with Margaret. He wanted to show her their new home first.

"Quickly," he ordered, and leaned back.

"It is not Raven Wood," he told her, "but wait until you see it."

The mules snorted, and Joshua, driving the carriage, pulled on the lines.

"We're here, Mister Sam," the slave said. "At least, I reckon we's here."

Sam pushed through the door, saw the home, and turned back, to help Margaret out of the wagon.

"There!" He wheeled around, took his crutch, and hobbled a few paces toward the house he had rented from Dr. Rufus Bailey, president of Austin College. Though short of breath, he beamed with pleasure.

"Oh," Margaret whispered, "my . . . word . . ."

CHAPTER TWENTY-SIX

March 2, 1863

No matter what Margaret said, he loved the damned house. Although called Buena Vista, folks around Huntsville had nicknamed it the "Steamboat House"—indeed, it resembled a sternwheeler in dry dock, narrow and long with twin turrets by the massive front staircase, galleries on either side, stained-glass windows, and outside stairways connecting the decks. Dr. Bailey had the home built for his son and daughter-in-law for a wedding place, but the girl wouldn't live there. She hated it. So did Margaret, but she must have seen how much pleasure the hideous monstrosity gave her husband. At least, she conceded, the rent came cheap.

This morning, he felt like hell—again—but dressed and made his way down the outside staircase.

"You need me to help you, Mister Sam?" Jeff asked from underneath the upstairs balcony.

"No." Houston grumbled and coughed, though he knew he could use all the help he could get. He turned seventy years old this day, and he felt like seven thousand. Halfway down the stairs, he stopped to catch his breath. He felt Jeff standing a few steps behind him, but the slave said nothing. He was just waiting for Houston to fall.

On that morning, Sam Houston scored another victory. He made it down in one piece.

"My crutch, Jeff." He held out his hand and took the crutch Jeff had carried down the steps.

"Where are they?" Houston asked.

"The spring, sir," Jeff answered. "You want me to drive you, Mister Sam?"

"No. I'll walk." After a few rods, Houston stopped, resting in the shade of crepe myrtles and fig trees. The spring lay perhaps a block from the Steamboat House, but he would never make it to the oak tree just a few yards away. "Yes. Yes, Jeff, fetch the surrey." He made up an excuse. "These are important visitors, and we should not keep them waiting."

Usually, Houston entertained guests at the Steamboat House, but for all her Christian upbringing and charity, Margaret felt uneasy when Indians came calling. Maybe she remembered the horror stories of the Red Stick War, or what the Cherokees had called Houston after he had resigned his governorship in Tennessee—The Big Drunk. She might have feared that Houston would revert to his wilder days, rollicking in the wilds with his Cherokee friends.

Billy Blount was no Cherokee. Blount was chief of the Alabama Indians, who had joined with the Coushattas and now lived on four thousand acres in the East Texas forests known as the Big Thicket. Houston had gotten that land deeded to the Indians.

After a warm greeting, Blount introduced his companions, and they passed the pipe while sitting at the spring's edge. The Alabamas and Coushattas were no different than the Cherokees, and quite a few politicians, in one regard. They talked about other things—the weather, the forests, the hunting, their children, and the stories they still loved to laugh about—before bringing up business. Houston's chest and head no longer hurt. Indian tobacco tasted sweet. He could not recall when he had last shared a pipe with his friends. Eventually, though, Blount came to the point. Houston listened with intent.

From newspaper reports, the Confederacy appeared to be winning most battles. Even back in October, Confederate General John Magruder led his command and reclaimed Galveston, sending Union ships back into the Gulf of Mexico and many Yankee prisoners to Huntsville, where they were locked into the state prison. Yet Houston saw the gloom in the faces of men and women he met, and the Union blockade remained strong.

And there was the Conscription Act, passed by President Jefferson Davis and the Confederate congress less than a year ago. White males between eighteen and thirty-five years old were to enlist in military service for a three-year term. Oh, the rich ones could hire a substitute, and Houston had toyed with that idea for Sam Junior, eager to return to service with the 2nd Texas.

"How many of your men have been conscripted into the army?" Houston asked Blount.

"Many," the Indian answered.

Houston found Jeff. "Return to the house. Bring back paper, pen, and ink. And an envelope."

"They take our young men far, far away," Blount said in Cherokee. "It is not our war to fight."

Nor is it mine, Houston thought. "Your brother Sam Houston shall send a letter to the Confederate War Department. The law says white men can be conscripted. It says nothing about our red brothers. If they listen, your young warriors will be home."

"Surely," Blount said, "they will listen to The Raven."

Houston felt his blood bubbling. "They have not listened to The Raven in many moons, my friend," he said, "but they will listen this time . . . else they shall rue the day."

After he had mailed the post and returned home, he struggled up the steps, thinking: *All I am good for these days is writing letters. Letters that get no answers.* Inside, removing his new hat— blue velvet with gold embroidery—Houston heard the pattering of feet as his young children came to wish him a happy birthday. He smelled lemon cake and coffee. Margaret and Aunt Liza would make him eat a slice, but all he really wanted was coffee, and little of that. Still, he let his boys, Temple and Andrew Jackson, hug him and guide him to the parlor. Margaret smiled warmly, and Temple begged him to eat the cake.

"Let me sit down, children," he said, and sank into the old wooden rocker. The presents came first, a new cane carved by Joshua, a scarf, a pair of boots, books. He loved the books. He hated the cane, but knew he would need it.

"Where is Sam?" he asked, after nibbling some cake and sipping coffee. He frowned. Even coffee did not rest well in his stomach.

"Father." The voice came from the hallway, and boot steps pounded as Sam Junior made his way into the room. Houston frowned. Margaret moaned. Having recovered from his wound at Shiloh, Sam Junior wore a new Confederate uniform. The boy who had returned after a prisoner exchange, resembling a skeleton, had put the weight back on. His limp had vanished. His belt of shiny black leather held a saber and a Navy Colt.

Yet Sam Junior could not stay at attention. He ripped an envelope from the inside pocket of his blouse and thrust it toward Houston.

"Father . . . my commission . . . I'm a . . ."—his grin widened—"a lieutenant!"

Margaret had to steady herself, but Houston nodded.

Houston looked at the letter, nodding and thinking: *Sometimes they do listen to me.* "Your orders intrigue me, Son."

As the smile faded, his son shook his head. "I don't know about those orders. I'm to go on a *geology* expedition. In *Mexico*. I thought . . ."

"Shave-tail lieutenants do not question orders." Houston grinned. Margaret's face lifted, the tears disappeared from her eyes, which closed as she bowed her head in a prayer of thanks.

"You have seen the elephant," Houston told his son, "but now you will learn that there is more to war than fighting. I warrant Rip Ford and others are thinking of a quick path to some Mexican port. The blockade strangles us. We cannot ship cotton to England from Texas. This is a mission of the utmost urgency."

"Geology?" his son asked.

"Geology is a science. Roads are not built without an understanding of the terrain. And Texas cotton growers need a fast route to a Mexican port. This is an important assignment, Lieutenant."

The smile returned, even wider, and Houston handed the commission and orders back to his son.

"I'm too full of cake and coffee to stand, and I've had quite the busy day for a seventy-year-old war horse. But allow me to be the first to salute you, Lieutenant Houston."

He raised his right hand to that receding hairline, and watched his son snap to attention and return a sharp salute.

Margaret cleared her throat. "You will write to us?" she asked hopefully.

"Of course."

"And," Houston said, "send some drawings of what Mexico looks like."

The boy accepted congratulations from his siblings and the Houston slaves.

"When do you report to Brownsville?" Houston asked.

"Oh, my." He spun on his heels. "I must pack." With Andrew Jackson and Temple saying—"Let us help, Sam."—Lieutenant Sam Houston Junior left the parlor, trailed by his first command, as his father settled back into his chair.

His appetite had returned. Reaching to the plate on the side table, he broke off another bite of cake.

A moment later, Margaret settled onto the footstool in front of her husband. The other children, home for Houston's birthday, excused themselves, leaving their parents alone.

"You have been busy," Margaret said, "haven't you?"

He found the coffee cold but satisfying, and washed down his cake.

"I called in some debts," he admitted.

"For my sake?"

He shook his head. "For ours." After another sip, he returned the cup to its saucer. "Sam has tasted battle. That is enough for him, for you, for me. Let him see Mexican rocks for the rest of this horrible war."

Rising, Margaret brushed away new tears. Leaning over, gently touching Houston's shoulder, she kissed his forehead. "I love you, Sam Houston," she whispered.

"Many have questioned your judgment," he said.

"I never did, though." She straightened. "I must go. Sam will leave without extra socks or unmentionables. Oh, what stories he will have to tell us when he returns from Mexico."

Suddenly then, Houston found himself alone, saddened. His oldest son, his pride and joy, would be leaving for Mexico, away from the horrors of war. Houston had done his job. He had maneuvered Lieutenant Sam Houston Junior out of harm's way. But he also knew that he would never see his son again.

CHAPTER TWENTY~SEVEN

April 6, 1863

This Monday morning, that nagging cough returned. Houston felt chilled, and he briefly thought that death would not be such a bad thing. He also remembered the prediction made two days earlier by an attorney in town.

"Old friend," Woody McKay had said with a warm smile, "Sam Houston shall never die."

McKay's joke had come after he had helped Houston finish his last will and testament. Houston had picked McKay not because he was a great attorney but because McKay had always been loyal to the Union, and loyal to Sam Houston, and he also knew how to keep his mouth shut. He also made pretty good catfish stew that smelled delicious, but Houston's stomach was not agreeable.

No, he thought while descending the stairs into the spring afternoon. *The people of Texas will not let Sam Houston die. Or even retire.* Margaret had sent Jeff off to Herbert Jordan's gristmill on the edge of town, so Joshua helped Houston down the steps. The black buggy waited. Houston knew he would need Joshua's help to get inside it, too. He offered no protest.

"Don't get old, Joshua," he told the slave as he gripped the edge of the surrey to catch his breath.

"Aunt Martha say . . . 'Don't it beat the alternative?' "

"When you reach seventy years, my friend," Houston said, "you wonder."

"You hush up. Let me boost you up. There. You comfortable, Mister Sam? Where we off to first this fine mornin'?"

Yes. Where to first? Margaret had scolded him, in a pleasant voice, over breakfast, or what seemed to be breakfast these days for Houston: half a piece of toast, black coffee, some foul-tasting medicines Dr. Warren Walkup kept sending to the Steamboat House—charging Confederate prices no less. "You are retired, my darling," Margaret had told him. "Why don't you act like you are retired?"

"Texas needs me," he had answered.

"Your family needs you, too."

"Texas needs me," he had repeated. "And I do not know how much longer she will need this old vagabond."

"Texas." She had sighed. "Sometimes I am jealous of this woman named Texas."

"Don't be." He had managed to eat another piece of toast, just to please her—and keep her and the other women off his back this day. "I made Texas. But you saved Sam Houston . . . from himself."

It had worked. She had even helped him dress, suggesting that he don his blue velvet cap, the leopard-skin vest, and that flamboyant crimson coat that she despised and he adored.

"To the spring," he directed Joshua.

He had never met the two Indians waiting for him at the spring, but he knew who they were. Butternut blouses and grimy kepis told him all he needed to know.

They spoke no Cherokee or English, and Houston had never met anyone, white or red, who could speak or understand Alabama and Coushatta tongue except Alabamas and Coushattas.

They used hands—after, of course, they smoked the pipe.

The Indians thanked him, and related that their chief, Billy Blount, thanked him. They offered him whiskey stolen from a Louisiana private, but Houston said his whiskey-drinking days lay far, far behind him. He did take the kepis and blouses as gifts, though, thinking that some damned provost marshal might shoot them as deserters on their way back to the reservation. He also told them that those uniforms were of too much value for what little he had done, so he handed them $250 in Texas notes—which would buy little these days. They accepted.

"Before you leave for your home," he signed

with his hands, "I ask for one thing in return."

"What?" the thinner of the two asked.

"Sing a song for me," he signed. "One of the old songs."

They did. Tears ran down his cheeks, and when they had finished, he embraced the two Indians. He asked that they tell Chief Blount it was his honor and duty to have helped them, and that he was glad the Confederate War Department had realized the mistake made when they had conscripted the Indian warriors into the army.

"Are all of your brothers returning home?" he signed.

The squat one with the missing left earlobe shook his head. Two, he signed, had gone to the other world.

"I wish," Houston whispered in English, "Billy had come to me sooner." After nodding farewell, Houston watched them disappear into the trees, then, sighing, he moved away to the surrey, where Joshua waited.

"That was a real sad song those Indians sang, Mister Sam," the slave said. "What was it about?"

Houston shook his head. "I do not know. It is one of the old songs, though."

"Sure was pretty."

"Yes. The Indians always sang beautiful songs, Joshua. Back in my younger days, I even sang a few with the Cherokees." He let himself be boosted into the surrey. "Today, all we hear are songs about war, about glory, about Yankee tyranny. The Indians sang songs of beauty."

"You must have sure enjoyed living with them." Joshua climbed into the driver's box.

"I was at peace with them," he said. *Even when I was The Big Drunk.*

"Where to next, Mister Sam?"

He sighed. "The prison."

The red-bricked gloomy structure called "The Walls" quickly came into view beneath pine trees.

Back in the late 1840s, Houston had helped get the state penitentiary established in town. Not that he wanted to live in a town that was home to a sprawling prison, but he did want to assist those in town who could use the business. Prisons always helped towns grow. Governments went broke. State pens prospered because men did stupid things. The Huntsville prison prospered better than most. A decade ago, a cotton and woolen mill had been established inside the prison, and convicts worked hard these days to produce uniforms for soldiers, even shirts, pants, and coats for civilians.

"Wait here," Houston told Joshua after he found his cane and adjusted his cap.

"I got no desire to go through that gate, Mister Sam."

Houston grinned. "There but by the grace of God, I could be behind those walls, myself."

"You'd be runnin' the place, Mister Sam, even if you was in chains."

He laughed, bent his withering frame against the cane, and hobbled toward the entrance.

"Hello, Cousin." Major Thomas Carothers, superintendent of the state penitentiary since 1859, held out his big right hand and grinned. Once he gripped Houston's hand, he pulled him into a hard embrace. It almost knocked the wind out of Houston, and he cursed himself as he sank into a settee in the warden's office.

"I'm sorry, Sam. Are you all right?"

At first, Houston could only nod, but eventually the shock and pain and damned old age passed long enough that he was able to smile. "You ambush all your guests this way, Tom?"

Carothers grinned. "We ambush them before they come here, Sam. That's how we get them here."

They exchanged pleasantries. Carothers's wife Mary had gone back to Kentucky, visiting family. The Texas General Land Office had given Carothers a third-class land grant of one hundred sixty acres, and he thought he might try raising stock. Houston updated his cousin on his family, then came down to the first part of business.

"Tom, I made out my will Saturday with Woody McKay. I've named you one of my executors."

Carothers leaned against his desk. "Sam . . ."

Houston raised his right hand. "I don't know

how this all will turn out, Tom. Well . . ." He snorted. "No, I do know. In the end, we lose. We all lose. But don't go off half-cocked. The way I keep gallivanting across Texas, I don't stop long enough in one place to die."

"Well, you look fit, Sam."

"Don't be a damned liar, Tom. I look like hell. And I feel worse."

Carothers's voice turned somber. "Sam, I will do everything to help your family and . . ."

His cousin stopped when Houston's hand raised again. "Don't tell Margaret. Don't tell Mary when she returns from Kentucky. And don't think I came here because I wanted to stay one step ahead of the Grim Reaper. I saw Doc Walkup yesterday . . . not for him to poke and prod me and hit my knee with a damned hammer. He came to see me."

"Yes." Carothers wet his lips. "He was here Friday."

"He told me. I would like to see the prisoners, Tom."

"Which ones?" Carothers's face told Houston that the warden already knew the answers.

"You know the ones, Tom. The prisoners captured from the *Harriet Lane*."

The copper-plated steamer had been captured in January during General Magruder's surprise attack on Galveston Island. Rammed by two "cotton-clads", the *Harriet Lane* had been boarded by Confederates. From what Houston had read in the newspaper accounts, the hand-to-hand fighting had turned gruesome, with the Yankee captain killed before he could blow up his ship, to keep her from falling into enemy hands. At least four other crew members had died, and the rest had been marched all the way to the Texas State Penitentiary.

In the prison hospital, Houston shook hands with gaunt men in nightshirts with hollow eyes. When they stepped into the yard, Houston said: "The others, Tom. Show me the others."

"I am," his cousin said, and walked away from the cells, past the whipping posts and to the sweatbox, an iron crate painted black on the inside and outside. Two guards standing by the entrance snapped to attention.

"Open it up," Carothers ordered.

The two men hesitated.

"Now."

It took both men to push the iron door open, and Houston started inside, but the stink stopped him. He almost gagged. Carothers struck a match and, holding a handkerchief over his nose, moved past Houston and stuck the Lucifer inside the box.

The flame flickered out a moment later, but Houston had seen enough.

"This," he roared, raising his cane as if to strike, "is how you treat prisoners of war?" For the past few days, he had been able to speak hardly past a whisper. Now rage enveloped him, and he spoke as Sam Houston of ten, perhaps twenty years earlier. One guard dropped his nightstick. The other stumbled back a full rod.

"Damn you, Tom Carothers, you are no kin to me." He pointed into the opening. "These are soldiers. Soldiers. Not banditti terrorizing our state with acts of robbery, murder, rapine. You put officers in with enlisted men. That's one thing. But you put these men of honor in a place I would not put a dog, or even my worst enemy. I would not even put you in such filth, although, by Jehovah, this is where you should be."

He shifted the cane toward the petrified guards. Other guards hurried from the cell-block. More stopped in front of the woolen mill.

"Get them out! Damn your miserable hides, I say get those prisoners out of this hole."

"Sam . . . ," Carothers started. "There's no place . . ."

"I don't give a damn, Tom. I do not give one tinker's damn where you put them. Put them in your own home. Hell, Mary is up in Kentucky. She won't mind. But you will not leave these brave men in this sweatbox for one minute longer!" He moved. He did not need his cane to move, not when he felt like this.

"Move, damn you insolent sons-of-bitches. By God, if these men are not out of this hole in two minutes, I will go back to the Steamboat House, I will load my revolver, and I will arm my sons . . . even Temple, all but two-and-a-half years old . . . my daughters, my wife, and my slaves, and you low-down, miserable excuses for Christian men will taste what war is truly like. We will slaughter you damned cowards!"

CHAPTER TWENTY~EIGHT

May 2–July 8, 1863

"And how was your supper last night with Tom?"

He finished pulling on his boots, surprised he could get them on at all, and straightened up on the footstool. Standing in the doorway to the upstairs bedroom, Margaret looked so damned lovely this morning that he hated to be leaving—again.

"Fine," he answered. "The first and second mates are staying with him these days. Doc Walkup has put up another officer. The whole town has come out to take in Yankee prisoners."

"Thanks to your . . . ahem . . . would tirade be an understatement?"

"I merely spoke my mind."

"Which you always do."

She offered her hands, and he let her pull him to his feet.

"But no Union prisoners here, Sam?" She gave him a mischievous grin. "I would think Yankee sailors would enjoy being imprisoned in a house built like a steamboat."

Bending down, he kissed the top of her head. "I would not like young sailors to be alone with my beautiful wife. Sailors cannot be trusted."

The laughter left her eyes, and she stepped away from him, sighing. "I wish you would not go, Sam. You travel too much. And you have not been well."

"Balderdash." He found his cane and the blue velvet cap. "Doc Walkup's concoctions have me feeling forty years old, and I have not coughed in at least a week." Margaret did not call him on that white lie. "Joshua and Jeff have loaded my grips?"

"Must you go?" she pleaded without answering the question.

"They have asked me to give a speech in Houston City, my darling," he told her. "You know that General Sam Houston cannot turn down the opportunity to say a few words."

"Still . . ."

He held up his hand. "No one has taken a shot at me in years, Margaret, and I have not been hanged in effigy in months."

"I would like to have you to myself, Sam." She handed him a cape. "Just once."

"That you would regret." Which, at least, got her to laugh, and she helped him to the door.

"How long will you be gone?" she asked as Jeff ran up the steps to help Houston down the staircase and into the top buggy.

"A few weeks. Your mother will arrive shortly. I'm sure you will enjoy her company whilst I am away."

"And her casket?" Margaret grinned.

"At eighty-two years and no sign of slowing down, Nancy Lea will live forever."

"You should slow down."

His head shook. "This will be a vacation. One speech in Houston. I would like to see the bay from Ben Lomond once more," he said. "And a stay at Sour Lake might do my leaking wounds well."

"Good," she said. "By all means, soak in the mud. It shall be my daily prayer that you find relief in those springs."

She followed him down the steps and to the buggy, where he turned, bent once more, and kissed her briefly on the lips. When Jeff and Joshua helped him into the wagon, she stepped closer, and put her hand on his. "Sam," she said.

He stared at her.

"Tell me again, that if a newspaper scribe has the audacity to ask you if you plan to run for governor, you will tell him no."

He patted her hand and felt his blue eyes twinkling. God had blessed him with a woman who knew his ego all too well.

"As I told that ink-slinger at the *Item* the other day, under no circumstances will I permit my name to be used as a candidate." He straightened, but kept his blue eyes trained on his wife. "A man of three score years and ten ought, at the very least, to be exempt from the charge of ambition." Then he barked at Jeff that they should be off.

Before they reached the street, he leaned out of the buggy and shouted back to her: "But were I to run for governor again, I daresay that I would receive the largest vote ever counted in the state of Texas!"

The trip to Houston City wore him out. He wasn't sure if he could make a speech, and he had to get past another sentry at White Oak Bayou. When they came to the railroad tracks, Houston told Jeff to stop, and wait. He pointed at the black smoke.

"Mister Sam," the slave said, "that train be a long way off. It ain't gonna run over us if I go now."

"I just want to watch it pass, Jeff," he said.

Five minutes later, Houston knew Jeff regretted that command, for the horses fought the driver, snorting, shaking their heads, stamping their hoofs on the hard road. Frightened of the locomotive, Houston understood, and he laughed.

Wouldn't that be a story to read in newspapers across the world? SAM HOUSTON KILLED. HORSES PANIC. TRAIN COLLIDES WITH RIG. WITNESSES PICK UP BITS OF FLESH AND CLOTHING AS SOUVENIRS.

He inhaled deeply the thick smoke, saw the embers, and lifted his hand in greeting at the man on the last car as the train rocked and moved on down the line toward Beaumont.

"We go now, Mister Sam?" asked Jeff, exhausted and drenched with sweat from keeping the team under control.

"When I was born," he said, "there were no steamboats. There were no locomotives. We traveled by horse . . . or canoe. Mostly, we walked. A pistol fired just once. If you wanted a likeness of yourself, you sat down for an artist. Daguerreotypes? No one dreamed of such inventions."

"Yes, sir. Can I go now, Mister Sam? Before the next train comes along?"

He laughed. "Yes, Jeff. Drive on." But he kept watching the smoke and disappearing cars of the locomotive as long as he could.

As he stared across the street at the crowd of men, women, and children, he waited before speaking, not to see if more people came to hear him, but to catch his breath. He thought of the train he had seen on the way into town, of looking across the bay when they had stopped at Cedar Point. Now, he thought of the gifted poet Robert Burns, and he began: "I have been buffeted by the waves, as I have been borne along time's ocean, until shattered and worn, I approach the narrow isthmus, which divides it from a sea of eternity beyond. Ere I step forward to journey through the pilgrimage of death, I would say, that all my thoughts and hopes are with my country."

Women put their hands to their ears. Others leaned forward. One, standing in front of Oliver's Saloon, called out: "Speak up, Houston! We can't hear you!"

Scarcely can I hear myself. He turned his head to cough.

"Once I dreamed of empire," he said after he had recovered, "vast and expansive for a united people. That dream is over. The golden charm is broken. . . ."

The drunk on the boardwalk hollered: "Hurrah for Jeff Davis! Down with the damned Yanks!"

Houston paused, glared, before continuing.

"Damn all the Yankees!" the drunk roared. "Damn them, and especially that bastard Abe Lincoln, all to hell's hottest flames. Hurrah for the gallant Southerner, Jeff Davis. Jeff Davis forever!"

He had heard enough. "My friend," he said, and felt his voice rising more than he thought possible. Everyone in the streets could hear him now. "I do not approve of cussing your worst enemy. There are ladies and children present. And as for us gallant Southerners, I would not call Jeff Davis one. The gallant Southerners are those, like my son, who wear the gray and have been tested in battle. My friend, you seem

299

to have been tested in saloons, and have yet to come out the victor."

The cough returned. He caught a cold. Jeff told him that they should head home, find Dr. Walkup, but Houston said a week in the springs at Sour Lake would do him good.

One week at Dr. Mud's Curing Water House & Inn stretched into another, and yet another.

Savvy Texas businessmen had transformed the Hardin County town into some sort of mecca for the infirm, and Houston sank into a basin and allowed servants to cover him with mud as thick as tar and as smelly as pitch pine. Dr. Mud washed off the mud with mineral water, and sold bottles of Sour Lake water for five Confederate dollars each.

Dark-skinned, black-haired, tattooed Dr. Mud claimed to be a Cherokee medicine man.

"I don't trust that doctor," Jeff told Houston after bringing him a newspaper.

"He is no doctor," Houston conceded. "Nor is he Indian. He cannot even speak Cherokee. He is a slave, I warrant, either having bought his freedom or escaped. Mostly, he is a charlatan." Seeing the blank look on Jeff's face, Houston explained: "A counterfeit. A fraud. A pretender."

"Then why you let him work on you so and spend money for that bottled water you're drinkin', Mister Sam?"

Houston set the drained bottle on his bedside table. "You believe anything when you ache as I do, Jeff." He opened a letter from Margaret, read it twice, and then asked to see the newspapers Jeff had bought in town.

Houston saw the headline, and what little color remained in his face, faded. "God help us now. Vicksburg has fallen."

They checked out the next day, and began the three-day journey home. Feverish and light-headed, Houston ordered Jeff to take him to the state penitentiary first, to make sure the Union prisoners of war had no needs, before returning to the Steamboat House.

"Sure is good to be back home, Mister Sam," Jeff told him as he helped Houston to the ground. "You feelin' any better, sir?"

"Jeff," he said hoarsely, "I will not last fifteen days."

Margaret hurried outside, stopping short and bringing a hand to cover her mouth.

"Sam," she whispered.

He stared at the towering steps that led to the upper deck and his bedroom. He had lost weight, resembled a ghost, and facing those stairs drained him of all willpower.

"Joshua." Margaret recovered from the appalling sight of her husband's condition. "Help General Houston to the front room on the ground floor. It is the coolest room in the entire house. Lewis, you and Jeff bring a couch from the parlor. And tell Aunt Liza to bring soup and hot tea for the general."

She followed Joshua and her husband, who moved weakly. The young Houston boys raced through the house, but Margaret stopped them from leaping onto their father. When Pearl stepped out the door, Margaret told her to find Dr. Walkup and bring him back immediately.

By the time Houston reached the room, Lewis and Jeff had dragged the couch in. Joshua eased the old man down, and Aunt Martha placed a pillow under his head. Lewis pulled off Houston's boots. Margaret sat on the edge of the sofa and gripped her husband's waxy hand. She nodded at Temple and Andrew Jackson and beckoned them to her.

"Is Pa going to be all right?" Andrew asked.

"It is up to the Lord," she answered honestly.

CHAPTER TWENTY-NINE

July 9–26, 1863

When Warren Walkup said there was nothing he could do, Margaret sent for other doctors—Pleasant Kittrell, an old friend of Houston, and J.W. Markham, who said that Houston had pneumonia. Unsatisfied, she summoned Ashbel Smith, who stayed four days.

"Doctor Markham was right," Smith told Margaret underneath the oak tree in the front yard. Having recovered from his wounds at Shiloh, Dr. Smith had returned with what remained of his Bayland Guards to the Texas coast. "Pneumonia, and a bad case. At Sam's age . . ." His head shook.

"He has moments," Margaret said. "Why, when Doctor Markham suggested that Sam have brandy, he raised his head off the pillow and said . . . 'By thunder, I am a teetotaler.' "

Smith's face warmed. "You reformed him, Margaret." He put his hand on her shoulder. "But, Margaret, even Sam Houston cannot live forever."

She stiffened. "He cannot . . ." Her voice broke.

"It is out of our hands, Margaret."

· · ·

She sent for the daughters. She gave a letter to Ashbel Smith to expedite to Sam Junior somewhere in Mexico. Oddly, she thought it might be better if her oldest son did not return until . . . until . . . after. At least one of her children could remember Sam Houston alive.

Jeff sat on a stool by the sofa, fanning Houston to keep him cool, to shoo away the flies. The slave rarely left his master's side.

Nannie, Maggie, Mary Willie, and Nettie arrived from Baylor University in Independence. From the parlor, Nannie played the Steinway piano Houston had given her for her sixteenth birthday—mostly hymns, at her father's request. Once, Houston asked her to play his favorite song.

"What is that, Father?" Nannie asked.

He answered in Cherokee and fell asleep.

Maggie and Mary Willie recited poetry when he was lucid—Burns and Longfellow, mostly, Lord Byron on occasion. Mary Willie relieved Jeff, fanning her father while humming "Will You Come to the Bower?", "Sit by the Summer Sea", and "The Indian's Prayer"—but she could not finish "The Dying Soldier", which her father requested.

His eyes opened to find Temple sitting on Margaret's lap in Houston's old rocking chair beside the couch. Margaret had fallen asleep, but the boy remained wide awake.

Jeff was on the stool, but had stopped waving the fan.

"Papa," Temple whispered.

Houston smiled.

"They moved your buggy to the barn," the boy said. "And they turned Horse-Horse loose in the corral."

Houston swallowed.

"They say you won't ride Horse-Horse or go off in the buggy no more, Papa." Tears filled the boy's eyes, and Houston reached for his youngest child, but could not keep his arm up.

Somehow, Houston smiled. Months had passed since he had even tried to ride Old Pete or any saddle horse, relying on the comfort of the top buggy or the faded yellow barouche. He wet his lips and said: "I might just fool them, Temple." With a wink, he drifted back into a deep sleep.

His wounds leaked badly. His nights rarely passed peacefully.

On a Sunday afternoon, he woke to find Nettie and Mary Willie beside him, and Andrew Jackson Houston playing jacks on the floor.

"Pa," Nettie said.

His mind seemed clear that day. "My pretty little flock of girls," he said. His voice was dry, and Nettie filled a cup with water from a pitcher, and Mary Willie raised his head to help him drink.

"I not a girl, Pa," Andrew said.

He swallowed, feeling the relief of the cool water, and Mary Willie laid his head gently back atop the pillow.

"No, but you are pretty."

"Boys can't be pretty, Pa."

He smiled, but suddenly Andrew buried his head in his father's chest and began sobbing. Tears cascaded down the cheeks of the girls, too. Houston ran his fingers through Andrew's head and whispered: "Boys don't cry, either, Son."

"You cried," the boy sobbed. "I . . . heard you. . . ."

"I'm a man full grown."

"Pa," Nettie wailed.

Mary Willie sniffled. "We don't want . . . you . . . to die."

"Listen." He tried to raise his head, but couldn't. Mary Willie helped pull Andrew off Houston's chest.

"You know what folks have told me?" Houston asked. "More than once, I think. They said . . . 'Sam Houston can never die.' " He forced a smile. "They were right." He managed to place his hand on Andrew's chest. "I will always be with you." He looked at Nettie, then Mary Willie. "With all of you. Whenever you need me . . . just call my name. I shall answer."

"Promise?" Andrew pleaded.

But Houston had fallen back into a deep sleep.

Sometimes he spoke with clarity. Other days he mumbled in unintelligible English or a tongue no one recognized. Cherokee? Who could tell?

On good days, he recalled stories from his childhood, his time in Washington City—as when back in 1832 he tracked down Congressman William Stanbery, who had questioned Houston's character in a letter published in the *National Intelligencer*, and beat that rascal with a hickory cane. He could recall his days as a senator or with President Andrew Jackson or debating his rivals in the Republic of Texas.

He told Temple: "I don't know who you are, but you are a handsome little cuss."

Temple cried himself to sleep that night.

The next morning, Houston had his youngest son crawl into the sofa with him, and he opened *The Iliad* and read several pages before he wore himself out, and slept.

"Mother is coming from Independence," Margaret told him one morning.

"I bet this time she doesn't bring that damned

old casket," he barked. "Because she thinks I'll steal it." He turned away. "I can't believe that old windbag is going to outlast me."

There had been days when he was not the Sam Houston Margaret had known, not even the Sam Houston who drank himself into drunken stupors. This might have been the worst, even more so than when he had barked at Aunt Martha: "You call this supper fit to eat? This is the worst meal I've ever had. What do folks say when they visit and you feed them such hog and hominy?"

When Margaret broke into tears, Houston reached up—with help from Joshua and Jeff—and pulled her into his arms.

"I am sorry," he whispered. "Please, forgive me. Please do not cry. I raise my Ebenezer because . . . I am . . . frightened."

On a few mornings, he spoke as the old Sam Houston, with wit, with charm. He doted on his young sons. He showered his daughters with compliments and kisses.

Mostly, he slept.

Others came to see the warrior—Judge Joab Banton . . . Anthony Branch . . . J. Carroll Smith . . . Judge A.B. Wiley . . . Colonel Robert Hays . . . Sometimes he was alert; more often, though, he tossed and turned in fitful sleep. The nights often proved the worst.

"Oh, my country!" he sang out in the middle of the night. "My country . . . my country."

Margaret tensed, closed the Bible, and reached for him, fearing this would be the end. Jeff fanned him all through the night. Sam Houston refused to die.

Margaret fell asleep at dawn, with Jeff waving the fan. At some point, exhaustion overcame Jeff, who dozed and dropped the fan on Houston's face.

Jeff jerked awake. So did Margaret. They blinked, surprised to find Houston awake and, apparently, cognizant.

"I'm sorry Mister Sam." Jeff grabbed the fan and started waving it, but Houston shook his head.

The sun crept through the leaves of the trees. It was just past dawn.

"Margaret . . ." His voice, though just a whisper, seemed strong. "You and that boy get some rest. There's no use in both of you breaking yourselves down."

A short while later, Houston again dropped into a deep sleep. Margaret gathered herself, told the kitchen slaves what to make for breakfast, dinner, and supper, and quickly tracked down Joshua.

"Go to Austin College and fetch the Reverend McKinney," she told him.

The slave's eyes widened.

"Tell him to hurry. Then tell Doctor Markham to please come here."

President of Austin College in Huntsville, the Reverend Samuel McKinney was Presbyterian. As a lifelong Alabama Baptist, Margaret frowned upon many aspects of the faith, but Houston and the minister had become friends over the years. Besides, the Reverend Rufus Burleson, who had baptized Houston back in 1854, could not leave Waco University for the time being but promised to keep the family in his nightly prayers. Robert Griggs, Margaret's own minister at the First Baptist Church, was visiting a daughter in Dallas.

Houston roused again when the minister knelt on the floor and began a prayer. The preacher did not even realize the old man had awakened until he ended his prayer.

"Amen," Houston said.

McKinney lifted his head. "Aye," he said in an Irish brogue, "the devil has awakened, I fear."

"You preaching to Indians, Parson?" Houston asked. "Or some backwoods settler?"

With a smile, the minister reached over and squeezed Houston's shoulder. "Seeing it's Sam Houston, I'd say I preach to both. Indian. And backwoodsman. In one body."

Houston closed his eyes, and muttered something in Cherokee.

The reverend leaned closer. He whispered into

Houston's ear: "Brother Sam . . . death is near. Are you right with God?"

At first, Houston did not answer. He began slipping into a deeper sleep. His eyes did not open, but after a few seconds, his lips moved. McKinney put his ear above Houston's lips.

"All is well," Houston said, his voice barely audible. "All is well."

Dr. Markham arrived forty minutes later. "He is in a coma," he told Margaret in the kitchen. "Keep the reverend nearby. Have your children gather. The time is at hand."

It was July 26th.

CHAPTER THIRTY

Oo-loo-te-ka

In the past, the ghostly but all too real visitors came to see him. In the Green Room. In an East Texas inn or South Texas campsite. On a rowboat. Wherever. This time, Houston finds himself not inside the Steamboat House, but on the banks of a river. An island, he understands, on the Hiwassee River in Tennessee. He fills his lungs with air, and cherishes wonderful scents from his boyhood: wood and tobacco smoke, roasting venison, pine sap, smoked fish. He recognizes the wooden structure before him.

It is the Town House, circular with a conical roof, covered with tree bark. The door, always on the left, opens, and a figure steps out. Comforted by the sight of the tall man, Houston smiles. Then, he cries. The man before him is *Oo-loo-te-ka*, known to the whites as John Jolly, whose Cherokee name means Man-Who-Beats-His-Own-Drum, but who Houston has always called *agidoda*. My father.

"*Osiyo*," his father says in Cherokee.

" *'Siyo*." Houston returns the greeting.

"I welcome you home, my Son." Houston and *Oo-loo-te-ka* enter the Town House, where his

Cherokee father fills the bowl of his pipe, saying: "You have come far."

"Yes," Houston agrees.

They pray to *Unetlanv*. *Oo-loo-te-ka* lights the pipe and takes seven puffs before passing it to Houston, who draws in the smoke seven times as well.

"You always come to us when you are in need, my Son," the Cherokee says.

Houston nods. "Yes. First when I was a child."

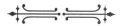

Cherished memories race past him. Picking strawberries and peaches. Digging up sweet potatoes. Afternoons of a *ne-jo-di*, a game of stickball; cornstalk shooting; hunting; fishing. Sitting underneath a tree and reading *The Iliad*.

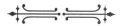

"I gave you your name," *Oo-loo-te-ka* says.

"*Co-lo-neh*," Houston whispers.

"The Raven," *Oo-loo-te-ka* says, "to us means good luck."

"Which I desperately needed," Houston says.

"The Raven often wanders, too," *Oo-loo-te-ka* says.

"And I wandered away from you, my Father."

His father whispers: "Things change."

"I changed." More tears stream down his face.

"No. You had a star to follow." He points. "I knew the star to be that of destiny. And I knew you would return to us, for we are your people. You are a white man by birth, but a Cherokee by heart."

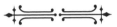

He remembers his return to these great people, when he helped negotiate the treaty that would send *Oo-loo-te-ka* and others to the country west of Arkansas. He has always told himself that he saved the Cherokees, or at least *Oo-loo-te-ka*, by doing this. But sometimes he wishes that he had fought against the Army, against his own people. At least *Oo-loo-te-ka* led his group west years before Jackson instrumented his most shameful act, sending the Cherokees on *Nu na hi du na tlo hi lu i*, The Trail Where They Cried.

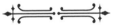

"And my heart rejoiced when you came back to me." *Oo-loo-te-ka* bobs excitedly. "The steamboat arrived and the moon had risen. I knew you were coming. *Unetlanv* had told me."

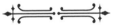

That memory is not one he cherishes. The last of the steamboats he has taken since leaving Nashville, the *Facility*, docks, and Houston sees the lights of torches. Drunk, shamed, he staggers into the light, hearing the Cherokee women whispering his name, and hearing his Cherokee father say . . . "My Son, eleven winters have passed since we last met, but my heart has wondered often where you were. We have heard that a dark cloud fell on the white path you walked, and when it fell in your way, you turned to my lodge. I am glad of it. It was done by *Unetlanv*. And we need you."

He will need them, too, although in those first years, he needs the whiskey more.

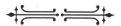

"I had been hurt," Houston tells his father.

"She was a dark spirit," *Oo-loo-te-ka* tells him. "We would have killed her had she been Cherokee."

Houston frowns, but even he cannot tell his Cherokee father not to speak ill of Eliza. He pictures another woman.

Oo-loo-te-ka reads his mind. "You think of Tiana."

Houston always called her Hina. Almost as tall as Houston himself, beautiful, hair so black it shines. He can never forget this daughter of a

Scottish trader named Hell-Fire Jack Rogers and a Cherokee woman.

"I hurt her," Houston admits. "I hurt you. Remember. I was no longer The Raven. I had become The Big Drunk."

That name fits him better than The Raven. Yet he weds Tiana. They open what he names Wigwam Neosho. He drinks himself into stupors. He drinks to forget all about Eliza . . . politics . . . Jackson . . . the wounds from Horseshoe Bend that never heal . . . everything. He drinks to kill himself. But he cannot die.

Another memory causes him to bury his head in his hands. He doesn't even remember even why he did it, but he had slapped his Cherokee father. "I'm . . . sorry. . . ." he sobs without any control. "I don't know why . . . I hit you."

"It was the whiskey," his father says.

He manages to dam the tears, and straightens, hating himself. "It was always the damned whiskey."

Oo-loo-te-ka stares beyond him, perhaps seeing that scene from all those years ago. "I remember our warriors were outraged. You had struck me, a vile insult. They wanted to tear you apart."

"You stopped them," Houston says.

"I stopped them with the truth. I told them . . . 'The Raven is troubled.' I told them . . . 'But he is my son and still I love him.' "

Sniffling, he manages to say: "I love you, too. And . . ."

He cannot look at his father any more. He remembers Tiana.

⊹══·══⊹

She will save him, too, before he even meets Margaret. He loves her. And he leaves her . . . but not because she has betrayed him as Eliza has done. Not because of any star, any sign from *Unetlanv.* But for his own glory.

⊹══·══⊹

"Even before you married, Tiana knew you would wander away," *Oo-loo-te-ka* says. "So did I. Eventually, the dark cloud was blown away. Your path, your true path, was no longer blocked. And you had to help your people. You went back to see Jackson, the Great White Father. Once more, you saved me. You saved your people."

"And I deserted you. I deserted Tiana. Because of Jackson. What he wanted." The truth chills him. "For what I desired in my heart. Glory. Fame. Immortality."

Oo-loo-te-ka's head shakes sternly. "No, my

317

Son. Jackson did not send you to Texas. *Unetlanv* did. He told you to go, to find your true place. Tiana knew you would not be hers forever. You were The Raven. You had to wander."

"She remarried," Houston says.

His father frowns. "Whose name is not worth remembering."

Houston brushes away his tears. He remembers hearing of Tiana's death of pneumonia in 1838. He had cried then, too.

"I failed at everything I tried," Houston tells his Cherokee father. "And now, all that I accomplished, all that I fought for, is laid to waste."

He cannot fight back the bitterness. "I am no hero. I was a drunk, a coward, a fool . . . but never a hero."

"You were a hero to me, my Son. You were a hero to many, white and red. No one is perfect. You stumbled, you fell, but you survived. You lived your life with honor."

His head lifts again. "Did I, Father?"

"Yes. All is well, my Son. All is well. You always return to us when you are in need. Do you know what you need now, *Co-lo-neh*?"

He does. He feels the chill. He asks: "Is dying hard, my Father?"

"I wouldn't know, ol' hoss."

Houston straightens, suddenly aware that he and *Oo-loo-te-ka* no longer sit inside the Town

House. They stand on the banks of a great river, surrounded by the mountains of Tennessee. A waterfall cascades. David Crockett rises on a rock in the middle of the river.

Cupping his hands over his mouth, Crockett shouts: "Let's go huntin'! I'll show you how to skin a b'ar!"

On the far side of the river, Tiana kneels at the bank, washing her midnight-colored hair. She wears her wedding dress. Soapy water drips from her black braids. She smiles at him. . . . Jackson is there, too, holding hands with Rachel, Old Hickory's wife, best friend, companion, champion. . . . Tears almost blind Houston when he sees his mother, his brothers, his sisters. *Muk-wah-ruh*, the great Comanche chief, gallops a pony underneath the waterfall, singing a fine song in a boisterous voice. Deaf Smith rocks in a chair. Gunter, the Cherokee scout from Horseshoe Bend, launches a canoe.

Looking back at *Oo-loo-te-ka*, Houston says: "I am frightened, my Father."

"There is nothing to fear, my Son." *Oo-loo-te-ka* says. "All is well. You have made it so." The old Cherokee's chin juts out, a signal, and Houston turns back.

He sees himself now, lying on the sofa in the downstairs room of the Steamboat House. The minister. His mother-in-law. All are there. Jeff fans the withered old man, the old man that is

Sam Houston. The gold ring on Houston's pinky reflects the fading sunlight. He touches the ring on his own finger. He sees his other slaves. He watches his children, some with heads bowed in prayer, others sobbing, Nannie reading a poem she has written for her father. Mostly, he focuses on his wife, his best friend, the love of his life. And he feels that, yes, perhaps *Unetlanv* did send him away from the Cherokees. To find Texas. To find his destiny. But, mostly, to find Margaret.

Sitting beside the dying old man, Margaret reads the Bible, and although her eyes glisten with tears, Houston understands that, yes, all is well.

All is well.

"What must I do?" he asks.

His Cherokee father answers, but Houston no longer sees him, or Crockett, or the waterfall, or the others. Even the river has vanished. He stares at the most beautiful light he has ever seen, brighter, more stunning than the sun, and is embraced by a warmth, a strength, a kindness.

"It is easy, *Co-lo-neh*," *Oo-loo-te-ka*'s voice tells him. "Say good bye to those you love. And step into the light."

CHAPTER THIRTY-ONE

July 26, 1863

She was reading from John 14—"Let not your heart be troubled: ye believe in God, believe also in me. In my Father's house are many mansions: if it were not so, I would have told you."—when Houston called out in a firm voice: "Texas!"

Margaret closed the Bible, and quickly moved beside him. She found his hand, gripped it.

"Texas," he said again, but softer this time, yet she felt his fingers tighten against her hand. She squeezed back. In a voice that warmed her, he spoke one more word.

"Margaret."

His fingers relaxed, his head sank deeper into his pillow, and he exhaled a final breath. Yet he appeared to be smiling. He looked at peace.

All around her, the children, the slaves, the Reverend McKinney, even Margaret's mother, cried harder.

The clock began to chime. It was 6:15 p.m.

"Is Papa . . . ?" Maggie started. "Is he . . . ?"

Somehow, Margaret could smile. "Yes, my darling children. He is with our Lord." She leaned over and kissed his forehead. "My gallant hero," she whispered, "you have earned your rest . . . and your reward. I love you."

Blocking the tears, she ran her fingers through his white hair.

"I don't want Papa to be with Jesus," Temple wailed. "I want him to be with us."

"He will always be with us." Margaret held out both hands. Temple took one. Nannie took the other.

"Join hands," Margaret said.

Maggie found Temple's other hand, and the Reverend McKinney took Nannie's. Other hands locked together . . . Houston's children, Nancy Lea, all the slaves.

Rain began to fall.

"Let us pray," Samuel McKinney said, but Margaret's head shook.

"Reverend," she said, "if you don't mind, I will lead us."

She did, praying not for Sam Houston's soul—for that had been taken care of years earlier—but for her children.

"Amen," she said, because her husband had always preferred short prayers. Now, she reached to his hand, and touched the ring on his pinky. She tugged, relieved as it slid off with little effort. It should not have surprised her. Houston had been lying on this couch for weeks, and he had lost much weight.

As far as Margaret knew, the ring had never

come off his hand—certainly not in their twenty-three years of marriage. She brought it closer, and found her reading glasses hanging on the ribbon across her chest. He had told her of the tiny gold band, but, until this moment, she had never read the inscription herself. Her heart swelled and she smiled as she lowered the ring and her eyeglasses.

"Children," she said, "this is the ring your father was given by his mother when he went off from home as a young, young man. There is an inscription inside. It was your father's creed. It was what drove him. It is what, I pray, will drive each of you . . . and me. I want you to read it now."

"Can I read it, Mama?" Temple said.

"Of course." Smiling, she placed the slim band in her youngest son's tiny hand.

The boy brought it up and said: "It says . . . 'This is my Daddy and he was . . .'" Temple sobbed. "'A really good person . . . and he loved . . . we loved him . . . and will . . . miss . . . him . . . very, very much.'"

Temple dropped the ring into Margaret's hand and, bawling, buried his face against Nannie's shoulder as his big sister swept him into her arms.

"Yes," Margaret said. "That's what it says, Temple."

Maggie sniffed. "What does it really say, Mother?"

She handed the ring to her daughter, and Maggie raised the ring, but quickly lowered it.

"I can't . . . read it . . . Mother." She returned the ring to Margaret, and put her balled fists against her teary eyes.

"It's all right." Margaret smiled, first at her children, and then at her husband.

"It is one word." Looking at her husband, at the ring, she found the strength she needed. Strength she drew from him. She returned the ring to Mary Willie to be passed around the children.

"Honor," Margaret said. "It simply reads 'Honor.'"

AUTHOR'S NOTE

Union prisoners of war at the Texas State Penitentiary made the coffin for Sam Houston, and carried it in the rain to the Steamboat House, where services were held in the upstairs parlor. Afterward, the cortège proceeded in the rain (a sign, according to folk tales, that the deceased is going to heaven) the few blocks to Oaklawn Cemetery, where Sam Houston was buried—and where he rests today.

Yellow fever would claim Margaret on December 3, 1867, in Independence, Texas. She had requested to be laid to rest beside her husband, but burial had to be immediate during yellow fever outbreaks, so she was interred next to the crypt that held her mother, who had died on February 7, 1864.

At some point, perhaps after the funeral, while alone in the Steamboat House in Huntsville, Margaret wrote in her family Bible:

> "Died on the 26th of July 1863, Genl Sam Houston, the beloved and affectionate Husband, father, devoted patriot, the fearless soldier—the meek and lowly Christian."

Houston's true epitaph, however, had been inscribed on the inside of that small gold ring his mother had given him back in Tennessee in 1813.

In the summer of 2014, on a combination boys baseball and magazine trip, I took my son Jack to the Sam Houston Memorial Museum in Huntsville, Texas. Researching an article on Sam Houston for *Wild West* magazine, I met with Michael C. Sproat, the museum's curator of collections, and director Mac Woodward.

I told them of my long fascination with the story of Sam Houston and his legendary honor ring, and Jack and I left Huntsville with a couple of cheap souvenirs: plastic orange wrist bands emblazoned with one word in white letters: HONOR.

The next day, our trip took us to La Porte, where Jack and I saw the actual ring at the San Jacinto Museum of History.

This must have made an impression on Jack. Over the next year, he wore that bracelet practically all the time, night and day. He slept with it. He showered with it. About the only time it came off occurred during Little League baseball games when an umpire would point out a rule prohibiting players to wear jewelry. He'd bring it to me, and I'd slip it on my wrist until after the ball game.

"If Jack can remember what that ring means," I told friends, "then I did my job."

This is a novel about the last years of Sam Houston's life, and most of it is taken from Houston's life. I've even used his own words, or close proximity, when possible. Yet this is fiction, and I've moved a few events around for the convenience of narrative. I made up stuff. Washington, Texas, reportedly became commonly known as Washington-on-the-Brazos after the Civil War, but it's Washington-on-the-Brazos here to avoid any confusion with Washington City, aka Washington, D.C.; likewise, Houston City got its 'City' surname tacked on to avoid confusion with Sam Houston the man. I also borrowed heavily from stories and memories involving my own father, my father-in-law, my grandmother, my mother, as well as from conversations with Bill O'Neal, the state historian of Texas and author of the invaluable *Sam Houston: A Study in Leadership* (Eakin Press, 2016); artist Thom Ross of Lamy, New Mexico; historian Paul Andrew Hutton, journalist Ollie Reed Junior, and novelist Max Evans, all of Albuquerque, New Mexico; and the late Robert J. Conley, Cherokee historian, novelist, and a good friend.

Much help came from Sproat, who let me hold a letter from Andrew Jackson to Houston, and Larry Spasic, president of Sam Jacinto Museum of History. David Marion Wilkinson of Austin, Texas, pointed me to the right sources when I ran into stumbling blocks, read the first five chapters, offered plenty of suggestions—and much-appreciated critiques—and his novel, *Oblivion's Altar*, helped spark an idea that became *The Raven's Honor*.

Sproat and I agreed on the two best biographies of Sam Houston: *The Raven*, Marquis James's Pulitzer Prize winner first published in 1929 (I own a well-read, ripped, battered but cherished Paperback Library version from 1971 that I picked up in a Denver suburb) and *Sam Houston* by James L. Haley (University of Oklahoma Press, 2002).

I also frequently turned to *Sam Houston: The Great Designer* by Llerena B. Friend (University of Texas Press, 1954); *Sword of San Jacinto: A Life of Sam Houston* by Marshall De Bruhl (Random House, 1993); *Sam Houston: A Biography of the Father of Texas* by John Hoyt Williams (Simon & Schuster, 1993); *Sam Houston with the Cherokees, 1829–1833* by Jack Gregory and Rennard Strickland (University of Oklahoma Press, 1967); *Sam Houston and the War of Independence in Texas* by Alfred M. Williams, originally published in 1893; and *The Life of Sam Houston* by Charles Edward Lester, originally published in 1855.

Likewise, *Sam Houston's Wife: A Biography*

of *Margaret Lea Houston* by William Seale (University of Oklahoma Press, 1970); *My Master: The Inside Story of Sam Houston and His Times by His Former Slave Jeff Hamilton* as told to Lenoir Hunt (State House Press, 1992); *From Slave to Statesman: The Legacy of Joshua Houston, Servant to Sam Houston* by Patricia Smith Prather and Jane Clements Monday (University of North Texas Press, 1995); *The Personal Correspondence of Sam Houston: Volume IV, 1852-1863*, edited by Madge Thornall Roberts (University of North Texas Press, 2001); *Sam Houston's Texas* by Sue Flanagan (University of Texas Press, 1964); and *Sam Houston: Hero of San Jacinto* (Texas State Historical Association, 2016) proved helpful.

Other sources included *David Crockett: The Lion of the West* by Michael Wallis (W.W. Norton, 2011); *The Blood of Heroes: The 13-Day Struggle for the Alamo—And the Sacrifice That Forged a Nation* by James Donovan (Little, Brown, and Co., 2012); *The Battle of San Jacinto* by James W. Pohl (Texas State Historical Association, 1989); *Ashbel Smith of Texas: Pioneer, Patriot, Statesman, 1805–1886* by Elizabeth Silverthorne (Texas A&M University Press, 1982); *Rip Ford's Texas* by John Salmon Ford and edited by Stephen B. Oates (University of Texas Press, 1987); *Ben McCulloch and the Frontier Military Tradition* by Thomas W. Cutrer

(University of North Carolina Press, 1993); *The Life of Andrew Jackson* by Marquis James (Bobbs-Merrill, 1938); *American Lion: Andrew Jackson in the White House* by Jon Meacham (Random House, 2008); *Andrew Jackson and the Creek War: Victory at the Horseshoe* by James Wendell Holland (University of Alabama Press, 1968); *Lone Star: A History of Texas and the Texans* by T.R. Fehrenbach (American Legacy Press, 1983); *Texas Culture, 1836–1846: In the Days of the Republic* by Joseph William Schmitz (The Naylor Company, 1960); *Seat of Empire: The Embattled Birth of Austin, Texas* by Jeffrey Stuart Kerr (Texas Tech University Press, 2013); *Galveston: A History of the Island* by Gary Cartwright (TCU Press, 1991); *Texas: The Dark Corner of the Confederacy: Contemporary Accounts of the Lone Star State in the Civil War* edited by B.P. Gallaway (University of Nebraska Press, 1994); the online edition of *The Handbook of Texas*; and various issues of the *Texas Monthly*, *Wild West*, *True West*, and *Southwestern Historical Quarterly*.

I cannot give enough credit to the staffs at the Sam Houston Memorial Museum and the San Jacinto Museum of History, plus Horseshoe Bend National Military Park near Daviston, Alabama; Star of the Republic Museum in Washington, Texas; Texas Governor's Mansion and Bob Bullock Texas State History Museum in Austin; Texas Prison Museum in Huntsville; Fort Gibson (Oklahoma) Historic Site; Tennessee State Museum in Nashville; Historic Washington (Arkansas) State Park; and the friendly Texans in Brenham, Goliad, Gonzales, Nacogdoches, Salado, and San Antonio.

And one final big thank you to Hugh Hennessey of Dallas, for putting Jack and me up on our research-baseball road trips.

This novel could not have been written without all their help.

Johnny D. Boggs
Santa Fe, New Mexico

ABOUT THE AUTHOR

Johnny D. Boggs has worked cattle, shot rapids in a canoe, hiked across mountains and deserts, traipsed around ghost towns, and spent hours poring over microfilm in library archives—all in the name of finding a good story. He's also one of two Western writers to have won seven Spur Awards from Western Writers of America (for his novels, *Camp Ford*, in 2006, *Doubtful Cañon*, in 2008, and *Hard Winter* in 2010, *Legacy of a Lawman*, *West Texas Kill*, both in 2012, *Return to Red River* in 2017, and his short story, "A Piano at Dead Man's Crossing", in 2002) as well as the Western Heritage Wrangler Award from the National Cowboy and Western Heritage Museum (for his novel, *Spark on the Prairie: The Trial of the Kiowa Chiefs*, in 2004). A native of South Carolina, Boggs spent almost fifteen years in Texas as a journalist at the Dallas *Times Herald* and Fort Worth *Star-Telegram* before moving to New Mexico in 1998 to concentrate full time on his novels. Author of dozens of published short stories, he has also written for more than fifty newspapers and magazines, and is a frequent contributor to *Boys' Life* and *True West*. His Western novels cover a wide range. *The Lonesome Chisholm Trail* (2000) is an authentic cattle-drive story, while *Lonely Trumpet* (2002) is an historical novel about the first black graduate of West Point. *The Despoilers* (2002) and *Ghost Legion* (2005) are set in the Carolina backcountry during the Revolutionary War. *The Big Fifty* (2003) chronicles the slaughter of buffalo on the southern plains in the 1870s, while *East of the Border* (2004) is a comedy about the theatrical offerings of Buffalo Bill Cody, Wild Bill Hickok, and Texas Jack Omohundro, and *Camp Ford* (2005) tells about a Civil War baseball game between Union prisoners of war and Confederate guards. "Boggs's narrative voice captures the old-fashioned style of the past," *Publishers Weekly* said, and *Booklist* called him "among the best Western writers at work today." Boggs lives with his wife Lisa and son Jack in Santa Fe. His website is www.johnnydboggs.com.

Books are produced in the United States using U.S.-based materials

Books are printed using a revolutionary new process called THINKtech™ that lowers energy usage by 70% and increases overall quality

Books are durable and flexible because of smythe-sewing

Paper is sourced using environmentally responsible foresting methods and the paper is acid-free

Center Point Large Print

600 Brooks Road / PO Box 1
Thorndike, ME 04986-0001 USA

(207) 568-3717

US & Canada:
1 800 929-9108
www.centerpointlargeprint.com